RED
ORC'S
RAGE

TOR BOOKS BY PHILIP JOSÉ FARMER

The Cache

Dayworld Breakup

Father to the Stars

Greatheart Silver

The Other Log of Phileas Fogg

The Purple Book

Stations of the Nightmare

Time's Last Gift

Traitor to the Living

RED ORC'S RAGE

Philip José Farmer

TOR
fantasy

A TOM DOHERTY ASSOCIATES BOOK

New York

RED ORC'S RAGE Copyright © 1991 by Philip José Farmer

A Tor Book
Published by Tom Doherty Associates, Inc.
49 West 24th Street
New York, N.Y. 10010

Library of Congress Cataloging-in-Publication Data

Farmer, Philip José.
　　Red Orc's rage / Philip José Farmer.
　　　　p.　cm.
　　"A Tom Doherty Associates book."
　　ISBN 0-312-85036-0
　　I. Title.
　　PS3556.A72R4　1991
　　813'.54—dc20   91-20577
　　　　　　　　　　　　　　　　　　　　　　　　　　　　　　　CIP

Printed in the United States of America
First edition: September 1991

0　9　8　7　6　5　4　3　2　1

Dedicated to A. James Giannini, M.D., F.C.P., F.A.P.A., Clinical Professor of Psychiatry at Ohio State University, the consultant during the writing of this novel.

In 1977, Doctor Giannini was in residency as a psychiatrist at Yale when he got the idea for what herein is called Tiersian therapy. Its actual development began in 1978 when he was in private practice in Youngstown, Ohio. In a letter dated December 28, 1978, he informed me that he was using a novel method of psychiatric therapy to treat troubled adolescents. This technique was based on my five-volume, science-fictional World of Tiers series. The patients, all volunteers, read the series and chose which character or characters to identify with and to try, in a sense, to become. The goals and methods of this therapy are outlined in this novel.

At present, Doctor Giannini and colleagues are preparing for publication the technical papers describing the actual therapy and its results.

Wellington Hospital Medical Center, Belmont City, Tarhee County, and all the people and events in the work at hand are fictional.

My thanks to David McClintock of Warren, Ohio, for the Youngstown area data.

CHAPTER

1

November 26, 1979

Jim Grimson had never planned to eat his father's balls.

He had not expected to make love to twenty of his sisters. He could not foresee that, while riding a white Steed, he would save his mother from a prison and a killer.

How could he, seventeen years old in October of 1979, know that he had created this seemingly ten-billion-year-old universe?

Though his father often called him a dumbbell and his teachers obviously thought he was one, Jim did read a lot. He knew the current theory of how the universe was supposed to have started. In the very beginning, before Time had started, the Primal Ball was the only thing existing. Outside of it was nothing, not even Space. All of the future universe, constellations, galaxies, everything, was packed into a sphere the size of his eyeball. This had gotten so hot and dense that it had blown up, out, and away. That explosion was called the Big Bang. Eons afterwards, the expanding matter had become stars, planets, and life on Earth.

That theory was WRONG, WRONG, WRONG!

Matter was not the only thing that could be put under tremendous heat and pressure. The soul could be squeezed too much. Then: BOOM!

God Almighty and then some! Less than a month ago, he had reluctantly entered the mental ward of Wellington Hospital, Belmont City, Tarhee County, Ohio State. Then he had become, among other things, the Lord of several universes, a wanderer in many, and a slave in one.

At this moment, he was back on his native Earth, same hospital. He was freezing with misery, burning with fury, and pacing back and forth in a locked room.

Jim's psychiatrist, Doctor Porsena, had said that Jim's trips into other worlds were mental, though that did not mean they were not real. Thoughts were not ghosts. They existed. Therefore, they were real.

Jim knew that his experiences in those pocket universes were as real as his pain when, not so long ago, he had driven his fist against his bedroom wall. And was not the blood flowing from the whiplashes on his back a witness to quell all doubts of his story? However, Doctor Porsena, scientist, rationalist, and rationalizer, would explain all puzzling phenomena with superb logic.

Jim usually loved the doctor. Just now, he hated him.

CHAPTER

2

November 3, 1979

"**A**ll previous patients," Doctor Porsena said, "have tried other types of therapy. These failed to improve the patients, though part of that might be attributed to the patients' hostility to psychiatric therapy of any kind."

"Old Chinese saying," Jim Grimson said. " 'You have to be nuts if you go to a psychiatrist.' Another celestial proverb. 'Insanity is not what it's cracked up to be.' "

L. Robert Porsena, M.D., F.C.P., head of the Wellington Hospital psychiatric unit, smiled thinly. Jim thought that he was probably thinking, Another smart-ass kid I got to deal with. Heard his rest-room-graffiti quotations a thousand times. 'Celestial proverb' indeed. He's trying to impress me, show me that he isn't just another ignorant drooling pimpled drugged-up rock-freak youth who's gone off his rocker.

On the other hand, Doctor Porsena might not be thinking that at all. It was hard to know what went on behind that handsome face that looked almost exactly like Julius Caesar's bust except for the black Fu Manchu mustache and the patent-leather mod haircut. He smiled a lot. His keen light-blue eyes reminded Jim of the Mad Hatter's song in Lewis Carroll's *Alice* book. "Twinkle, twinkle, little bat! How I wonder what you're at! Up above the world you fly, Like a tea tray in the sky. Twinkle, twinkle—"

Doctor Porsena's adolescent patients said he was a sha-man, a sort of miracle worker, a metropolitan medicine man with control over magical forces and far-out spirits.

Doctor Porsena started to say something but was inter-rupted by his desk intercom. He flipped a switch and said, "Winnie, I told you! No calls!"

Winnie, the beautiful black secretary sitting at her desk on the other side of the wall, evidently had something urgent on the line. Doctor Porsena said, "Sorry, Jim. This won't take more than a minute."

Jim only half listened while he gazed out the window. The psychiatric unit and Porsena's office were on the second story. The window was, like all windows in this area, covered with thick iron bars. Past breaks in the buildings beyond, Jim could see the tops of the waterfront structures. These were on the banks of the Tarhee River, which ran into the Mahoning River a mile to the south.

He could also see the spires of St. Grobian's and of St. Stephan's. His mother had probably attended early morning Mass at the latter today. That was the only time she had now to go to worship. She was working at two jobs, partly because of him. The fire had destroyed everything except the painting of his grandfather, which had been brought out of the house along with him. His parents had moved into a relatively cheap furnished apartment some blocks from the old house. Too close to the Hungarian neighborhood to suit Eric Grimson. That ungrateful attitude was just like his father. Eva's relatives—in fact, the entire Magyar area—had contributed money to help them out of their plight. A large part of the cash had been raised by a lottery. This was remarkable, for charitable donations had dropped considerably in the past few years because of the economic distress in the Youngstown area. But Eva's family and friends and church had come through.

Though she had been a semioutcast because of her marriage, she was still a fellow Hungarian. And, now that she was down, she should have learned her lesson and be properly contrite, as the old phrase went.

The Grimsons had not been able to buy the insurance to cover property damage or loss from the collapse of underground structures. Though they did have fire insurance, they would not be paid if the fire had been caused by an act of God. That had not yet been determined.

Eric Grimson could not afford a lawyer. But one of Eva's cousins, an attorney, had volunteered to take the case. If he won, he got ten percent of the payoff. If he lost, he got nothing. Clearly, he was donating his time because of clan unity and because he felt sorry for his cousin. That she was married to a non-Magyar who was also a shiftless bum and an atheist who had been a Protestant was bad enough. But to lose her house and all her possessions and to have a son who'd gone crazy . . . that was too much. Though a lawyer, he had a big heart.

The money needed to keep Jim in therapy was provided by the medical insurance, but the quarterly payments were very high. Eva Grimson had taken on another job to pay for them. The two times she had visited Jim, she had looked very tired. Her weight had gone down swiftly, her cheeks were hollowing, and her eyes were ringed with black.

Jim had felt so guilty that he offered to quit therapy. His mother would not accept that. Her son had been given the option of taking the therapy or being sentenced to jail. The district attorney had wanted to treat him as an adult, which would have meant a more severe sentence. She would do all she could to prevent that. Besides, though she did not say so, she could not hide her belief that Jim was genuinely crazy and would remain so unless he was treated by a psychiatrist.

Jim's father had not visited him. Jim did not ask his mother why Eric Grimson stayed away. One reason was that Jim did not wish to see his father. Another was that he knew that Eric was deeply ashamed because he had a "crazy" child. People would think that insanity ran in the family. Maybe it did in Eva's family. All Hungarians were crazy. But not the Grimsons, by God!

Actually, Jim had been very fortunate in being taken into therapy so quickly. Because of the lack of funds in the area, programs for treating the mentally disturbed had been cut far back. Normally, Jim would have been in the back of the long waiting line. He did not know why or how he had been jumped ahead to favorite-son status.

He suspected that Sam Wyzak's uncle, the judge, had used his influence. Also, his mother's cousin, the attorney, maybe brought some pressure to bear, probably not all of it with strictly legal procedures. Though Doctor Porsena would not comment on how Jim had been leapfrogged over others, he may have had something to do with it. Jim had the impression that the psychiatrist thought that he was a very interesting case because of his history of stigmata and hallucinations.

Maybe he was just being egotistical. After all, he was really nothing unusual, just another jerkoff, blue-collar, mongrel, squarehead-Hunkie punk. When he got down to the ungilded basics, that was what he was.

Doctor Porsena finally hung up the phone.

He said, "We were talking about other patients now in this program who had previously tried other types of therapy. Those had not succeeded with these patients, all of whom were hostile to psychiatric therapy of any kind.

"What I'm offering you—there's no pressure or force used

here—is immediate entrance into a type of therapy we've had much success with."

Doctor Porsena spoke very rapidly but clearly. He was remarkable in that his speech had very few of the pauses or hesitations halting most people's talk. No uh, ah, well, you know.

"It's not easy; no therapy is easy. Blood, sweat, and tears, and all that. And, like all therapy, the success depends basically upon you. We don't cure the patient. He or she cures himself with our guidance. Which means that you have to want to be able to handle your problems, genuinely desire to do so."

The doctor was silent for a moment. Jim looked around the office. It seemed quite luxurious to him with its thick (Persian?) carpet, overstuffed leather chairs and couch, big desk of some kind of glossy hardwood, the classy-looking wallpaper, the many diplomas and testimonials on the wall, the wall niches with busts of famous people in them, and the paintings which seemed abstract or surrealistic or whatever to Jim, who knew little about art.

"You understand everything I've said?" Porsena asked. "If there's anything you don't comprehend perfectly, say so. Patient or doctor, we're all here to learn. There's no shame in exposing one's ignorance. I expose my own quite often. I don't know everything. Nobody does."

"Sure, I understand. So far. At least you're not talking down to me, just using monosyllables, none of that psychological gobbledygook. I appreciate that."

Doctor Porsena's hands were flat on top of Jim's opened case file. They were slim and delicate and had long thin fingers. Jim had heard that he was an excellent pianist who usually played classical music, though he sometimes played jazz, dixie, and ragtime. He would even knock out some rock now and then.

He only had two hands but could have used four. He was

very busy, which was to be expected. Not only did he run the psychiatric unit of the hospital, he had a private practice in an office a block away on St. Elizabeth Street. He was also head of an organization of northeast Ohio psychiatrists and a teacher at a medical college.

Porsena's accomplishments awed Jim. But what most impressed him was the doctor's 1979 silver Lamborghini. Now, that was in the WOW! category.

The doctor turned a page of the file and read a line or two. Then he leaned back.

"You seem to be a wide reader," he said, "though you prefer science fiction. So many young people do. I have been a fan of science fiction and fantasy since I started to read. I began with the Oz books, Grimms' and Lang's fairy tales, Lewis Carrol's *Alice* books, Homer's *Odyssey*, the *Arabian Nights*, Jules Verne, H.G. Wells, and the science fiction magazines. Tolkien quite captivated me. Then, while I was in residency in Yale, I read Philip José Farmer's World of Tiers series. Do you know those books?"

"Yeah," Jim said. He straightened up. "Love them! That Kickaha! But when in hell is Farmer going to finish the series?"

Porsena shrugged. He was the only man Jim had ever seen who could make a shrug seem an elegant gesture.

"The point is that, while I was at Yale, I also read a biography of Lewis Carroll. A phrase in the commentary on the chapter in *Alice in Wonderland* titled 'A Caucus Race and a Long Tail' sparked something in my mind. I then and there got the idea for Tiersian therapy."

"What's that?" Jim said. "Tiersian? Oh, you mean from the World of Tiers?"

"As good a word as any and better than some," Doctor Porsena said, smiling, "It was only a glimmering of an idea, a zygote of thought, a brief candlelight that might have been blown out by the hurly-burly winds of the mundane world or by common sense and logic rejecting divine inspiration. But I clung to it, nourished it, cherished it, and at last brought it to full bloom."

This guy is really something, Jim thought. No wonder they call him The Shaman.

However, Jim had been misled and deceived by adults so many times that he did not entirely trust the psychiatrist. Wait. See if his words matched his deeds.

On the other hand, Porsena was this side of thirty. Old but not real old. Young-old.

It was a good thing that he was in biology class, Jim thought. Otherwise, he would not have known what the doctor was talking about when he had spoken of "zygote of thought." A zygote was any cell formed by the union of two gametes. And a gamete was a reproductive cell that could unite with another similar one to form the cell that develops into a new individual.

He had started out as a zygote. So had Porsena. So had most living creatures.

As he listened to the doctor explain the therapy, Jim understood that, in a psychotherapeutic sense, he was a gamete. And the object of the therapy was to become a zygote. That is, a new individual composed of the old personality and another one which was, at this moment, imaginary.

CHAPTER

3

"The Tiersian therapy patients form a small and elite volunteer group," Doctor Porsena said. "Usually, they start out with volume one, *Maker of the Universes*, and read the rest in proper sequence. They choose a character in the books and try to BE that character. They adopt all the mental and emotional characteristics of the role model whether they're good or bad. As therapy progresses, they come to a point where they start getting rid of the bad qualities of the character they've chosen. But they keep the good features.

"It's rather like a snake shedding its skin. The patient's uncontrolled delusions, the undesirable emotional factors which brought him or her here, are gradually replaced by controlled delusions. The controlled delusions are those which the patient adopts when he or she becomes, in a sense, the character in the series.

"There's much more to the treatment than this, but you'll understand that as therapy proceeds. You follow me?"

"So far," Jim said. "This really works, right?"

"The failure rate is phenomenally low. In your case, even though you've read the series, you will have to reread it. The *World of Tiers* will be your Bible, your key to health if you work with it and at it."

Jim was silent for a while. He was considering the series and also wondering which character—some of them were really vicious—he would like to adopt. To become, as the doctor said.

The basic premise of the series was that, many thousands of years ago, only one universe had existed. On one planet only in that universe was there life. The end of its evolutionary path was a species that resembled humans. These had attained a science vastly exceeding anything Earth had ever known. Eventually, the humans had been able to make artificial pocket universes.

So knowledgeable and powerful were these beings, they were able to alter the laws of physics governing each individual pocket universe. Thus, the rate of acceleration in a fall toward the center of gravity could be made different from that in the original world. Another example, one pocket world might contain a single sun and a single planet. The World of Tiers, for example. This was an Earth-sized planet shaped like a terraced Tower of Babylon. Its tiny sun and tiny moon revolved around it.

Another universe contained a single planet which behaved like the plastic in a lavalite bottle. Its shape kept changing. Mountains arose and sank before your very eyes. Rivers were formed within a few days and then disappeared. Seas rushed in to fill quickly forming hollows. Parts of the planet broke off—just like the thermoplastic in the liquid of a lavalite bottle—whirled around, changing shape, then fell slowly to the main body.

Many of the Lords, as the humans came to call themselves, left the original universe to live in their artificial pocket universes or designer worlds. Then a war made the planet unfit for life forever and killed all those then living on it. Only the Lords inhabiting the pocket worlds were saved.

Thousands of years passed while more artificial universes were made by the Lords living in those already made at the time of the war. These were inhabited by the life forms that the Lords had introduced on the planets of their private cosmoses. Many of these forms had been made in the laboratories of the Lords. There were other humans than the Lords on these. But these lesser beings had been made in the laboratories, though their models were the Lords themselves.

Access to these pocket worlds was gotten through "gates." These were interdimensional routes activated by various kinds of codes. As the Lords became increasingly decadent, they lost the knowledge of how to make new universes. The sons and daughters of the Lords wanted their own worlds, but they no longer had the means to create them. Thus, as was inevitable, there was a power struggle among them to gain control of the limited number of worlds.

By the time *Maker of the Universes* began, in the late 1960s, many Lords had been killed or dispossessed. Even those who had their own universes wanted to conquer others. That they could live without aging for hundreds of millenia meant that most of them had become bored and vicious. Invading other worlds and killing the Lords there had become a great game.

If they could not create, they could destroy.

The *World of Tiers* series was clearly an anticipation of the "Dungeons and Dragons" games which were so popular among youths. Its gates, the traps set by the Lords in the gates, the ingenuity necessary to get through the gates, and the dangerous worlds in which a wrong decision would land a character prefigured the D-and-D games. Jim was surprised that the series had not been adapted to such a game.

He was even more surprised to find that the books had

become a tool used in psychiatric therapy. But it seemed like a great idea. It certainly appealed to him far more than conventional therapy, Freudian, Jungian, or whatever. Though he did not know much about any of the various psychiatric schools, he nevertheless did not like them.

Rest-room graffiti flashed across his mindscreen.

"Mental illness can be fun." "Over the edge is better than under it." "Nobody catches schizophrenia from a toilet seat."

Doctor Porsena looked at the clock on his desk. A puppet of Time, Jim thought. Doctors and lawyers, like railroads, ran on Newtonian time. They knew nothing of Einsteinian. No loafing and inviting your soul, to hell with relativity. But that was how they got things done.

The psychiatrist rose, and he said, "On to other things, Jim. *Excelsior!* Ever upward and onward! Junior Wunier will give you the books, no charge. He'll also acquaint you with the rules and regulations. May you be safe from the curving carballoy claws of Klono, and may the Force be with you. See you later."

Jim left the room thinking that the doctor was really something. That reference to the Force. That was from *Star Wars*, and any kid in America would recognize it. But that bit about Klono. How many would know that Klono was a sort of spaceman's god, a deity with golden gills, brazen hooves, iridium guts, and all that? Klono was the god whom space-farers swore by in E. E. Smith's Lensman series.

Jim found Junior Wunier at the officer of the day's post near the elevators. Junior Wunier! What a name for parents to stick a kid with! Handicapped him from birth. As if he wasn't handicapped enough. The eighteen-year-old had hair like the Bride of Frankenstein's, a curved spine like the Hunchback of Notre Dame's, a dragging foot like Igor's, and a face like the Ugly Duchess's in the first *Alice* book. Besides the hump, he had a monkey on his back. He was a speed freak. Jim hoped that he had been caught before his brain had been burned out.

Worst of all was his tendency to drool.

And he, Jim Grimson, had thought he was born with two strikes against him.

Jim pitied the poor guy, but he couldn't stand him.

Wouldn't you know it? Junior Wunier had chosen Kickaha as his role model. Kickaha, the handsome, strong, quick, and ever-tricky hero. Whereas Jim would have thought that Wunier would pick Theotormon. That character was a Lord who had been captured by his father and whose body had been cruelly transformed in the laboratory into a monster with flippers and a hideous and bestial face.

Wunier went into the storeroom and brought out five paperbacks for Jim. "Read 'em and weep," he said.

Jim put the stack of Farmer's novels under his arm. Were they to be his salvation? Or were they like everything else, full of promises that turned out to be hot air?

Wunier led Jim to his room through halls that were, at this moment, empty. Everybody was in his own room, in the recreation room, or in private or group therapy. The long wide halls with their white walls and gray floors echoed their footsteps. Jim had been assigned, for the time being, to a one-person room, small and very hospital-looking. The tiny closet was more than large enough, however. The only clothes Jim had were on his back, and these had been brought by his mother, who had gotten them from Mrs. Wyzak. Being Sam's, they fit him too tightly. The shoes were embarrassing, square-toed oxfords that Sam would have worn only if his mother had threatened to kill him if he didn't, which she probably had.

Junior Wunier pointed to a niche in the wall. "You can put the books there. Now, here's the rules and regulations."

He leaned against the wall. Holding the paper with both

hands close to his face, he read it aloud. A spray of saliva moistened the paper.

Jim thought, Suffering succotash! This guy was another Sylvester the Cat.

He sat down in the only chair, a wooden one with a removable cushion. He wished he had a cigarette. His teeth ached slightly; his nerves were drawn as tightly as telephone cables; his temper badly needed tempering.

Wunier droned on as if he were a Buddhist monk chanting the Lotus Sutra. The patient had to keep his or her room neat and orderly. The patient had to take a shower every day, keep his nails clean, and so on. The patient could use only the telephone by the officer of the day's desk and must not tie it up for more than four minutes. Smoking was permitted only in the lounge. Graffiti was forbidden. Those patients caught with nonprescription drugs or booze or tearing off a piece (Wunier's words) would be subject to being kicked out on his or her ass.

"And when you jack off," he said, "don't do it in the showers or in the presence of anyone else."

"How about before a mirror?" Jim said. "Is the image another person?"

"From Sarcasmville," Wunier growled. "Just obey the rules, and you'll get along fine."

Wunier dragged his foot across to the wall and tore off a taped-up paper. Jim read the words on it before it went into the wastebasket.

DON'T BE AFREUD OF YOUR SHRINK.

Beneath the phrase was a Kilroy-was-here drawing.

"There's some wise guy puts this stuff up in all the rooms," Wunier said. "We call him the Scarlet Letterer. His ass'll be scarlet if we catch him."

Besides some framed prints that looked as if they came out of the *Saturday Evening Post*, the only thing hanging on the wall was a calendar.

Jim said, "How about the mantras? A lot of the rooms have them up on the walls."

"That's OK, part of the therapy. Some people need them to get into the World of Tiers." Wunier paused, then said, "You decided yet what character you'll choose?"

He obviously wanted to stay and talk. Poor guy must be lonely. But Jim didn't feel like sacrificing himself for someone who was the last person he wanted to talk with.

"No," Jim said. He was about to get up but then drew back into the chair. He pointed at the space below his bed.

"What's that?"

Wunier's eyes widened. He started to bend over to look under the bed, then changed his mind.

"What do you mean, 'What's that?'"

"It just moved. I thought it was just the shadows. But it's very dark, blacker than outer space. It looks like if you put your hand in it, the hand'd freeze off and float into the fourth dimension. Sort of spindle-shaped. About a foot long. Hey, it moved again!"

Wunier stared briefly at the bed and a longer time at Jim.

"I have to get going," he said. Attempting nonchalance, he added, "I leave you to entertain your guest." But he got out of the room as swiftly as he could.

Jim laughed loudly when he thought that Wunier would not hear him. The thing he had claimed to see was out of a novel by Philip Wylie—he didn't remember the title—but he didn't know if Wunier had really thought there was one under the bed or if he was scared that Jim was about to freak out.

However, he was, a minute later, in a mixed black and red mood. A sort of AC phase. Depression alternating with anger. The psychologists said that depression was anger turned against yourself. So, how could he, like a light flashing off and on, suffer from both states within a minute's time? Maybe he really was about to freak out.

IT'S DEPRESSING TO BE A MANIC.

He'd tape that to the rest-room wall. He'd show them that the demmed elusive Scarlet Letterer wasn't the only one who could strike from the shadows.

He didn't even have clothes of his own. And he had no money. Strip a man or woman of his possessions and money, and you see a person who's lost his manhood or her womanhood. That person was no longer a person. Not unless he or she were a Hindu fakir or yogi, part of a culture that considered such people to be holy. Not in this world where clothes and money made the man, where the emperor was the only one who could go naked and still be a person.

He had nothing.

While sitting in the chair, staring at nothing, a nothing looking into a mirror, he felt the blackness recede. It was followed by red, red that surged into every cell of his body and mind.

But a man who was angry was a man who had something. Rage was a positive force even if it led to negative action. A poem he'd read a long time ago said—how'd it go? couldn't remember it verbatim—rage would work if reason wouldn't.

Gillman Sherwood, a fellow patient, stuck his head in the doorway. "Hey, Grimson! Group therapy in ten minutes!"

Jim nodded and got up from the chair.

He knew then what character he was going to choose. To be.

Red Orc. A villainous Lord in the series, Kickaha's most dangerous enemy. One mean and angry Ess Oh Bee. He kicked ass because his own was red.

CHAPTER

4

October 31, 1979, Halloween

Something had awakened Jim just before the alarm clock had gone off. His eyes still sleep-blurred, he had stared upwards. The cracks in the ceiling were slowly forming a map of chaos. Or were they preliminary strokes of a drawing of the image of a beast or some cryptic symbol? Several new cracks had shot out from the old ones since he had gone to bed last night.

The alarm clock startled him. Twirrruuup! Up and Adam! Rise from bed, sluggard! Roll 'em! Roll 'em! Once more to the breach!

The early-morning sun shone through the thin yellow curtains on white dust motes falling from the cracks.

The earth had moved below the house and shaken his bed. Somewhere directly below him, one of the many long-ago abandoned mine tunnels or shafts under Belmont City had shifted or crumbled, and the Grimson house had sunk or tilted a little more.

Three months ago, four blocks from Jim's house, two houses, side by side, had fallen into a suddenly born gap two feet deep. They now leaned toward each other, their front and back porches torn off. Once six feet apart, they were jammed together, stuck in the hole like a couple of too-large and too-hard suppositories in the Jolly Green Giant.

A tremor a minute ago had yanked him upward, like a trout on a hook, from a nightmare. But it was no dream of a monster that had made him moan and whimper. It had been a black-on-black dream in which nothing, nothing at all, had happened.

He told himself to haul his weary ass out of bed and get it in gear. "With a song in his heart." Yeah. A song like "Gloomy Sunday." Only this was Wednesday, All Souls' Day.

The room was very small. Seven big posters were taped to the faded red-roses-and-light-green wallpaper and the back of the door. The largest was that of Keith Moon, Moon the Loon, great and late mad drummer for The Who. The most colorful displayed the five members of the Hot Water Eskimos, a local rock group. There was "Gizzy" Dillard vomiting into his saxophone; Veronica "Singing Snatch" Pappas shoving the microphone up under her leather miniskirt; Bob "Birdshot" Pellegrino jacking off one of his drumsticks, Steve "Goathead" Larsen looking as if he were humping his guitar; Sam "Windmill" Wyzak tickling the ivories. Above the unsavory crew hovered a dozen cowbells resembling UFOs in flight. Up close and in bright light, you could see very thin wires connecting them to the ceiling.

Clad in torn green pajama tops, red pajama bottoms, and black socks, he got out of bed and opened the door. Yes, it did stick more than it had yesterday. Turning to the left, he went down the unlit hall. Its carpet was thready and a dull green. Inside the narrow bathroom, he turned on the light. When he looked in the mirror, he winced. A third pimple was bulging redly under the skin. His reddish whiskers were sticking out a little more than they had yesterday. By weekend, he would have to shave. The dull razors his father insisted on keeping because new ones cost too much would scrape his skin raw, cut off the scabs over the recently squeezed pimples, and make them bleed.

He urinated into the washbowl. By doing this, Jim was helping his father, Eric Grimson. Eric was always hollering about too many flushes running up the utility bill. Jim was also getting a small, if secret, revenge on that domestic tyrant and all-around prick, his father.

While standing there, he studied his face. Those large deep-blue eyes were inherited from both his Norwegian father and his Hungarian mother. The reddish hair, long jaw, and prominent chin were handed down from Eric Grimson. The small ears, long straight nose, high cheekbones, and slightly Oriental cast of the eyes were the gifts of his mother, Eva Nagy Grimson. His six feet and one and a half inch of height came from his father. Jim would grow three more inches if he became as tall as his begetter. His old man was wiry and narrow-shouldered, but Jim had gotten his broad shoulders from his mother's side of the family. Her brothers were short but very wide and muscular.

God Almighty and then some! If he could get rid of the damn pimples, he might be good-looking. He might even get some place with Sheila Helsgets, the best-looking girl in Belmont Central High, his unrequited love. Jim meant to look up "unrequited" in the dictionary someday and find out what it meant exactly. To Jim, it meant that his love was one-sided, that she felt no more for him than an orbital satellite did for the radar beam bouncing off it.

The only remark she had ever directed his way had been to ask him to stand downwind of her. That had hurt him but not enough to make him quit loving her. He had started bathing twice a week, a big sacrifice of time on his part, considering how little he had to spare for trivial matters.

Those pimples! Why did God, if He existed, curse teen-agers with them?

After splashing water on his face and penis and drying them off with the towel only his father was supposed to use, he headed for the kitchen. Despite the darkness of the hallway, he could see white plaster dust on the carpet. When he got to the kitchen, he noticed that new cracks were in the greenish ceiling. There was white dust on the gas stove and the oilcloth cover on the table.

"We're all going to fall into a hole," he muttered. "All the way to China. Or Hell."

Hurriedly, he made his own breakfast. He swung open the door of the forty-year-old refrigerator, the cooling coils atop it looking like an ancient Martian watchtower. From it he took a jar of mayonnaise, a Polish sausage, a Polish pepper hot enough to burn the anus when it came out the next day, half a browned banana, wilted lettuce, and cold bread. He forgot to close the refrigerator door. While water boiled for the cup of instant coffee he would make, he sliced the sausage and banana and slapped together a sandwich.

He turned on the radio, purchased by his father's father the day after the first transistor radios came on the market. The vacuum-tube GE was gathering dust up in the overbur-dened attic along with piles and piles of old newspapers and magazines, broken toys, old clothes, cracked china, rusty silverware, broomless brooms, and a burned-out 1942 Hoover vacuum cleaner.

Eric and Eva Grimson found it painful to throw anything away except garbage, and sometimes not even that. It was as if, Jim thought, they were cutting off pieces of their own bodies when they parted with a possession. Most people put their past behind them. His parents put it above them.

He bit deeply into the sandwich and followed it with a

piece of Polish pepper. While his mouth burned and his eyes watered, he turned the gas off and poured the boiling water into a cup. As he stirred the instant coffee, WYEK, Belmont's only rock station, blasted into the kitchen with the tail end of the weather report. After that, it began to blare out number sixteen of this week's local hit list. "Your Hand's Not What I Want!" was the first song by The Hot Water Eskimos that Jim had ever heard on the radio. It would also be the last.

While he was bent over the sink and filling a glass with cold water, he heard a growling which did not come from the radio. Then the set went off. For two seconds, there was no sound except that of running water. The growl behind him came again.

"Goddamn! I told you and I told you! Keep that fucking noise down! Or, by God, I'll throw the goddamn radio through the window! And close the fucking refrigerator door!"

The voice was low in volume but deep in tone. It was his father's, his legal master's. The voice that had filled Jim with dread and wonder when he was a child. It had not seemed to be human. Jim still found it hard to believe that it was.

Yet, he could remember moments when he had loved it, when it had made him laugh. That was what confused his attitude toward his father. But he was not mixed up now.

He straightened up, turned the faucet off, and drank from the glass as he wheeled slowly around. Eric Grimson was tall, red-faced, red-eyed, puffy-lidded, fat-jowled, and big-paunched. The broken veins in his nose and cheeks reminded Jim of the cracks in the ceilings.

Jesus, Mary, and Joseph!

Another parent-child confrontation, as the school psychologist called it. One more time locking horns with a shithead, as Jim thought of it.

His old man sat down. He put his elbows on the table and then his face between his hands. For a moment, he looked as if he were going to cry. Then he straightened, his open palms striking the tabletop loudly and making the sugar bowl dance around. He glared. But his hands, when he lit a match to a cigarette, were shaking.

"You turned it on loud on purpose, didn't you? You won't let me sleep. God knows, you know, too, your mother knows, I need it. But, no will you let me sleep? Why? Goddamn nastiness, pure orneriness, the mean streak you got from your mother, that's why! And I told you to close the refrigerator door! You . . . you . . . snake! That's what you are! A goddamn snake!"

He slammed his right hand against the table. The cloud of stale beer issuing from his mouth made Jim wrinkle his face.

"I won't put up with that crap from you anymore! By God, I'm going to throw that goddamn radio through the window! And you after that!"

"Go ahead!" Jim said. "See if I care!"

His father would not take him up on that dare. No matter how furious Eric Grimson got, he would not destroy anything that might cost him money to replace.

Eric rose from the chair. "Get out!" he yelled. "Out, out, out! I don't want to see your fartface around here, you long-haired freak-weirdo! Get out right now or I'll kick your ass all the way to school! Now! Now! Now!"

His old man was trying to provoke him to hit him, Jim thought. Then he could break a few bones in his son, bloody his nose, slam him in the belly, kick him in the balls, kidney-punch him.

Which was exactly what his son wanted to do to his old man and was going to do some day.

"All right!" Jim screamed. "I'll go, you drunken bum, hopeless welfare case, parasite, loafer, loser! And you can shut the door yourself."

Eric's cement-mixer voice got lower but louder. His face

was red, and his mouth was wide open, showing crooked tobacco-yellowed teeth. His eyes looked like blood clots.

"You don't talk to me like that, your father! You fucking hippie, stinking . . . stinking . . ."

"How about pink Commie bastard?" Jim said as he sidled by his father, facing him, ready to strike back but trembling violently.

"Yeah! That'll do fine!" his father roared.

But Jim was running down the hall. Just before he entered his bedroom, he saw a door open at the far end of the corridor. From the narrow rectangle between door and wall came a flickering light and a strong odor of incense. His mother's face appeared. As usual, she had been praying and fingering her beads while kneeling before the statues in the room. Then, hearing the uproar, instead of coming out to defend her son, she had hidden behind the door until peace and quiet came again or, at least, seemed about to break out.

"Tell God to shove it!" Jim shouted.

His mother gasped. Her head disappeared, and her door closed slowly and softly. That was his mother. Slow and soft, quiet and peaceful. And no more effectual than the shadow she resembled. She had lived so long among ghosts that she had become one.

CHAPTER

5

Jim, now dressed and holding his school book bag in one hand, leaped through the front doorway. Behind him, standing in the doorway, shouting insults and threats, was his father. He was not going to pursue his son outside his territory, on which he felt safe. He was the cock of the walk and the bull of the woods on his own land. Which, actually, was the bank's, if you wanted to get technical about it. Which, if the tunnels and shafts under the house kept collapsing, might soon be Mother Earth's.

The sky was clear, and the sun promised to warm the air up to around the low seventies. A great day for Halloween, though the radio weather report had said that clouds were supposed to appear later in the day.

That was the outside weather. Jim felt as if lightning was banging around in him like an angry ogre cook throwing pots and pans around. Black clouds were racing across his personal sky. They bore news of worse to come.

Eric Grimson kept on shouting though his son was now a block down the street. A couple of people were sticking their heads out their front doors to see what the commotion was. Jim plunged ahead, swinging his bag, which held five textbooks, none of which he had opened last night, pencils, a ballpoint pen, and two notebooks the pages of which mostly bore Jim's attempts to write lyrics. It also contained three tattered and dirty paperbacks, *Nova Express*, *Venus on the Half-Shell*, and *Ancient Egypt*.

His mother had not had time to fix his lunch for him. Never mind. His stomach hurt like a fist gripping red-hot barbed wire.

Too much too long.

When was he going to blow up in his own Big Bang?

It was coming, it was coming.

In a notebook was his latest lyric, "Glaciers and Novas."

> *Burn, burn, burn, burn!*
> *Nothing tells how hot I am.*
> *Words're shadows; fury's the substance.*
> *Uncle Sam will blacken my fire.*
> *Uncle Sam's a grinding glacier,*
> *Five miles high, a-grinding*
> *Mountains down to flatness.*
> *Glacier wants everything flat,*
> *Glacier wants to quench all fire.*
> *Pop and Mom are ice giants*
> *Coming to get me, cool my fire.*
> *White house frost giant,*
> *FBI trolls,*
> *CIA ogres,*
> *Werewolf Fuzz are circling me.*
> *Jailhouse fridge'll freeze the fire.*
> *Ahab chasing Moby Dick,*
> *Chasing his own dick, it's said,*

Ahab tearing the mask from God,
Bombshell heart about to explode,
His anger's a candle, mine's a klieg.
Eons on, ages on, eons on, eras on,
Old switchman Time reroutes the tracks,
Express-train Sun rams head-on
In destined doom the Nova Special,
Blows, explodes, incinerates all,
Splattering Pluto with pieces of Mars.
Glacier gives up my frozen corpse,
Glacier gives itself to fire.
Frozen corpse will burn again.
Righteous fire is never quenched.
Burn, burn, burn, burn!

That said it all, yet it was not enough.

That was why movies, paintings, and the beat of rock—above all, the beat of rock—were sometimes better than words. The unsayable was said. Better said, anyway.

For a moment, the street around him seemed to become wavy. It was as shimmering and as unstable as a mirage in a desert. Then it cooled off and became unmoving again. Cornplanter Street was as solid as it had been a few seconds ago. Just as squalid, too. Seven blocks away, above the roofs of the houses, the gray-black smokestacks and upper stories of the Helsgets Steel Works mills were metal giants. Dead giants because no stinking and black smoke poured from them. Jim remembered when they had been alive, though that seemed so long ago that it might have been in another century.

Cheap foreign steel had shut down the area's industrial-steel complex. Since then, or so it seemed to Jim, his parents' troubles and, thus, his own troubles, had started. Though the busy furnaces had poured clouds of dirt and poison over the city, they had also showered prosperity. Now, hand in hand with cleaner air had come poverty, despair, rage, and violence. Though the citizens could now see a house two blocks away, they could not see the future and were not sure they wanted to.

This street, the whole city, was Bob Dylan's "Desolation Row."

Jim shuffled along the cracked sidewalk in his dirty and scarred cowhide boots. He passed two-story bungalows built just after World War II ended. Some of the front yards were fenced in; some of these fences were white with paint and had been repaired not too long ago. Some of the yards sported nice-looking lawns. Those with little grass or none at all were occupied by old cars up on blocks or motorcycles partly torn apart.

The morning sun was glorious in the unflecked blue sky. Yet the light in Belmont City had seemed for a long time to Jim to be unlike the light elsewhere. It was particularly harsh and, at the same time, gritty. How could sunlight in clear air be gritty? He did not know. It just was. He did not know when it had first seemed so to him. He suspected that it was about the time his pubic hair began to grow. SPOING! There It was, the irrepressible It. SPOING! It rose and swelled like an angry cobra at just about anything, as long as that anything hinted of sex. Anything in movies, photos, ads, you name it, unaccountable stray thoughts and mental images—all called It up like a witch waving a magic wand. SPOING! There It was, no matter how embarrassing.

That was when the sunlight in Belmont City had started to be harsh and gritty.

Or was it?

Maybe it had begun when he had had his first "vision." Or when his "stigmata" had first appeared.

Jim saw his best buddy, Sam "Windmill" Wyzak, a half block away down Cornplanter Street. Sam was standing by the white picket fence on his front yard. Jim stepped up his pace. Only Jim's grandfather, Ragnar Grimsson, the Norwegian sailor and locomotive engineer, and Sam Wyzak really loved him. All three had souls like forks attuned to the same pitch. But his grandfather had died five years ago (maybe that was when the light got harsh and gritty) and now only Jim and Sam vibrated on the same frequency.

Sam was six feet tall and very skinny. His sharp and pointed face could have been a model for that of Wile E. Coyote of the "Roadrunner" cartoons. He looked just as hungry and desperate, but his deep-brown and close-set eyes lacked Wile E.'s never-quenched light of hope. His glossy black hair was unruly and bushy, almost an Afro.

When Jim got closer, Sam called out, "Jimbo! My man!" in a high-pitched and whiney voice. He danced a shuffle-off-to-Buffalo while he sang the first six lines of a lyric of Jim's. Jim thought it was good, but the Hot Water Eskimos had rejected it as "not rock enough." Its first line was a phrase used by Siberian Eskimo shamans when they worked magic, words that organized chaotic lines of force into powerful instruments for good or evil.

The song in its entirety went thus:

ATA MATUMA M'MATA!
You in trouble, deep in crap?
Hire the ancient Siberian shaman.
Wizard magic guaranteed to work.
Shaman chants a Stone Age spell:
ATA MATUMA M'MATA!
Gather all these witchy items!
You don't get these at Neiman Marcus!
Angel's feather, Dracula's breath,
Polar bear's malaria,
Politician's unbroken promise,
Scream from Captain Hook's toilet stall,
Earwax from Spock of far-off Vulcan,

Nielsen rating of Tinker Bell,
Turnip blood—Rh-negative,
Jack the Ripper's love for women,
Needle's eye which traps the rich,
Belly buttons of Adam and Eve,
Visa stamped by Satan himself.
Mix them like you're Betty Crocker.
Stir the bubbling brew around!
When it cools and when it shrieks,
Drink it down, drink it down!
ATA MATUMA M'MATA!

"The 'Ata Matuma M'Mata' spell won't work, Sam'" Jim said. "I'm down, way down. I'm also pissed, really got the red-ass."

Mrs. Wyzak was looking out a window at him. She was big and had Mother Earth breasts and was a mighty big mother herself. She was, unlike his mother, the powerhouse in the family. Mr. Wyzak was no wimp, but he was his wife's shadow. When she moved, he moved. When she spoke, he nodded his head.

Mrs. Wyzak had a peculiar expression. Was she wishing that Jim was also her son? She had wanted at least six kids, a brood, a pulsation of progeny. But she had had a hysterectomy after Sam, her firstborn. Mr. Wyzak, in his less charitable moments, and he had many, said that Sam had poisoned her womb.

Or was her face set so oddly because she thought that Sam's friend was so odd? A boy who had had such strange visions and who suffered from stigmata was not your normal playmate for your child.

Jim's mother . . . that was a different case. She had thought at first that Jim was a latter-day St. Francis because of the unearthly things he had seen and his unexplainable bleedings. But when Jim got older she had put aside her dreams of sainthood for him. Now she was not so sure she had not mated with the devil when she was sleeping and Jim was their child. She had never said so, though Jim's father had. But Jim believed that his father was repeating what she had told him. However, his father could have made it up. He did not put in full time hurting his son, but that was only because he had other things to do. Like getting drunk and gambling.

Jim waved at Mrs. Wyzak. She stepped back as if startled, then moved to the window again and waved at him. Since she was not afraid of anyone—he wished to God that his mother was like her—she must have been thinking something bad about him. For a moment, she had been ashamed. Or was he, he thought, too damn sensitive and self-centered? That was what his father and his school counselor had told him.

Jim and Sam walked away. Sam shook his head, and his near-Afro waved like the plume on the helmet of a Trojan warrior.

"Well?" Sam whined in Jim's ear.

"Well, what?"

"Jesus, you said you were down, way down, and we've walked a whole block, and you ain't said a word! Down about what? Same old story? You and your old man?"

"Yeah," Jim said. "Sorry. I was thinking, lost in my thoughts. One of these days I'm going to lose my way and never come back. And why should I? Anyway, here's my sordid and sad tale."

Sam listened, interjecting only a grunt or a "Weird, man! Weird!" When Jim was finished, Sam said, "Ain't it the shits? What can you do now? Nothing—according to The Man. But it won't be long 'til you're eighteen, and you can tell your old man to go fuck himself."

"If we don't kill each other first."

"Yeah. *Th-th-that's all, f-f-folks!* Period. No Continued Next

Chapter. You're pissed off? Listen, me and Mom got into it this morning, about some of the same things you and your Dad argued about. But, you know, with Mom it's always the music.

"'I worked my ass off,' she says, 'so you could take music lessons, and now you can play the piano and the guitar. But I didn't work myself to a frazzle as a grocery clerk and a baby-sitter and God knows how many other jobs and pinch my pennies so you could be a rock musician. And now you want to dress up like a punk, look like some drunken murdering redskin, embarrass me and your father and my friends and Father Kochanowski! The saints help me, the Virgin Mary help me! I wanted you to be a classical musician, play Chopin and Mozart, be somebody I could be proud of! Look at you!' And so on. Same old shit.

"Then I said what I should've never said, but I was seeing purple by then."

Sam rotated both arms several times, the lunch bag in one hand. "Windmill" Wyzak was really going into action.

"'Worked your ass off?' I said. 'What do you call that? A camel?' I pointed at her big ass. God forgive me, I do love my mother even if she's mostly a pain. Anyway, I had to run for my life. Mom threw dishes at me and took after me with a broom. I had to run through the house and then into the backyard with her screaming at me and the old man laughing like crazy, rolling on the floor, glad to see somebody besides him being picked on by her."

Jim was hurt by Sam's seeming not to care about his troubles with his father. Jim was open, panting and slavering, for sympathy and understanding and advice. So what was his supposed best friend doing? Ignoring his friend's absolutely pressing crises to talk about his own problems, which Jim had heard too many times.

CHAPTER

6

They turned off Cornplanter Street onto Pitts Avenue, which led straight for six blocks to Belmont City Central High School. Cars loaded with students sped by them. No one in the vehicles waved or shouted at the two pedestrians, though all knew them. Jim felt like an outcast, a leper whose only skin disease was acne. That made his mood blacker, his anger redder.

Jesus H. Christ! Those uppity snobs didn't have any right to look down on him because his father was out of work and the Grimson family was pisspot poor and lived in a run-down low-class blue-collar area. The students who had their own cars were not so rich themselves, except for Sheila Helsgets, and her family wasn't doing so well either. The closing of the steel mills had socked it to her father. He probably wasn't now worth more than a million or so, and that would be mostly just property and low-value stocks and bonds. At least, that's what he had heard about the Helsgets.

Sam had no idea how madly and badly in love with her Jim was. Jim held some things back from his old buddy because he didn't want to be laughed at. Like his passion for Sheila Helsgets and his writing "straight" poetry at the same time he was writing rock lyrics and reading many books and his vocabulary, which was much larger than Sam's and that of the other guys he hung around with though he wasn't always sure of the precise meaning of the words he used.

". . . a cigarette?" Sam said.

Jim said, "What?"

"Christamighty!" Sam said. "Get with it! Where are you? Lost in space? Beam me back to Earth, Scotty. I asked if you want a coffin nail."

Sam was holding in a dark hand, the fingernails dirty, two nonfilter Camels. Jim should have been grateful for the offer; he was so short of money he couldn't buy a pack. But, for some reason, he did not want to smoke.

"Nah! How about an upper?"

Sam slipped a Camel into the right corner of his lips, put the other in the pocket of his black shirt, and dipped his hand into the outside pocket of his blue jacket. It came out with three capsules.

"Yeah. Black beauties. Guaranteed to give you a balloon ride to the moon. But watch out for the landing."

"Thanks," Jim said. "I'll take one. I'll have to owe you."

"That's seven dollars you owe," Sam said. He quickly added, "Just keeping the books up to date. No hurry. Your credit's always good with me, you know. I ain't billing you for the cigarettes I been giving you, either. I know when you get them, you'll help me in my distress. Like you always say, we're Damon and Pithy-ass, whoever they might be."

Jim popped one upper into his mouth and swallowed it dry. He worked his mouth to generate saliva to help it on down.

The Biphetamine worked far faster then usual. Zap!

Where there had been tired blood, as the ads said, was now a river of molten gold. Coursing through his veins, not to mention his arteries, each molecule racing the others to get back to his heart first and then back to the merry-go-round for another race at breakneck speed. The harsh and gritty light melted into a soft smoothness.

Sam had put a black beauty into his mouth before stopping to cup his hand and then flicking the Bic. He drew in deeply and blew out smoke as he resumed walking. Jim, waiting for him, looked around as if he had never seen this place before. He could see the top of Belmont Central over the scrungy houses (Pitts Avenue *was* the pits). Beyond that, to the northeast, was the two-story building of earth-colored brick and Tuscan columns, Wellington Hospital. To the southwest was the spire of St. Stephan's, smack in the Hungarian neighborhood. His mother bypassed St. Grobian's, the Irish church, to attend St. Stephan's even though she had to walk an extra mile.

Looking north again, Jim could see the dome of City Hall. Lots of action there, most of it dirty, if what Sam Wyzak's drunken uncle, a judge, said was true.

And straight north went Pitts Avenue, ending at the foot of Gold Hill. Up above, so high in the sky, were the homes of the kings and queens of Belmont City. While they sipped their martinis and counted their money, they could look down on the rabble, the proletariat, the salt of the earth, those who would inherit, not trust funds but the earth, that is, the dirt itself.

What made Jim's father especially angry about Gold Hill people was that his wife worked there. Her job was only part-time, and the wealthy did not pay much (the tight-assed skinflints!), but the money was better than none. Eva Nagy Grimson was employed by a small company to houseclean on Mondays, Wednesdays, and Fridays. Eric's unemployment checks had long ceased to come in. Reluctantly, Eric had applied for and gotten welfare. He was of a generation that regarded welfare as shameful. He also believed that a wife should not work. The husband was humiliated if she did. He was a failure as a man and a provider.

Jim could understand why his father writhed with shame and despair and frustration. But why did he have to take it out on his wife and son? Did he think they liked the mess they were in? Were they responsible for the bad things in their lives?

Why did his father spend the precious money his wife made on booze? Why didn't he just up and pull anchor, leave the doomed house behind, take his family to California or some place where he could get a job? However, if he did that, he was up against his wife. She went along with everything he did, no matter how rotten it was, never complained or argued. Except once. When he had suggested leaving Belmont City, she had told him firmly that she would not obey him. She would not move away from the Nagy clan and their friends.

"Jesus Christ!" Eric had shouted. "If you got a Hungarian for a friend, you don't need an enemy!"

Jim and Sam were now two blocks from Central High, a huge old three-story redbrick building. At least, Jim thought, my body is two blocks from it. My mind, Jesus, where's my mind? All over the place. I got to get with it.

The day you were living in was the present. But the past was often with you, poking a sharp-nailed finger in the tissue of your brain and gouging out a piece, then pressing on a nerve to remind you that the bottom line of life was pain, then groping around other parts, feeling your dick, giving you a proctological examination, thumping your heart's naked flesh to make it beat like a hummingbird's wings, tying your intestines into a running sheepshank knot, vomiting hot acid into your stomach, whipping up nightmares with the blender of old Morpheus, ancient Greek god of sleep.

A title for a lyric. "The Dead Hand of the Past." Nah. A cliché, though that never stopped most rock lyricists. Anyway, the past was not a dead hand. You carried it with you like it was a living thing, a tapeworm. Or like Heinlein's parasitic slug from Titan, the ice-moon of Saturn, the slug growing tendrils in your back and sucking the life and brains out of you. Or like a fever no pills could cool down until you were cold-dead, and you didn't need pills then.

". . . trying to get a gig tonight, no soap," Sam was saying. "Got one Saturday night at the Whistledick Tavern out on Moonshine Ridge, but that's redneck territory, and we gotta play that godawful country-western. We might cancel. Anyway, we couldn't get one tonight, and my cup runneth over. Halloween's for fun. Remember how we pushed over old man Dumski's outhouse when we was fifteen? Maybe it was when we was fourteen. Anyway, remember how Dumski came out of his house screaming and shooting his shotgun? Man, did we run!"

"Sounds good," Jim said. "I'll call work and tell them I'm sick. I'll probably get fired, but what the hell."

CHAPTER

7

J ust before he and Sam joined the gang, Sam slipped him a stick of chewing gum. "Take it. You got a breath would knock down King Kong."

"Thanks," Jim said. "Must be the Polish sausage, too much garlic. Anyway, my stomach's upset."

Three guys were waiting for them. Hakeem "Gizzy" Dillard, a short chunky black suffering from yellow jaundice. Bob "Birdshot" Pellegrino, a big youth with a huge black walrus moustache and one glass eye. Steve "Goathead" Larsen. They gave each other five fingers, Jim noticing that the greeting only seemed a hundred percent natural when Gizzy did it. Goathead brought out a marijuana butt from which each took a puff while keeping an eye on the big front entrance for an appearance of Central's principal, Jesse "Iron Pants" Bozeman, or one of his teacher snitches.

"Hey, man, you hear about what Kiss did in that hotel room in Peoria?"

"I got an upper trade you for a downer."

". . . said Mick Jagger caught the clap from the mayor's wife . . ."

"The old man said, 'You get a Mohawk, I cut off your balls.'"

". . . think Lum'll spring a surprise exam today?"

". . . and I thought, You can drive the point of that I-saw-Cele's triangle all the way up your ass. Define it, shit, I can't even pronounce it. But I was cool. So, I told Mister Slowacki, geometry ain't my fortay. That's for Republicans, and my folks always vote straight Democrat."

". . . sent to Iron Pants's office again. But he wasn't there. Probably balling his secretary in the xerox room."

". . . so he says, 'I knew you was long, and I knew you was black, but where did you get them googly eyes?'"

"Man, I swear you wasn't my asshole buddy, I don't take those racist jokes. Lemme tell you about the white woman—a mouse ran up her snatch so she go see this black doctor. And he say . . ."

Chattering fast, seeming to talk out of both sides of their mouths at the same time, giggling, butt-slapping, shadow-boxing, the group danced into the front hall. Jim was silent, his only responses a grunt or a forced grin. The black beauty wasn't working the way it was supposed to. The guy who'd sold it to Sam must've cheated him. Probably had just a little Biphetamine in it. The rest of it was ground-up aspirin or something.

While on his way to his locker, he saw Sheila Helsgets leaning against the wall. She was talking to and smiling at Robert "Ram-'Em" Basing, a very big and very good-looking blond who was Central's foremost tackle and captain of the football and the rhetoric teams. A six-letter man. Lots of money, drove a Mercedes-Benz, and lived on Gold Hill. An A-minus average. A clear and tanned complexion. Naturally, he was pinned to Sheila, probably in more ways than one,

Jim thought. But reliable reports said he was cheating on her. He'd even been seen in a nightclub in the nearby city of Warren with Angie "Blow-Job" Calorick.

Seeing him pat the egg-shaped cheek of Sheila's ass made Jim want to puke.

He slammed his locker door shut with a big bang. Sheila looked away from Basing and at him. She quit smiling. Then she turned her head back to The Winner. She smiled again.

Shelia baby, you think he's Jesus H. Christ Himself! I'd like to crucify him, preferably with rusty nails that wouldn't be hammered through only his hands and feet. Wouldn't make any difference, though. She'd still look at me like I was a leper. "Unclean! Unclean!"

Jim sang softly to himself as he trudged down the hall toward Biology 201. It was his own creation, titled "Here's Looking Up at You."

> *Scruff me, scurve me,*
> *Deck me out with pimples and fleas.*
> *Feed me beans, then bitch about*
> *Gas a-boiling in your face.*
> *Step on me, and call me flat.*
> *Squeeze me dry, and call me husk.*
> *Say I got no class at all!*
> *Trip-hammer sky's ramming me down,*
> *Knocking the dandruff off my head,*
> *Thumpa-thumpa-thumping me,*
> *Drilling rock and liquid iron.*
> *Earthworms, moles, and buried bones,*
> *God, the Devil, Mrs. Grundy,*
> *Who's not looking down at me*
> *Spinning in the core of Earth?*
> *Any way from here is up.*
> *Can't believe that's not a lie.*
> *Every way looks down to me.*

Raunch me, sleaze me,
Rip my soul with taloned scorn.
Call me ragged, light a candle,
Say for me a ragged mass.
    Scruff me, scurve me,
Deck me out with pimples and fleas.

He followed Bob and Sam into the big classroom and took a chair in the rear row corner with the other losers. There was the usual loud talk, poking fun at each other, sailing paper airplanes, and throwing spitballs. Then silence and rigidity came down like a guillotine blade as the aged but not venerable Mister Lewis "Holy Roller" Hunks walked in. Grim and crusty and obnoxiously religious described Mister Hunks. Add to that that he was a creationist who was forced by law to teach evolution, though it was called "development," and you had one frustrated and miserable white-haired old man.

Hunks checked off the students present and absent as if he were taking the roll call on the Day of Judgment. After pronouncing each name, he looked up from behind very thick glasses. He grimaced when he spoke the name of a student he did not like, and he smiled thinly when he uttered the name of a student who was not going to Flunkers' Hell. He smiled three times.

Having designated a favorite student to carry a list of the absent to the principal's office, Hunks launched into today's lecture. It continued the previous lecture, which was on the reproductive system of the frog. Jim tried to listen intently and to take notes because the subject was interesting. But his stomach hurt, and he had a headache. To make conditions worse, Hunks managed to combine droning with a squeaky voice. Jim felt like he was on an oxcart with an unlubricated wheel going across a flat and treeless plain. The view was putting him to sleep, but the wheel was keeping him awake.

Sam Wyzak, who was sitting by Jim, leaned over and whispered, "I'm going to fall asleep. Whyn't you tell him he's full of shit? At least we won't be bored to death."

"Why don't you tell him?" Jim whispered back.

"Hell, I don't know nothing about this and couldn't care less. You're the expert. You start the fireworks. Old Sam just wanta make things jump. Geeve eet to heem!"

A silence in the room alerted Jim. He straightened up and looked at Mister Hunks. The old guy was glaring at him, and the students had turned their heads to look at him and Sam. Jim's heart felt like a squirrel thrown into a wheel-cage. It began running just to stay in one place. The thuds of its feet against metal were also drum signals. "Man, you done it now!"

"Well, Mister Grimson, Mister Wyzak," Hunks squeaked. "Would you mind sharing with us your private thoughts about the subject at hand?"

Jim said, "It was nothing."

His own voice was squeaky. He was angry because he had been caught, and he was angry with himself because he was afraid to speak out against Hunks. The old man would make a fool of him for sure.

"Nothing, Mister Grimson? Nothing? You two were disturbing me and the class because you were just making nonsensical noises? Or perhaps you were imitating the apes you claim you're descended from? Were you imitating ape calls, you two?"

Jim's heart beat even harder, and his stomach swung back and forth, sloshing acid from one end to the other. But, trying to look cool, he stood up. He also was trying to keep his voice steady.

"Well," he said. He paused to clear his suddenly phlegmed throat. "No, we weren't imitating ape language. We . . ."

"Ape language?" Hunks said. "Apes don't have a language!"

"Well, I mean . . . ape signals, whatever."

Sam whispered, "*Umgawa!*" He writhed with silent laughter.

"When your fellow simian recovers from his fit, you may continue," Hunks said. He squinted through his thick glasses as if they were a telescope and he, the astronomer, had just discovered some worthless asteroid that had no business being where it was.

Sam quit moving, but he was biting his lips to keep from exploding with laughter.

"Uh," Jim said, and he cleared his throat again. "Uh, I had some thoughts on what you just said, uh, that about life developing, no, I mean originating, in the primal soup, and its, uh, statical, I mean, statistical improbability. But I got to think more about that before I say anything.

"What I was thinking was about something you said last week. Remember? You, we, talked about why, for example, uh, dog embryos and human embryos were so similar. In the early stages of their development, anyway. You explained why human embryos have tails, that is, according to the theory of development. You evidently didn't believe that theory. Then you tried to explain why, uh, if the Creator made all creatures in just a couple of days . . . you said, you tried to explain why all male mammals have nipples even though they don't need them, why, uh, flightless insects have wings."

His throat felt dry. Hunks's grin was mean, mean, mean. The students were watching him. Some had tittered when he mentioned nipples.

"Also, why do snakes have rudimental . . . rudimentary . . . limbs when they never need them any more than males need nipples and insects that can't fly need wings? They wouldn't have nipples, limbs, and wings if they were

43

created in a single day. You said that the wings, nipples, and limbs were created for the sake of symmetry. The Creator was an artist, and It had to make Its creatures symmetrical."

Jim referred to the Creator as It because it bugged Hunks. Now his voice was stronger and deeper, and he was speaking without the awkward hesitations. He was on a roll. Devil take the consequences.

"That 'symmetry' explanation, if you'll pardon me, Mister Hunks, doesn't ring true. It doesn't seem to be logical. Anyway, I was thinking about it. Here's what I'd like you to explain to me, sir. If the Creator was so keen on 'symmetry,' why, on the day of Creation, didn't It make males who also had female genitals and vice versa? Why don't us men have vaginas, too, and why don't women have penises?"

Laughter from the students. Explosion from Mister Hunks.

"Shut up and sit down!"

"But, sir!"

"I said shut up and sit down!"

Jim should have been happy because he had triumphed. But he was shaking with rage. Hunks was just like his father. When he had lost in a battle of words, he refused to listen any more, and he evoked the gag law that adults used against children. It was unappealable to a higher court because Hunks was also that court.

Fortunately, the end-of-the-class bell rang just then. Hunks looked as if he was going to have a stroke, but he did not tell Jim to see him in his office that afternoon. Jim felt as if his own blood vessels were going to erupt. However, a few seconds later, as he walked down the hall, he began to feel exultance mixing with the rage. He had really given it to the old fart, the living fossil, the Ku Klux Klanner of Kristians.

Bob Pellegrino and Sam Wyzak were walking with him through the crowd of students. Bob said, "It don't matter if you win every argument with that dirty old man. He's gonna flunk your ass."

Jim understood the description of Hunks. To the young, anybody over sixty was dirty. No matter how physically clean the old were in actuality, they were dirty because they were close to death. Old Man Death was the ultimate in filthiness, and anybody in his neighborhood was deeply soiled.

There was also something that Jim could not know then and would not know until much later. That was that Hunks was much closer to the truth than the evolutionists.

CHAPTER

8

Lunch hour came. Jim had no money to buy food, and his anger had subsided enough for him to feel very hungry. Sam Wyzak split his lunch with him, and Bob Pellegrino gave him half a tuna fish sandwich and half a pickle. Jim cooled off even more during Mister Lum's course in Advanced English and Composition. This was the only subject in which he had a B average. Well, pretty close to a B. A few A's on the compositions he was going to write, and he would get a B average. But if Jim didn't ever master the difference between a dangling participle and a dangling particle, he wouldn't pass the course.

"Knowing that won't help you become a better writer, and you'll never use that item of academic knowledge," he had said. "However, it's not so hard to understand, and you're not a moron, no matter what your other teachers say. I'm not going to pass you until knowledge of the difference is embedded in your bones. Now, I'm not current with the latest discoveries in physics. What the hell is a dangling particle?"

After biology class, Jim and Sam headed for the rest room. They went past the elderly guard outside the room and entered. The place was busy, noisy, and stinking. There, leaning against the wall by the washbowls were Freehoffer, "The Blob," and his buddies, Dolkin and Skarga. They were passing around a roach as if they didn't give a damn if the guard caught them, and they didn't. Freehoffer was huge, six feet four, close to three hundred pounds, double-chinned, balloon-bellied, pig-nosed, and weasel-eyed. His blue-black facial hair should have been shaved three days ago. A ponytail bound his black greasy hair. Egg yolk stained his red-and-black striped shirt.

Dolkin and Skarga were both short but very wide, and their yellow-brown hair looked like viper nests.

Freehoffer and his buddies would have been shaking down his victims, mostly scared freshmen or nerds, if the room hadn't been so crowded. Jim had been forced to give them money at least a dozen times during his four years at Central. But this year he had never been caught alone in the rest room by them, and the last time he had coughed up his change for them, he had told Freehoffer, "Never again!"

Having eased themselves at the urinals, Jim and Sam started to leave the room. Freehoffer stuck a foot out and tripped Jim, who fell forward and banged his head against the exit door. The pain was a hammer blow on a detonator. Jim yelped and, cursing, straightened up, turned around, and swung with his right fist. He did not think about what he was doing; he was scarcely aware that he was doing it. His fist sank into the big belly. Freehoffer's laughter became a deep grunt, and he doubled over.

A surfer of rage carried on by a red wave, Jim brought his knee up against The Blob's chin. The Blob fell on the tiled floor, but he got up on all fours. Jim snarled, "Don't ever touch me again, Pus-Face!"

Sam said, "Let's get going, Jim!"

Freehoffer got to his feet. "You won't get away with this, shithead!"

Dolkin and Skarga started to move in. Sam tugged on Jim's arm. "For Christ's sake, let's get outa here!"

"This ain't the place!" Freehoffer bellowed. "But if you're a real man, Grimson, you'll meet me back of Pravit's after school's over! You won't get no chance to hit me when I ain't looking! I'll beat you to a bloody pulp if you got the guts to stand up to me, and I don't think you got 'em!"

Jim started to shake, but he said, "Fair fight? Man to man? Fists only?"

"Yeah! Fair fight! Fists only! I don't need nothing except my fists to stretch you out, you spindly little fruitcake!"

"I don't like to dirty my hands on you, but I'll do it, you heap of shit," Jim said. With Sam behind him, he swaggered out of the rest room.

"Jesus Christ, man!" Sam said. "What got into you?"

"I just won't take any more of his shit!"

"You must be mad at everybody and everything," Sam said. "You ain't thinking straight. You know he ain't going to fight fair, and Dolkin and Skarga'll be there to jump on you, too."

"What'd you do if you were in my place?" Jim snarled.

"Me? I wouldn't show, no way. I'm not crazy!"

"You gonna be there, or you gonna let me take them on by myself?"

"Oh, I'll be there," Sam said. "I won't let you down, old buddy. But I better tell Bob and the others about this. The more the better. You'll need backup. I'll bring a brick, too. But this is crazy!"

By the time that school was out, the entire student body seemed to know about the scheduled fight. Jim was still mad but not so much that he was not also scared. Sam's advice to stand The Blob up instead of standing up to him was making more sense. But he was not going to back out now. Everybody would think he had a yellow streak down his back.

Pravit's Confectionery and Drugstore was a block away from the high school. Trailed and preceded by students, Jim went down the alley along the side of the store and then went a few paces along the alley behind the old redbrick building. With him were Wyzak, Pellegrino, and Larsen. Jim had hoped that Freehoffer would be a no-show. No. There was The Blob, leaning against the wall near the back door, a toothpick in his blubber lips, seeming most nonchalant. By his side stood Dolkin and Skarga.

"There's the rest-room mugger, the bully of the crapper!" Jim called out. His voice started out loud and firm enough, but it cracked near the end of his sentence. He stopped a dozen feet from Freehoffer while the crowd shifted around to form a semicircle. Jim's three cronies stood just behind him.

The Blob sneered. He said, "Sticks and stones, big mouth." He continued to lean against the wall.

Jim dropped his book bag, screamed, and ran forward. Freehoffer straightened up, his eyes wide. Jim ran and then launched himself. He had seen karate fighting in many movies but had never practiced any. This was a first-time, all-or-nothing effort, do or die. His body came close to leveling out as he slammed the bottom of his shoe into Freehoffer's nose. He had tried for the chin, but his aim was off. Not so bad, though. The Blob's head snapped back, and he staggered against the wall. Blood gushed from his nostrils.

Then Jim fell straight backward, tried to twist, but fell heavily on his side. Pain shot through his shoulder. The wind was knocked out of him. Despite this, he was up on his feet and charged Freehoffer with his head down. He drove it into the big belly. More pain lanced through him, but down his neck this time.

Freehoffer gasped. Blood ran down his face, and he bent over, clutching his belly. The attack had caught both him and his buddies by surprise. Dolkin and Skarga, however, unfroze and jumped on Jim, who still had not gotten his wind back. Sam Wyzak, though fight-shy, did not hold back once he got into a battle. He brought out from under his jacket a brick. He slammed it against the side of Dolkin's head. Dolkin went down onto his knees, a hand clamped to the injured part. Skarga brought his fist out of the pocket of his jacket. Brass knuckles gleamed as he pulled his arm back to drive them into Jim's ribs. Bob Pellegrino stepped in and slammed a fist against the side of Skarga's jaw. Sam hit Skarga on his shoulder with the brick. Skarga went down, yelling with pain, then tried to crawl away into the crowd. Pellegrino kicked him hard in the butt. Steve Larsen jumped on Skarga and bore him all the way to the ground.

The Blob had a lot of flesh to absorb the damage done to him. He was far from being out of the fight. Bellowing, he lunged forward, drove into Jim, locked his arms around him, and carried him down to the hard black pavement. Since Jim had his arms free, he was able to strike Freehoffer as they rolled around, though not effectively. When The Blob bit him in his stomach, Jim cried out, but the pain gave him strength to tear himself loose. He was still on his back when Freehoffer rose to his feet and drew a foot back to kick Jim.

Jim kicked first. His foot slammed into The Blob's crotch. Yelling, holding his testicles, Freehoffer fell forward. Before he hit the ground, he gushed yellow vomit. Jim rolled away and escaped the crushing weight of the near three hundred pounds. But the puke showered his hair and the left side of his face and body.

He got to his feet. Then the stench and the feel of the stuff sticking to him and the thought that it came from The Blob's belly made him retch. Bent over Freehoffer, he sprayed him in the face with his own vomit.

Some of the spectators were delighted. Others got nauseated, and a small number of these threw up. Their example caused more to puke. But neither the enjoyers nor the loathers had much time to express their reactions. Nearby sirens announced the coming of the cops. Most of the crowd hurriedly left the scene.

CHAPTER

9

As a black-and-white squad car pulled into the alley, Freehoffer croaked out his threats between sobs and long-drawn-in breaths.

"I'm going to get you! I'll use the old man's shotgun, Piss-Face! I'll blow out your crazy queer brains, then I'll jam the Polack's brick up his ass before I blow off his head, too!"

Dolkin and Skarga had fled. Bob Pellegrino and Steve Larsen had reluctantly left after Jim had told them it made no sense for them to stay to face the music. Sam, however, had refused to desert Jim.

"Bullshit!" Jim said. He was breathless, too, though not nearly as much as Freehoffer. "You've had it, puke-face! Your reign of terror is over! Anytime I see you extorting money from some scared kid, I'm going to jump you, right then and there! I'll beat the piss out of you!"

He was shaking so much that his muscles seemed to be trying to tear themselves loose from his bones. Yet he still felt as if he were riding a gigantic surf wave. It was lifting him up and up, and when he reached the crest, he would soar off into the wild blue yonder. The fight had spurted out much of the rage and the urge to do violence that had possessed him all day.

The cops came then, strolling up slowly, looking around but grinning. They were relieved that they did not have to handle a riot. Jim thought that whoever had reported the fight had exaggerated. Old man Pravit? Maybe. In any case, the police department was understaffed and overworked, like every other department in money-poor Belmont City. It was a wonder that any police car had shown up.

It was good that Sam had not gone with the others. The cops recognized his name. One of them knew that Sam was the nephew of Stanislaw Wyzak, a night court judge, and of John Krasinski, an alderman. The two patrolmen treated the whole incident as just a heated argument among high school kids.

Normally, the cops would have spread-eagled them against the wall and frisked them. But they did not want to get the stinking mess on their hands or, indeed, come any closer to Grimson and Freehoffer than they had to. Nor could they get out of the youths the true story of what had caused the brouhaha. Jim refrained from telling them about Free-hoffer's extortions and his threats to kill him and Sam. The Blob evidently wanted to accuse Jim of all sorts of things, but he, too, abided by the unwritten law: Don't tell the fuzz nothing about nobody. Though the cops knew that they were being lied to, they did not care. If they let the three go with a warning, they would avoid paperwork and getting in Dutch with Judge Wyzak and Alderman Krasinski. However, they added, this incident would have to be reported to the boys' parents.

In effect: Go, children, and sin no more. And for Christ's sake wash your clothes and take a bath. Haw! haw!

Just before the cops left, one of them scowled and said, "Grimson? Where've I heard . . . oh, yeah . . . I think I hauled your old man in one night on a drunk and disorderly. But there's something else. Oh, yeah! Didn't I read a couple of years ago about you? Something to do with some strange visions and you bleeding in your palms and forehead. It made quite a to-do, didn't it? Some people thought maybe you was a saint, and others thought you was touched in the head."

"That was years ago. I was just a kid then," Jim said sourly. "Everything's cleared up since then. Anyway, it didn't mean much. The paper exaggerated. Anything to get news."

He had a flash of the doctor who'd examined him after the stigmata came. Old Doc Goodbone, believe that name or not. "It's just his overactive imagination coupled with a tendency to hysteria," the physician had told his mother. "The weird things he saw, the stigmata, they're explainable, and not by the introduction of supernatural elements. Not common, these cases, but there have been many such reported in medical journals. It's all psychological. The mind can do strange things. Even the bleeding, which seems purely physical, can be produced by the mind. Especially by the minds of children and adolescents and hysterical women. Little Jim will probably get over this, be quite normal. We'll just have to keep an eye on him. Don't worry."

His mother should have been relieved and probably was. But she was also disappointed. She had been convinced that the visions and the stigmata were God's signals that he was destined to be a saint.

The cop made them promise that they would not start fighting again and that they would go home immediately. A call came in, and the fuzz left hurriedly. Freehoffer looked as if he would like to keep threatening Jim and Sam, but he shambled away down the alley. Jim looked for his book bag. It was gone.

"For God's sake, what next?" he cried. "Someone stole it! The books . . . I'll have to buy new ones!"

That was going to make his father even madder. It had been hard enough to get the money for the textbooks at the beginning of the semester. Eric Grimson would have more to raise hell about than just the fight. And Eva Grimson would have to take the purchase money out of what she brought home from her cleaning job. No. His father would insist that his son pay for it. Where would he get the cash?

Did bad things never end?

Jim's mother was still working up on Gold Hill when Jim arrived home. But his father was waiting for him. He began yelling at him to get his clothes into the washer in the basement and to take a shower. Right now. The shock of the shower might kill him, but Jim and the world would be better off then. Jim tried to tell him why he got into the fight. Eric Grimson paid no attention to his explanation. He stood at the top of the basement stairs while Jim shucked off his clothes and put them in the old washer.

"That'll take extra soap and water and gas heat and run up the bills, and they're high enough now, though I can't say you generally raise the water bill much," Eric said. "Maybe I should look at this as a God-given chance to force you to take a shower."

Jim waited until he had put on clean clothes before he decided to tell his father about the stolen books. But, when he reluctantly left his room, he found that his father was not around. Eric Grimson had gone some place, probably five blocks away to Tex's Tavern. He'd be spending the money on booze that he could have used to buy the schoolbooks. That reminded Jim that he had forgotten to call in to the fast-food place where he worked. If he told the manager he was

sick—which he had done too many times—he would probably be fired.

Well, so what?

It wouldn't be easy finding another job, that's what.

But he had promised Sam that he would go Halloweening
tonight, and he did not want to miss out on the fun.

If he could get his mother to one side, away from his
father, he might get pocket change from her. She'd dredge it
up from some place; she almost always did. However, he
knew how hard it was for her to do that. Though she would
not complain, her big sad eyes, her air of suppressed
reproach, disappointment, and defeat would make him feel
like a bum, a parasite, a bloodsucker, a failure, and a really
rotten son.

Her silence and her quiet manner made him feel far worse
than his father's ravings and rantings. At least he could blow
off steam when he argued with his father. But her unwill-
ingness to fight frustrated and wore him out. A termite must
feel that way when it was chewing merrily along in wood
and then ran slam-bang into iron.

The house was quiet except for a slight groan or a very
faint murmur now and then. Those could be the voices of
small shiftings of earth in the tunnels and shafts below. They
were warning the heedless humans above of the coming big
collapses. Or were they, as in the poem "Kubla Khan" by
Coleridge, "ancestral voices warning of war"? Or trolls
working away in the abandoned coal mines so they could
hasten the ruin of Belmont City's houses?

Man, I'm a case, Jim thought. My brain is like a bullet that
missed its target. It richochets all over the place, envisions a
hundred scenarios where only one could be real. I'm cut out
to be a writer or a poet, not a garage mechanic.

He sat in a chair in the living room. He faced the fake
fireplace and the mantel, which held two glass balls with
Christmas scenes inside (turn the balls upside down and

then right side up and snow fell on the little houses and people therein), statuettes of the Virgin Mary and St. Stephan, two incense candles, a can of furniture polish spray, an ashtray with a pile of cigarette stubs, and a music box on top of which was a circle of white-clad but nicotine-stained ballet dancers.

On the wall above the mantel was a large photograph of Ragnar Fjalar Grimsson, Jim's dearly beloved grandfather, dead for eight years now. Though Ragnar was smiling, he looked as fierce as his namesake, the legendary Viking king, Ragnar Hairy Breeches, whom he claimed to be descended from. His white and bushy beard fell to below his chest. His white eyebrows were as thick and as splendid as God's must be (if there was a God), and the blue eyes were as penetrating as the edge of a Norse pirate's war ax. When the old man had died, his son, Eric, had taken down the big painting of Jesus, despite his wife's pale protests, and had put up the picture of his father.

It was, Jim had thought, a satisfactory substitute.

The old Norwegian was a real man. A far voyager on sea and on land, an adventurer, tough, no complainer, a go-getter, largely self-educated, a wide reader, afraid of nobody and of no thing, a quoter of Shakespeare and Milton and of the old Scandinavian sagas, yet one who enjoyed the cartoon strips and who had read them to Jim before Jim could read, stubborn, convinced that his way was the only way but with a sense of humor and wit, and also convinced that most of the present generation were degenerates.

It was a good thing old Ragnar had died. He'd be deeply disgusted with his son and even more so with his grandson. As for Ragnar's daughter-in-law, Eva, he'd never liked her, though he had always treated her politely. She was scared of him, and he scorned people he could scare.

His grandfather had at first been disturbed by Jim's visions and dreams and stigmata. After a while, he had decided that these were not necessarily signs that Jim was mentally sick. Jim had been touched by the Fates, who gave him second sight, a gift the Scotch called "fey." Jim could see things invisible to others. Though the old man was an atheist, he did believe, or professed to believe, in the Norns, the three Fates of pagan Scandinavia. "Even today, out in the rural and forest areas, you'll find Norwegians who believe in destiny more than they do in their Lutheran God."

His grandfather had taken Jim's small hands in his huge and work-gnarled hands. He held them up so that the faint whitish marks on Jim's fingernails shone in the light. Jim was keenly aware of them and somewhat shy about people seeing them. But Ragnar said, "Those are the marks the Vikings called Nornaspor. They've been given to you by the Norns as a special sign of their favor. You're lucky. If the marks'd been dark, you'd be cursed with bad luck all your life. But they're white, and that means you're going to have good fortune most of your life."

Destiny. Mister Lum had said more than once in English class, "'Character determines destiny.' That's a quote from Heraclitus, ancient Greek philosopher. Remember that, and live by that. 'Character determines destiny.'"

That had deeply impressed Jim. On the other hand his grandfather thought that character was given you by destiny. Whatever the truth, Jim knew that he had been doomed to be a loser. Never mind what old Ragnar had said about Nornaspor. Jim Grimson was a hopeless case, everything a hero was not. As the school psychologist had told him, he had low self-esteem, could get along only with a few of his peers, all as messed up as he was, couldn't relate to his superiors, hated authority in whatever form it took, had no drive to succeed, and was, in short, without brakes and on the steep road to hell. Having said that, the psychologist had added that Jim did have great potential even if his character was chaotic and self-defeating. He could pull himself up by his bootstraps. And then the psychologist really piled on the crap.

Jim sighed. For the first time, he became aware of something wrong with his surroundings, something maybe not so wrong as missing. It took him a minute to realize that he was enveloped in silence. No wonder he had been feeling uneasy.

He went to the kitchen and turned the radio on. WYEK was into "The Hour of Golden Oldies" and was playing "Freak Out," the 1965 album in which Frank Zappa made his debut with the Mothers of Invention. Jim had been three then, ages ago.

Before the album was finished, Eric Grimson came home. And the gates of hell opened.

10

At 6:19, an hour after sunset, Jim raised his bedroom window and crawled out. Thirty minutes ago, he had eaten the supper stealthily given him by his mother.

Eva Grimson had arrived a few minutes before her husband came home and had started cooking supper. She had asked Jim to turn the radio down, and he had done it. He had said nothing about his troubles that afternoon. Eric Grimson had reeled in at half past five, red-faced and breathing fumes that would've floored a dragon. The first thing he had done was to turn the radio off, yelling that he didn't want that damn crap on when he was in the house. Then, of course, he had started in on Jim. Eva had been confused about it all until her husband told her of the telephone call he had gotten from the police about Jim's fight with the Freehoffer kid and the pukey mess on his clothes.

One thing led to another—didn't it always?—and very quickly father and son were shouting at each other. His mother, facing the stove, her back to them, her shoulders slumped, said nothing. Now and then she quivered as if something inside her had bitten her. Finally, Eric had commanded his son to go to his room. He sure as hell wasn't going to get supper, he added.

Presently, silence settled throughout the house. Jim took a tattered and yellow-paged paperback, Mary Shelley's *Frankenstein*, from a shelf and tired to read it. Reread, rather. He was in the mood for this story about the monster made of dead human parts, the doomed outsider hated by all humans and hating all humans, the rejected, the killer of the natural-born and the would-be killer of his maker, a man who was in a sense his father.

But the godawful old-fashioned prose style had always tended to throw him off. It certainly did now. He dropped the book on the floor and roamed around the narrow room. After a while, the TV in the living room began blaring. Eric Grimson was sitting there, a beer in his hand, watching the boob tube. A few minutes later, Jim heard a knock on the door. He opened it and saw his mother holding a tray with supper on it.

"I can't let you go hungry," she whispered. "Here. When you're done, put it under the bed. I'll get it . . . you know."

He said, "I know. Thanks, Mom," and he leaned over the tray as he took it and kissed her sweaty forehead.

"I wish," she said, "I wish . . ."

"I know, Mom," he said. "I wish, too. But . . ."

"Things could be . . ."

"Maybe, someday . . ."

When they did talk to each other, they usually spoke in fragments. Jim did not know why. Perhaps it was because the pressures on them broke off their sentences. But he just did not know.

He closed the door and devoured the mashed potatoes and gravy, the fried ham, the beans, the celery, and the black

Hungarian bread. After hiding the tray under the bed, he sneaked down the hall and used the bathroom. And, about an hour after sunset, he crawled out of the window. If his father discovered that he was gone, too bad.

The air temperature had warmed up to the seventies in the late afternoon but had by now plunged into the upper fifties. Though the stiff western breeze had softened somewhat, it was still strong enough to make the air nippy. Clouds had begun to form. The half-moon was draped in thin fleece. It was a good night for Halloween.

He ducked down when he passed the living room window. The TV was still blaring. When he got to the sidewalk, which was well lit by a streetlamp, he saw that the cracks in the cement had widened. He did not know when this had occurred, but it seemed to him that they were broader and more numerous than when he had entered the house. However, he had been too agitated then to pay heed to them.

Here came a group of trick-or-treaters, children costumed as witches, demons, Klingons, skeletons, ghosts, Draculas, Frankenstein's monsters, robots, Darth Vaders, and a single punk—painted face, earrings, and Mohawk, probably his parents' idea of a real monster. One kid, however, wore a giant naked brain. That seemed right-on to Jim. The true horrors of this world were spawned in the human mind.

Since the group was heading toward his house, Jim walked faster. Though his father would not be answering the doorbell, his mother might see him when she came out to the porch to drop a Hershey's Kiss apiece into the sacks held out by the kids. (This neighborhood was slim pickings.) She would not say a word to her husband about it unless he asked her if she'd seen their son. Then she'd feel compelled to tell the truth. Otherwise, the saints, not to mention the bogeymen, might get her.

Sam Wyzak was waiting for him on the front porch of his

house. He was smoking a cigarette, which meant that his mother must be busy in the back of the house and wouldn't see him. Sam's father, unlike Eric Grimson, would be dropping candy into the kids' sacks. He'd be bitching because it interfered with his TV-watching, but he'd do it. He didn't give a damn if his son smoked as long as it didn't make any trouble for him.

Sam gave Jim a cigarette, and they walked down the street talking about the fight with The Blob and his buddies. Then Sam slipped Jim an upper. Jim felt more than just an upsurge of spirits and nerves. The drug hit him in the center of his brain like an atomic missile striking dead on target. He had never been hit so suddenly or with so much force by so little. He was abnormally wide open, the walls broken, the army in the castle sound asleep.

He was able a few days later to recall slices of what happened in the next six hours. The rest of the nightmare pie was gone, eaten up by the black beauties, marijuana joints, beer, whiskey, and angel dust his friends had given him. Until then, no matter how tempted, he had always refused even to try dust. It had sent three of his friends into convulsions and then fatal comas. But the deluge of the lesser drugs and the booze had washed away his fear.

Jim and Sam went first to Bob Pellegrino's house. Here they waited until Steve Larsen and Gizzy Dillard came, then drove away in Bob's 1962 Plymouth, which, for a wonder, was running. On the way to Rodfetter's Drive-In, Bob opened a fifth of moonshine "white mule." Steve provided a six-pack of Budweiser he had gotten his older brother to buy for him. Half of the liquor and all of the beer was consumed by the time that, whooping and yelling, they got to the drive-in. A joint was half gone by then, and each had swallowed a black beauty.

Rodfetter's was the hanging-out place, the "in" site, for the Central crowd whose parents were blue-collar workers.

Jim and his friends did a lot of horseplay and monkeying around there for several hours. They did not, unlike the other students there, do much carhopping. Outside of their small group, they had no friends or even close acquaintances. They were the pariahs, the untouchables, and the unbearables, and they claimed to be proud of it.

Jim did not remember just how long they were there. During this somewhat hazy time, he had smoked more joints and drank the warm beer Pellegrino produced from the trunk. Then Veronica Pappas, Sandra Melton, and Maria Tumbrille had shown up with some LSD. Veronica was the lead female singer for the Hot Water Eskimos; Maria, her understudy. Sandra was the rock group's manager. Her nickname was "Bugs," but her close friends used it only when she was not present. Sandy took offense when she heard it. Unless, that is, she was in one of her deep-blue, very deep and blue, depressions, lower than the mud at the bottom of the Pacific Ocean, farther out than the cold and dead planet, Pluto.

Tonight, she was in a way-out talkative and jumping-up-and-down mood.

Sometime during the evening, while they were sitting on the Plymouth's hood or leaning against it, Steve Larsen brought out some LSD in sugar cubes.

"I been hoarding this," he said. "Saving it for the right time. Tonight's the night, Halloween. We can go ride broomsticks with the witches, ride all the way to the moon."

Jim later remembered that he had said something about it being hallucinogenic, though he had trouble pronouncing it.

"I mean, it gives you visions, makes you see the fourth-dimensional worlds, things that aren't there, scary things, all of space and time at once. I don't need that. I get visions naturally, and I don't like them. No, thanks."

"It ain't like heroin and cocaine," Steve said. "It don't hook you, ain't habit-forming. Anyway, you ain't had them visions for years."

"Oh, well, why not?" Jim had said. "What've I got to lose besides my mind, and I don't have one, anyway."

"It's a ticket to heaven," Steve said. "I never been there, but this shit'll take you to a place even better."

"All the way around the universe faster'n light, so they say," Pellegrino said. "Coming back you meet yourself going."

Jim ate the cube and then inhaled deeply from a brown stick. They passed it around until it was a short butt. Steve put it in his jacket pocket.

It must have been after that that someone suggested they drive out to old man Dumski's apple orchard and push over his outhouse. It was an old Halloween tradition that the ramshackle wooden crapper be turned over. Or that an attempt be made to do so since not many had succeeded. The orchard farm had been in the county. But, as Belmont City spread out, it had annexed the area around it.

Dumski's was at the end of a dirt road that led for half a mile from the main highway. It was surrounded by a barbed wire fence. The house had burned down years ago. Dumski lived alone in the barn. The city had been trying for some time to make him build a house, one which would have indoor plumbing and a flush toilet. But the old recluse had defied the city authorities and taken them to court.

He had a huge dog, a rottweiler, one of that black-and-tan, huge-headed, sinister-looking, and terrifying breed used in the film *The Omen*. The brute roamed the farm area day and night and was only tied up when harvest time came. Since Dumski had gotten the dog, nobody had trespassed on his land.

"Anybody got downers?" Jim had said. "Put a bunch in a hamburger and feed it to the dog. He falls asleep, then we go in."

Those were the last words of good sense uttered that night. Bob Pellegrino purchased a big hamburger, hold the onions. He put a dozen downers in the bun, rewrapped it, and they were off, eight jammed into the Plymouth like circus clowns in a trick car, giggling and screaming while WYEK lobbed the barrage of "A Day in the Life" throughout the car, its quicksilver shrapnel shells exploding inside their young souls. The Beatles had sung that thirteen years ago, shook the world with it in the primeval rock-dawn when Jim had been only four years old. Bob "Guru" Hinman, the ancient disc jockey who loved the hoary old stuff (so did Jim) would be playing next Chuck Berry's "Maybellene," which Guru claimed had started rock 'n roll.

Veronica sat on Jim's lap in the back seat. He was to remember vaguely that she was messing around with his fly but not what happened when she opened it. Probably nothing. He had not had a hard-on for two weeks, that's how depressed he had been. And he was supposed, at seventeen, to be at the peak of his sexual drive.

Dumski's apple farm was on the other side of Gold Hill. It took about twenty minutes to get there because of all the red lights they hit, though Bob went through some. Then they were on the highway. The headlights showed trees on both sides. There was no oncoming or passing traffic. Jim kept waiting for the hallucinations, but they did not come. Or were they already here? Maybe this mundane Earth was the basic hallucination?

Bob slowed the car down but not quickly enough. They had passed the turnoff road to Dumski's. After Bob had backed the car up and got it heading down the dirt road, Sandy said, "Hadn't we better turn the radio off? It's loud enough to wake up the dead!"

They all protested because Bob Dylan was in the middle of "Desolation Row," and they wanted to hear it to its end. They compromised by turning the volume down. As soon as the classic song was over, Bob turned the set off. A moment later, he turned the headlights off. The moonbeams coming through gauzy clouds and gaps between them were enough to show them their way.

The car moved slowly out of the tree-lined and shadowy roadway and stopped in front of the gate in the barbed wire fence.

CHAPTER

11

Jim did not remember much of what had happened since they had been at the drive-in. Many details were long afterward given by Bob Pellegrino, who had not boozed and drugged it up as much as the others because he was driving. But he was not in what could be called a chemically unsaturated state.

The barn loomed dark and sinister in the intermittent moonlight. If Dumski was inside, he either had no lights on or the shutters fit tightly over the windows. There was neither sight nor sound of the rottweiler. The outhouse, said to be a three-holer, was an indistinct shape about eighty feet from the barn and to the left of the group. It had been somewhat distant from the house, the remains of which were a tumulus. Old Dumski had to trudge a long way to use the outhouse.

They piled out of the car. Bob had cautioned them to be quiet, but Gizzy slammed the door after getting out of the car. Before he could be reprimanded by Bob, Gizzy got sick. He went back down the road and into the woods so that the sounds of his vomiting would be muffled. Even so, they were too loud for Pellegrino, now the mother hen of the group. Just after he started to walk after Gizzy to tell him to pipe down, he stopped. A deep growl came from the darkness on the other side of the fence. That hushed the youths.

After a few seconds of looking around frantically, they saw the huge dog behind the gate. That it only growled and that it was such a shadowy shape made it more menacing. Pellegrino, murmuring, "Here, doggie! Nice doggie!" approached it slowly. When he got close to the gate, he threw the hamburger over it. It landed with a plop. A few seconds later, he turned and whispered, "He bolted it down."

Sandy Melton had added acid to the hamburger while they were on the highway. She had said something about wondering what kind of hallucinations a dog would have. Jim remembered that later because it had struck him as very funny. The dog kept on growling. Then, after a few minutes, the growls began to get weak. Presently, it started to wander away, staggering. Before it was thirty feet away, it collapsed.

The gate was bound with a heavy chain, the ends of which were secured by a big lock. Jim went over the gate, the top of which bore strands of barbed wire. He helped Pellegrino over, and they assisted Sam Wyzak and Steve Larsen over. All of them had bloodied hands but did not feel pain.

Sam said, "Holy Mother! The barn just turned into a castle! It's made of glass and diamonds, and it's shimmering in the moonlight!"

Nobody thought to tell him that there was, at that moment, no moonlight.

Jim was having no visual hallucinations, but he did feel as if his legs had stretched out, like the kid in the fairy story with the seven-league boots, and that he could reach the outhouse in one stride. He was distracted, though, because the girls refused to go over the gate. They could feel the barbs, and they had seen the rips in the boys' clothes. "Besides," Sandy Melton said, "who's going to take care of Gizzy? We might have to run like hell. We don't want to leave Gizzy behind."

"You're right," Bob said. "OK. This won't take long; we don't need you, anyway. You get Gizzy into the car."

The three boys walked along the gravel road running from the gate to the heap that had been the farmhouse. Before they got to it, they angled across toward the outhouse. Just as they reached the stench-emitting crapper, a break in the clouds flooded moonlight around them. They could even see the crescent carved in the door.

Jim was surprised that Bob, Sam, and Steve also had reached the structure with only one stride. They did not look as if their legs were elongated. Then Bob said, "Where's Sam?"

Jim turned to indicate Sam, who had been by his side. But Sam was no longer there. He was standing at a point halfway between the gate and the outhouse and was staring fixedly at the barn. Later, Jim would figure that he had just thought that Sam had walked all the way with him. Or had someone else, someone unknown, been at his side?

"OK," Bob said. "We don't need him. But don't forget to bring him along when we go back."

They went to the north side of the outhouse, and all three began pushing on it. The structure rocked back and forth but would not tip over.

"Man, it's heavier than my mother's doughnuts!" Bob said. "Listen up. We gotta get it oscillating, get it into the right frequency, then, when I give the word, all shove together hard as hell!"

They began rocking it again. Just as they finally heaved and the wooden shack toppled over, they heard a yell. They started to whirl to see who was making the noise. Then a shotgun boomed, and they heard pellets cutting through the leaves of a nearby tree. Steve, yelling, ran away. Pellegrino grabbed Jim when he fell backward. They screamed as, locked together, they hurtled into the hole and bounced off the slimy dirt wall and into the godawful excrement. They hit feet first and were quickly up to their necks in the loathsome stuff.

The shotgun boomed again. Faintly, Jim could hear the shrieks of the girls. Steve Larsen was no longer yelling. Jim and Bob screamed for help. For a second afterward, there was silence. Then he heard a growling. The next he knew, the dog was in the hole. It came down like a vengeance from the gods, landed right in front of Jim and Bob, splashed their heads and open mouths, came up like a cork, and began struggling.

Jim's toes touched the bottom or what he hoped was the bottom. Bob, who was taller, had his whole head sticking out from the muck. Jim was up to his chin. But the crazed dog knocked him back, and he went under again.

Later, Jim knew that the rottweiler had recovered somewhat from the drugs and run, or maybe walked, since it was still weak and dazed, to the hole. Not very alert yet, it had fallen, or maybe jumped, into the hole.

Now, he and Bob had to keep from being bitten by the dog—those powerful jaws had a 600-pound pressure—or being scratched by its flailing forefeet or being thrust under by its weight. They could see only very dimly because the moonlight did not reach to the bottom and their eyes were covered by the slime. Then Bob got sick and was vomiting, and that caused Jim to throw up also. The puke didn't make things any worse—nothing could—but it certainly did not help their situation. Moreover, it was very difficult to avoid the dog while heaving their guts out.

Finally, though weak from his efforts, Jim reached out and

grabbed the dog by its ears. Frenzied, he shoved its head under the surface.

At that moment, a flashlight shone from above, and a cracked old voice yelled at him.

"Leave the dog alone, or I'll shoot you! Don't touch him, you . . . !"

Jim did not understand the following words. Dumski had switched to Polish.

"Don't shoot, for God's sake!" Jim cried. He released the dog. It emerged, sputtering and growling, but it no longer tried to attack him. It had occurred to the dog that it had better save its strength to keep from drowning. Or to keep from choking to death. It dog-paddled furiously just to stay above the surface.

"Yeah, you damn fool!" Bob yelled. "You'll kill the dog, too!"

Pellegrino was not worried about the rottweiler, but he had wits enough to know that Dumski was in a terrible rage, out of his mind, if he did not think about what a shotgun blast in that narrow shaft would do to its occupants.

"Oh!" Dumski said. "Don't go away! I'll be gone for a minute."

"Sure. We'll just leave," Bob said. He groaned. "Oh, God, what a mess!"

It seemed like a long time before Dumski returned, though it must have been only two minutes. Puffing and panting, the old man kneeled at the edge of the hole. Then something struck Jim, not hard, across his face. He did not know what it was until Dumski shone the flashlight down on the rope he had dropped.

From far away but still loud enough to be heard over the screams of the girls came the wail of a siren. The cops were coming.

"Tie the rope around the dog!" Dumski said.

"How about us?" Bob shrieked.

"The dog comes up first!"

"Are you out of your mind?" Jim screamed. "How are we going to do that? It'll bite our hands off!"

"Get us out of here!" Pellegrino shouted. "I can't breathe! This stuff's choking me to death! I tell you, I'll die if I don't get out of here soon!"

"Serves you assholes right," Dumski said. "Tie the rope around the dog, then maybe I'll think about getting you out."

"We're gonna die!" Bob bellowed, then choked as a wave of excrement caused by the animal's struggles slapped him in the mouth.

"Get the rope around the dog!" Dumski shrieked. "Quick about it, or I'll leave you to die!"

That just could not be done without getting bitten. But the siren, which had been getting nearer, died. A door slammed. A man yelled something. Dumski muttered something and then was gone. Jim thought about shoving the dog under again. If it was dead, it would be easy to tie the rope around it. But Dumski would shoot them if the dog died.

Another stretch of seeming-forever passed. Then Jim heard voices approaching. Dumski had unlocked the gate and let the cops through it. Jim had never been glad to see the police before this; now, he was very happy. Never mind what was going to happen to him after he got out of the hole.

A flashlight held by a cop illuminated the hole. The cop laughed loudly for a while, then said, "For God's sake, Pete, look at this! You ever see such a sight!"

Pete looked down and laughed. "Man, you boys're in deep shit, and that's a fact!"

They went away with Dumski. After another long time, they came back with a ladder. They let it down and told Jim and Bob to climb up it. But the dog was between them and the ladder, and it would not allow them to get on it. Meanwhile, Dumski complained that the dog had to be gotten out, and, if the boys came out first, who'd tie the rope around it?

"We're not getting down there," a cop said. "You can go down and tie him up. But the kids gotta be got out first."

Dumski argued without success. The ladder was moved to the other side of the hole. Jim went up first. He was so weak and his hands were so slippery on the rungs that he had a hard time getting up. He had to drag himself out of the hole and onto the ground. The cops would not help him. Bob came up then and lay down, breathing hard, by his side. Old man Dumski, grumbling, went down the ladder after it had been moved back to the wall near the dog. Then the cops hauled up the rottweiler. When it tried to bite one of them before it was halfway out of the hole, it was dropped back into the mess. Dumski screamed at them that the splash had gotten him even filthier. Finally, the dog was hauled up again, the cops bitching about how disgustingly slimy the rope was. Dumski came up at the same time and pulled the dog off to the barn, where he hosed it off. The dog howled as the cold water struck it.

"You two better go over there and get hosed off, too," the cop called Pete said. "No way are you going to get into the squad car stinking like you do now."

Jim by now really did not care about anybody except himself. Sam was still in a trance, enthralled by the barn, the glittering Emerald City of Oz in his mind. The squad car had driven through the gate to a place near the barn. Its headlights shone on the huddled-together and forlorn-looking girls. Evidently Steve had escaped, and Gizzy had stayed in the woods.

Pete went to the squad car and called for backup. His partner, Bill, started Bob and Jim toward the barn so that they could be hosed off. Before they got there, the dog attacked its owner. The events of the night, plus its drug-dazed condition and its resentment of the cold water, had confused it. Or perhaps it knew that it was attacking Dumski. It may never have liked the old man.

The dog knocked Dumski over and fastened its teeth into his left arm. Dumski screamed as the jaws clamped down and its teeth struck bone and blood soaked through the sleeve of his jacket. The cops could not get the dog to let loose. They shot it dead. That made Dumski furious. He attacked the cops, who had to handcuff him before arresting him. Then Pete called for an ambulance.

Afterward, Bill hosed off Jim and Bob. They yelled with the shock and danced around, begging for mercy. None was given. Then Pete went inside the barn and got some towels for the boys so they could try to dry themselves off.

"We'll get pneumonia!" Pellegrino cried.

"You're lucky if that's all you get," Pete said.

CHAPTER

12

"**A** hell of a mess you got us into," Eric Grimson said.

His mother murmured, "Jim, how could you?"

He restrained his desire to say, "It was easy."

He was wrapped in a blanket and on the back seat of their 1968 Chevy. He had not stopped shivering since the cop had doused him with cold water. His father, out of pure meanness, had refused to turn the car heater on. Though Jim had sloshed water around in his mouth in the courthouse and had spit it out a dozen times, his mouth tasted of human excrement. Well, why not? He'd eaten shit all his life.

"It's a lucky thing for you that Sam's uncle is the night judge," Eric growled. "Otherwise, you'd be in jail."

"Juvenile hall," Jim said.

"What the hell's the difference?" Eric said loudly, gripping the steering wheel as if he wanted to tear it off the column. "It's just a station on the way to prison, anyway! I've known since you was twelve years old you was hell-bound for prison!"

"Please, Eric," Eva Grimson said softly. "Don't say that."

The car traveled through deserted streets and by dark houses. Halloween had long been over, and everybody had gone to bed even though, in this area, very few had work to go to in the morning. The time from when the cops had appeared at Dumski's to his release in his parents' custody had been long. After being frisked, he and his friends had had to walk a line to test their sobriety. Afterward, they were tested with a breath analyzer. All flunked. Two more tests which I couldn't pass, Jim had thought. Their rights were read, and they were handcuffed, jammed into two squad cars, and driven downtown. They had been in a holding cell for an hour before being marched to a room where blood and urine samples were taken. Jim's brain was fogbound but not so much that he did not realize that traces of the drugs would still be in his bloodstream.

An hour later, they were again taken to a holding room, and a half hour after that, they were in night court. The culprits' parents were also there, except for Sandy Melton's father, who was out of town. Jim's mother was weeping; tears dripped on her rosary beads as she told them. Eric looked hung over and very furious.

Sam's uncle was an old shriveled-up bald man with a long face and a big beaked nose with many broken veins. Those features and his long skinny neck, his whiskey-shot red eyes, his bald head, the black gown, and his hunched-over shoulders made him look like a vulture. However, Jim thought, the judge must have felt more like a canary who sees a cat. His nephew Sam was facing some serious charges: trespassing, destruction of private property, drunk and disorderly, under the influence of drugs, and breaking the curfew law. He was possibly involved in injury causing loss of a limb and, if Dumski died, aiding and abetting manslaughter. He could be charged with contributing to the dog's death. Dumski was in the hospital, and he might lose his arm.

These were not issues to take lightly. Judge Wyzak couldn't let his nephew and the other long-haired freaks off easy. But if he dealt with them as they really deserved, his sister-in-law, Mrs. Wyzak, would wring his neck. Not figuratively but literally.

The alleged culprits were minors, and that gave the judge a way out for the time being. He lectured them severely and then released them into the custody of their parents.

At least, Jim thought, possession of drugs and alcohol was not one of the charges. The girls had gotten rid of the bottles and capsules as soon as they heard the siren in the far distance. Sandy Melton had frisked Sam Wyzak, removed his pills, and tossed them into the woods. Jim had never had any drugs in his pockets, and Bob Pellegrino had dropped his while he was still in the outhouse hole.

After the judge dismissed them, Sam's mother had grabbed him by his ear and pulled him along behind her while he whined and windmilled one arm. Jim thought that she must think she was Aunt Polly and Sam was Tom Sawyer, for God's sake!

The car pulled up into the oil-stained gravel driveway by the house. "Home, sweet home," Eric Grimson said. "Ain't it something? An out-of-work crane operator, a Holy Roller Catholic cleaning houses for rich people, and a hippie loser who's stupid and crazy. I could stand the stupid if he wasn't crazy, and I could stand the crazy if he wasn't stupid. Now he's gonna be a jailbird. His bimbo sister's got two bastard kids whose father she can't name, and she's living in sin with a man old enough to be her father, a nut who makes a living reading palms and tea leaves and doing astrology charts!

We're living in a shack that's gonna drop all the way to China one of these days, not that I give a damn! Where did I go wrong, God?"

"God doesn't care for us pissants," Jim said as he got out of the car. He slammed the door hard.

His mother said, "Jim! Don't blaspheme. Things are bad enough."

"He's got a big foul stupid mouth, your son has!" Eric yelled. "Why in hell couldn't he have been one of your miscarriages?"

"Please, Eric," Eva said softly, "you'll wake up the neighbors."

Eric howled like a wolf. Then he said, "Wake 'em up? Who cares? They're gonna read about your son in the papers anyway, know all about us, as if they didn't already know! Who cares?"

Jim opened the side door. His father began chewing out Eva because she was supposed to have made sure that all the windows and doors were shut and locked. Jim turned in the doorway and said, "What's the difference? What do we have that's worth stealing?"

He went into the house, but his father stormed in after him and grabbed him by the shoulder. Jim lunged ahead and ran up the stairway to the hallway, leaving the blanket in his father's hand.

Eric shouted after him, "I might have something worth stealing if it wasn't for you and your mother!"

Jim ran into the bathroom, closed the door, and locked it. He brushed his teeth with the salt and baking powder from the rusty cabinet above the bowl. Then he cleaned his fingernails and shucked off his clothes, which were still wet. While his father stood in the hall by the door and yelled, now and then thumping his fist on the door, Jim showered. It took a long time for him to feel clean.

He did not turn off the water until it suddenly became cold. That would anger his father even more. He was always stressing the need to conserve on water and gas. At the same time, of course, he was always yelling at Jim to take a bath.

Despite the cooling-off effects of the shower, Jim still felt hot inside himself. If his anger could be seen, he'd be glowing in the dark. Everything had gone wrong today, like it did most days. Gone wrong? That was an understatement. It had been one humiliation after another. Shame after shame, failure after failure.

He stood in the fog-filled and warm room for a minute or so. As soon as he left it, he'd have his father on his neck. And, sure as cause and effect, he'd hit his father whether or not his father struck him first. The red cloud building up in him made that certain.

Reluctantly, he unlocked and opened the door. Eric Grimson was not there. Voices came from the kitchen along with the odor of coffee. His father's tones were subdued, and his mother's were barely audible. Maybe the old man had quieted down, though that did not seem likely. The furnace came on, its fans drowning out the kitchen noises. The heat struck Jim's legs. He was grateful for that since he had started shivering again as soon as he had left the muggy bathroom.

Naked, his damp clothes draped over his arm, he walked quickly to his room. He closed the door behind him, dropped the clothes on the floor, and went to the closet. Just as he reached into it to take his pajamas from a hook, he was startled by a loud bang. Whirling, he saw his father charging through the doorway. Eric's face was red, and his hands were clenched. Whatever had gone on in the kitchen, it had not pacified him.

"Get your clothes on!" he howled. "Don't you have no decency!"

The unfairness of the insult—after all, his father had burst in without asking permission—squeezed the anger in Jim down to a tiny hot ball. A little more heat, a little more pressure, and it would go up, out, and away. But it would take Eric Grimson with it.

"From now on, things're gonna be different!" his father yelled. "You'll either shape up or ship out, that's for sure! First thing . . . !"

He looked wildly around, then reached into his back pocket and brought out a jackknife. He opened the blade and began slashing at the posters of the rock groups and stars. Before Jim could yell in protest, he saw the Hot Water Eskimos being cut into strips. Then Eric attacked the poster of Keith Moon.

"All this shit's gotta go!" Eric screamed.

The red-hot ball exploded in white flame.

Shrieking, Jim jumped at his father, clamped a hand on his left shoulder, spun him around, and struck him in the nose. Eric Grimson staggered back against the poster, blood running from his nostrils. Jim hit him in the shoulder with his fist though he had meant to strike his chin. Eric dropped the knife and closed with his son. Face to face, wrapped in each other's arms, grunting, wheezing, they swayed back and forth.

"I'll kill you!" Eric screeched.

Jim screamed and tore himself loose. He leaped back. He was panting, his heart beating so hard that it seemed to him that it would tear itself apart. Then, piercing the drumming of blood in his ears, came the clicking of a lock. So loud was the sound, the lock had to be huge. The key turning in it also had to be gigantic. A groaning followed the clicking. It sounded like a very heavy door with rusty hinges being opened.

The floor dropped, the walls tilted, and books tumbled out

from the shelves. Jim and his father fell on the floor. They got up quickly, looking at each other with wide eyes. Plaster dust fell on them along with chunks. Jim saw them bounce off his father. The white dust covered Eric's head and shoulders and powdered the two streams of blood trickling down from his nose.

Eva Grimson screamed in the kitchen.

"Oh, my god!" Eric howled. "This is it!"

The house lurched again.

"Get out! Get out!" Eric shouted. He whirled and ran out of the room. He had to lean to one side to compensate for the slope of the floor. Even so, his shoulder struck the side of the doorway.

Jim began to laugh, and he kept on laughing. The house was going to fall deep into the earth. Maybe his parents would get out in time, maybe not. Whatever happened, it would come from fate, from the Norns. Justice and fairness had nothing to do with it. And he would stay here and go down with the ship. Let the earth gulp him down. It was better so, and it was also laughable.

Jim did not remember anything after that. He was told that his parents did get out of the house and scrambled across the front porch, which had been torn away from the main structure, and across the gapful yard and onto the sidewalk. But they then had to go across the street because the cement they were standing on was shoved even more upwards and made larger fissures. The house lurched and sank another foot. The neighbors on both sides of the Grimsons' house ran screaming from their leaning houses. The whole neighborhood came alive, lights going on, people coming out on the front porches and crying out questions, children being bundled up and put in cars for a quick getaway.

Sirens wailed in the distance as the police cars and the fire engines raced toward Cornplanter Street.

Eva Grimson began crying out that someone should go into the house and rescue her son. No one volunteered. Eric insisted, over and over, that Jim was just delayed because he was putting on his clothes. Eva said that Jim must be hurt, and he was probably trapped.

Just as the squad cars and fire engines and ambulances pulled up, Eva ran toward the house. Eric and two neighbors grabbed her and held her while she screamed and struck at them and begged them to let her go.

"You're a coward!" she said to Eric. "If you were a real man, you'd go after Jim!"

The lights had gone out in the house; the power lines had been torn from the house. Suddenly, two small lights appeared in the doorway. They were candles, one in each of Jim's hands, and they shed illumination on his wild face and naked body. He could not be seen below the knees, however. The house leaned so much that he had to stand on a floor which dropped steeply away from the bottom of the twisted doorway.

Jim shouted something unintelligible to the people across the street. He jumped up and down, waving the candles, which he had picked up from the floor in the room his mother used as a shrine.

Seeing these, Eva began struggling even harder. She shrieked, "The candles! The candles! They'll set the house on fire! He'll burn, burn, oh, my God, he'll burn to death!"

The cops and the firefighters had by then cleared away most of the crowd so that the engines could be moved closer to the house. A fire department lieutenant and a police captain questioned the Grimsons but got only hysterical and confused answers. They could, however, see Jim in the doorway.

"Nuts, completely off his rocker," the captain said.

Shortly after this, another light shone in the house.

"Fire! Fire! For God's sake, save him!" Eva cried.

That must have deepened her agony. The candles she had lit for the Holy Family and the saints were going to cause Jim's death and put him for eternity in the greater flames.

The firefighters had discovered by then that the pipe to the nearest fire hydrant had been broken by the shifting of the earth. They brought the water truck up close and attached their hoses to it. Meanwhile, the captain and the lieutenant had ventured as close as they dared. Using his bullhorn, the policeman was urging Jim to get out of the house.

The earth shrugged beneath the crowd. The beams in the house snapped with loud reports. The house slid down and tilted even more. Jim disappeared from the doorway, dropped down and backward. The spectators ran away.

"Son of a bitch!" the lieutenant said. "Someone's got to go in after the kid!" He looked around for likely volunteers.

The flames were getting big on the side of the house nearest the driveway. Smoke poured out and was caught by the wind. The house next to it was going to catch fire soon unless the hoses could stop it. And, since the gas lines to the house must be broken, the fire could cause a hell of an explosion.

The lieutenant could not see Jim Grimson, but it was evident that he was throwing objects through the doorway. The spotlights from the trucks showed him, a few seconds later, that these were statuettes of the saints and the Holy Family. Most of them were broken.

"The kid's crazy as a loon!" the captain said.

It was then that the name of Jim Grimson sparked the captain's recall. Pete and Bill had told him about the stoned-out and drunked-up youths who'd pushed over old man Dumski's outhouse and about two of them falling into the crap. Until now, the captain had failed to connect the hilarious incident with the people who owned this house.

"The kid's hopped up," he told the lieutenant. "I heard all about him earlier tonight. Maybe we should forget about him. He'll be better off if he doesn't make it."

The lieutenant looked reproachfully at the captain. He did not say anything, but he got what he was thinking across to the captain. No matter how worthless or vicious the subject was, he, she, or it had to be saved.

"Just kidding," the captain said. "But I'd sure hate to lose good men."

The lieutenant ordered that ropes and a ladder be brought out. He asked for volunteers and got four, from whom he picked two. One was a black fireman, George Dillard, Gizzy's father. He had long ago given up his hopes that his son would be a lawyer, and he knew Jim Grimson only too well. But he was brave. Moreover, if he rescued the kid, he would gain another handhold on the rung of the ladder to higher rank and pay. God knows he needed it, and if he had to put his ass in a sling to get it, he would. Black firepersons were not promoted very often despite affirmative action and equal opportunity quotas and all that. Not in Belmont City, anyway.

The man who accompanied him was a wild man of Irish descent who was eager to be in on the rescue attempt. The more dangerous it was, the better he liked it.

Ropes tied around their waists, the loose ends held by other men and two women, Dillard and Boyd moved across the broken yard. Their smoke masks made them look like two enormous insectine St. Francises on an errand of mercy. They could see that the insane youth inside the house was still throwing objects out through the front doorway—a coffee pot, coffee cups and drinking glasses, a skillet, table cutlery, a portable radio, albums of records, clothes, and photos.

By now, the flames were leaping from the side of the

house, though not from that part which was below ground. The hoses had been turned on it but, so far, without avail.

Before the two firemen got to the doorway, the barrage of stuff cast out of the house ceased. They could faintly hear the howling of Jim Grimson above the crackling of the fire, the sound of the water striking the house, and the cries of the spectators.

They halted when the ground moved again and the house dropped a few inches. Smoke suddenly billowed out of the front doorway and the windows, the glass of which had been shattered and fallen away. Dillard and Boyd did not have much time.

Jim was curled in the living room, holding the painting of his grandfather between his arms and his drawn-up knees. He was wedged in a corner formed by a wall, which was part floor now, and by the floor, which was part wall. His eyes were closed, but his mouth spat gibberish between fits of coughing. Smoke covered the white plaster dust on his body and face. A few more minutes of inhaling the smoke would have killed him unless the rapidly spreading fire had gotten to him first. As it was, he and his rescuers got out of the house only thirty seconds before the house fell inwards. Reduced in size suddenly, it disappeared entirely from sight. Flames and smoke leaped up from the hole. More than one spectator thought that it looked as if a gate to Hell had been opened.

Jim was rushed to Wellington Hospital. He did not recover consciousness for two days, though whether the smoke or his psychotic state, as the doctors called it, was responsible would never be known.

When Jim woke up, he remembered only one thing from the moment the house clicked and groaned. It was a vision, the first in many years. He had seen a tall and naked youth chained to a tree. He resembled nobody Jim had ever seen before. Just within the borders of this vision was a hand holding a huge silvery sickle. It did not move, but it was obviously threatening. It was destined to sweep up and then down, and Jim had no doubts about what it was going to cut off.

The sickle also looked to him like a giant question mark.

CHAPTER

13

November 9, 1979

Jim's wardroom wall now bore a large five-pointed star. Each arm was composed of five illustrated paperback covers taped to the wall. The topmost arm contained covers from Farmer's first book in the *World of Tiers* series, *Maker of the Universes*. The second, *Gates of Creation*, formed the horizontal arm on the left. Going counterclockwise, the next arm held covers from the third novel, *A Private Cosmos*. The next, *Behind the Walls of Terra* covers. The fifth arm of the star was formed by *The Lavalite World*.

This was to be Jim's third serious attempt to get into a Tiersian universe. The five-pointed star was his gateway. Most patients called their gateway a mantra. The others, a sigil. Tragil was Jim's name for his entrance device. By combining both symbols in a portmanteau word, he made it twice as powerful as an ordinary gateway.

It was half past eight in the evening. His room lights were out, but the insurance company building across the street provided a twilight strong enough for him to see the tragil. The door to his room was closed. Though it had no lock, it displayed on its hallway side a taped notice that he was "gating." He could hear, very faintly, Brooks Epstein chanting in Hebrew in the next room.

Jim sat in the chair that he had pulled up next to the bed. Staring at the vacant space in the center of the star, he also began chanting.

"ATA MATUMA M'MATA!"

Over and over, the words coming faster and faster and getting louder and louder, he launched the ancient vocal mantra at the center of the star, the round white blankness.

"ATA MATUMA M'MATA!"

Just as a laser structured wild-running photons into a channeled beam, so the chant arranged force lines as a blaster to open a hole in the wall between two universes.

It also was a carriage to transport the chanter through a universe.

He had not found it easy to do. The first time, he had felt himself borne by a soundless but very strong wind toward and then through the hole. He was in a blackness which felt very cold and, at the same time, very hot. These and the sense of being lost and out of control had frightened him even more than his childhood visions. He had lost his courage and striven to swim back against the wind. For a few seconds, he had feared that he would not make it.

Then something had snapped like a rubber band stretched too far, and he had awakened sitting in the chair. He was shivering and moaning and sweating. The clock told him that he had been gone for two seconds. Yet, he had had a sense of many hours having passed.

That was the end of his first expedition.

He had told about this during the group therapy the next day. No one had scoffed at his experience or accused him of cowardice. Anyone who did this would be sat upon at once by the staff member supervising the group. It was strictly against policy for anyone to voice disbelief in the narratives of others. That could invalidate the belief of the traveler in his or her journey and, thus, slow down or even end progress in therapy. Besides, all had gone through obstacles which were different in form but similar in emotional content.

The second time, he had conquered enough of his panic and fright to persist. Up to a point, that is. The blackness and the cold and heat had suddenly vanished. The wind became much weaker. He was surrounded by walls—lines of force?—that came up at many angles from some abyss and down from a vast space. They glowed whitely and intersected each other, then continued their extensions through other walls. They formed a jigsaw puzzle in four, maybe more, dimensions. But he could not grasp their extradimensionalness, their essences. Across, along, and up were dimensions that his brain knew. These other extensions, however, were beyond his comprehension. Yet he knew that they were there.

That was so weird that he almost surrendered to his fears and went back "home" before he lost his way forever.

Abruptly, the walls fell away. They did not collapse as walls on Earth would. They just disappeared in some fashion he could not fathom. Their afterimages glowed briefly, then were gone.

He was in one of the worlds of the Lords. He did not know how he knew this. But he did. Though he was still frightened, he was too curious to allow himself to be sucked up by the winds of return.

Though he could see, he was not in a body with flesh and organs. Perhaps he was an astral soul. It did not matter. That he was out of Earth's universe and in a Lord's was enough for him.

He seemed to be high above a planet which had the same shape and size as Earth. The sun was green, however. Later, he would find that the color of the sky varied according to the day of the week. A week here was nine days long. And the Lord who had made this world had arranged for the sky color to change every day.

He descended swiftly while hoping that he was going toward his goal. He had selected Red Orc as the one in whom he would be incorporated. But if he could pick the person and the place for his otherworld rendezvous, he could also pick the time. It seemed logical.

He had concentrated, while chanting, on a time many thousands of years in the past, hoping to zero in on Red Orc when he was still a child of seven. The events in the Tiers series would not take place until much much later. He was the only one in the therapy group who had chosen not to travel into the present.

Porsena had asked him why he had done this. Jim had said that he did not know why. It just seemed the right thing to do. The doctor had not continued questioning him about it, but he undoubtedly would note this development for future investigation.

Like Earth seen from the top of the atmosphere, the continents and seas of this planet were nowhere near as clearly distinguishable as on a map. Great cloud masses roamed it, but he could see the roughly cross-shaped continent toward which he was drawn as if he were connected to invisible and spiderweb-thin cables. Down he went, and the land spread out below him as if it, not he, were moving.

Then he was above a gigantic ring of mountains in the center of which was a plain, in the center of which was a single enormous mountain. The top of this was a relatively flat plain with rivers and creeks and many forests. Here and there were clusters of round, cone-roofed houses. He was too high to see any people or animals.

In the center of the plain was a structure so huge and strange that his already almost-overpowering awe became greater. Nine vast pylons two miles high curved inwards like elephants' tusks. Inside the pylons were three floors, the bottom one of which was a half-mile above the ground. It was transparent, thus allowing the few tenants there to see below the villages and farms of the non-Lords. These were along a river at least two miles broad which ran from a lake formed by cataracts from the mouths of vast crystalline statues placed along the edges of the bottom floor. Mists swirled up from the cataracts but did not reach the floor.

The second floor, also transparent, had less area than the first, though it covered at least seven square miles. Like the bottom level, it contained small dwellings and some large buildings and walled-in areas of earth on which grew trees and other plants. Some were fields bearing plants or enclosing pastures on which animals grazed.

The third floor was only two miles square. On it were houses and some gigantic structures the function of which Jim did not know. Many of these resembled somewhat the ancient temples of Karnak in Egypt as they looked when first built. Yet, though they reminded Jim of the Egyptian structures, they differed in many respects. The hundreds of statues at their entrances and sides were not Egyptian or like anything on Earth of which he knew.

At the apex, held within the curve of the inward-curving pylons, was a green emerald. This seemed larger than any cathedral on Earth. It had been carved to make doors and windows and was hollow. Or perhaps it had been made in a mold which provided the openings and the empty space. He would learn that it was tiny compared to the diamond on one of the planets of one of Urizen's worlds. That Brobdingnagian gem was a dam for a river that made the Mississippi seem a trickle in a child's mud pie.

Down he went. Though the emerald reflected the rays of the sun from its huge facets in a glory of many-beamed light, Jim was not blinded. He could see, but he had no eyes to be dazzled. The jewel shot out as if it were exploding, and he was dwarfed by a facet directly ahead of him and then was through it and inside the temple. That, he now realized, was what the gem was—a temple.

The vast interior was shadowy except for the very center of the floor. A ray of bright light coming from an unseen source illuminated the floor in the middle. Outside its area were very large and somehow ominous statues. They crowded the floor and were set in a rising series of niches on the curving walls. As they neared the apex of the temple, they became vague figures. Some could not be seen at all from the floor, but he felt their presence.

It was a very scary place for Jim. How it affected the seven-year-old boy standing in its center, Jim could not know. The child, Orc, might have been there several times, but he would perhaps find it frightening. Awing, at least.

Jim called the boy Orc because he knew, without knowing how he knew, that the boy was not yet called Red Orc.

The boy and two adults were the only human beings in the temple. Some other being was there, yet it was hidden. It filled the entire chamber with a brooding menace.

The man was tall, handsome, blond-haired, and blue-eyed. His name was Los, and he was Orc's father. The woman was as tall as he, statuesque, auburn-haired, and green-eyed. She was Orc's mother, Enitharmon. Both wore ankle-length gauzy robes which concealed little. His robe had a purple hem band; hers, a blue. He held a censer in his right hand and swung it back and forth slowly while he chanted in a language Jim could not understand. (Though Jim had no ears, he could hear.) From the censer came an orange smoke with an odor that was a mixture of bitter almonds and sweet apples.

Enitharmon held a wand at the end of which was a circlet containing a large and scarlet uncut gem. She waved it in a ritualistic manner.

The boy stood rigid, his green eyes rolled up to look at the ceiling, his arms held close to his sides, one hand a fist, the other open. Now and then, Los stopped his chanting to ask the boy a question. Once, when Orc could not respond properly, the father struck him across his face with the back of his hand. A red mark appeared on Orc's cheek, and tears came.

Jim had expected, for some reason, that Orc would look like him. He did not. His body was stockier, and his arms seemed longer. His nose was snub, his lips fuller than Jim's, his chin less pronounced, and his hair was black. Moreover, the eyes were wider and gave him a look of innocence.

He wore no clothing except a blue headband printed with symbols unfamiliar to Jim. One looked like a trumpet of some sort. Did that represent the Horn of Shambarimem, which Jim had read about in the series and which was supposed to open all gates among the worlds when it was blown?

Now, the father and the mother slowly began to circle the child counterclockwise. Los continued to swing the censer, and he questioned his son only when he was in front of him. Jim could see the boy tighten up when this happened. Twice, he responded successfully. The third time, he stammered. Again, the father struck his son on the face.

The woman frowned and opened her mouth as if to say something to her husband. But she closed her lips. Los shouted something. Perhaps the anger was required by the ceremony, but it seemed to be far more personal than ritualistic.

Orc quivered. His face and body shone with sweat, and his lower lip trembled. His signs of stress seemed to make Los more furious.

Jim hated the father.

Though he had come here to enter Orc and to be one with him, he hesitated. His sympathetic anger was making his mind whirl, and he needed all the coolness and self-control he could master to be able to enter Orc. That step was frightening enough. He had no way of knowing, of course, but he felt that he could err during the incorporation procedure and find himself in a very bad situation.

The father, whose face had been getting redder and more twisted, swung the censer hand against the side of Orc's head. The boy went down to his knees. Both of his arms remained down. Jim guessed that, if the boy had moved his arms, he would completely fail to fulfill his part in the ceremony. What the result of that would be, Jim did not know.

The woman said something. Los glared at her and spoke one word. The woman glared back and spoke one word. Jim did not think that they were complimenting each other.

Orc rose unsteadily to his feet. He stared upward while blood trickled from the wound. Tears swept down his cheeks, but he had locked his jaws together.

Enitharmon shrieked. She sprang toward Los and swung the end of her wand against the side of Los's head.

She certainly did not react as his mother would, Jim thought.

Then he was whisked away, up out of the temple, up above the mountains, the continent, the planet, the sun, back to the gate to his room on Earth, and through the gate with a soundless explosion.

CHAPTER

14

November 8, 1979

When Jim entered the next time, he did not see the scary, intersecting, glowing, and many-dimensional walls. Instead, he was confronted by a great swarm of figures that alternately flashed green and red. They looked like spermatozoa with human faces, all grinning malignantly at him.

He flew through the horde, those in his path wriggling swiftly away, and was quickly in Orc's universe. But, before he had started chanting, he had decided to enter Orc when he was seventeen years old.

The youth was in a forest hundreds of miles beyond the city. Orc had grown into a tall and very muscular young man. He was standing behind the massive bole of a tree, his left hand grasping the shaft of a spear. He wore a blue cap shaped like Robin Hood's. A scarlet feather stuck out of its side. Except for the cap, a short blue kilt, and sandals, he wore nothing. A belt held a scabbarded short-sword and a holstered throwing ax. It was an hour or so into the afternoon. The sky, crimson today, was clear, and the sun, also crimson, blazed down on top of the forest. It was, however, cool below the thick canopy of vegetation connecting trees seven hundred feet high.

The layer of tangled plants far above him held a multitude of insects, birds, and animals. From a branch fifty feet above him, a raccoonlike creature with a green beard hung by its prehensile tail and scolded him. Orc was listening intently to something, but it would have been difficult to hear anything above the uproar of the forest life.

Orc turned his head. His father, Los, and his mother, Enitharmon, had appeared from the shadows of the trees behind him. His parents were clad only in kilts and sandals, and they, too, carried weapons. Though Los had a spear and an ax, he was armed also with a bulbous-ended handgun, a beamer.

Jim was again suffering from fear. To project himself into Orc's mind and possibly never get out again was to dare a danger such as he had never encountered before. But he had to do it or live as a coward forever after. Do or die. And maybe die, anyway. Worse, be absorbed by Orc or be only partially absorbed but forever a prisoner in that alien body.

Never mind. Get into Orc's mind. Become partly Orc. Not completely Orc, dear God!

It was done. For a second or more, he seemed to have fallen into a silo of wet oats. Slimy and squidgy matter pressed around him. He was blind. The darkness and the loathsome substance drowning him came close to making him turn back. He gritted his figurative teeth and shouted voicelessly at himself. "Go on!"

The frightening muck was behind him, though the darkness remained. He had a sensation of plunging into a furiously running stream of a mercury-heavy liquid, of being shot through many winding and twisting tunnels, and of hearing a noise like that of the beating of giant wings or a vast heart.

That was behind him. Now, he floated in a silent chamber. Then, he heard a faint crackling. Sparks showered around him.

Suddenly, the sparks expanded and coalesced. They became a bright light. He could see and hear and smell and taste as he had in his body on Earth.

He was enfleshed and enbrained, almost entirely Orc. He was like a tiny parasite hanging on to its host's artery wall and hoping that it would not be swept away by the raging current of blood. Meanwhile, it tapped into its host's nervous system and shared all thoughts, memories, emotions, and sensations.

That one-way input was, as he was to find out, very confusing for him. It would take some time to be able to handle at the same time his own thoughts and identity and Orc's.

Orc saw his Uncle Luvah and Aunt Vala as they came from the shadows of the trees. Behind them walked a dozen natives, slaves of the Lords, trackers and beaters. They were somewhat darker than the Lords but only because they spent more time in the sunlight. They wore loinclothes, were heavily tattooed, and bristled with feathers stuck in their long dark hair and in holes in their ears. Their only weapons were bamboo air guns which expelled darts with anesthetic-coated tips. Their leader carried a signal horn made from the doubly curving horn of a giant bovoid animal.

Los's voice was deep and growling.

"Any luck, son?"

"I think one of them is holed up in that cluster of *shinthah* trees," Orc said. "He's been wounded. I've trailed him partly by his blood, though he doesn't seem to be bleeding heavily."

"He must be the one who killed the two slaves," Los said. "The others are all accounted for, dead or gotten away."

Jim was vaguely amazed that he could understand the speech of the Lords, or Thoan, their name for themselves. If his reaction was diluted, it was because all his own feelings were, so far, shadowy. But everything funneled through to him from Orc was bright and hard.

Luvah and Vala moved up to stand beside Los. They had been invited by Orc's parents to be their guests at the palace and to go on a manhunt. Los had opened the gates between their worlds long enough for them to pass through.

Los would never have done that on his own. His wife had insisted that Luvah of the Horses and his wife and sister, Vala, be invited. Enitharmon needed more than the company of her family and slaves.

Orc adored the beautiful and warm-natured Vala. As it turned out, though, he had been kept too busy to talk to her. The hunt had been furious and intense and had few pauses.

Los said, "Is the man still armed?"

"I don't know," Orc said.

All the quarry were natives who had been sentenced to death by their own people for serious crimes. Los had decided to override the sentences and use the convicted as prey. He did this now and then when he got bored with other amusements. Seven men, all dangerous, had been taken to this jungle, given spears and knives, and let loose. After twenty minutes of waiting, the Lords and their retainers had started tracking them. The Lords were, except for Los and Vala, armed only with primitive weapons. That ensured that the hunt would be dangerous for the hunters. Orc's father and his aunt carried the beamers to shoot any beasts of prey that might attack the party or a human quarry if he got the upper hand in a fight with a Lord. Manhunt rules, as determined by tradition, were never broken. Or, if a Lord had broken them, he or she had kept quiet about it.

"Who wants to go after the beast?" Los shouted.

"I will be happy to do it," Orc said. He was aware that he had volunteered because he wanted to get his father's respect even though he did not like his father. Also, a stronger reason, he wanted to show off before his aunt.

"It's true that you do need more practice," Los said. "You haven't killed many beasts yet, man or animal. But it's only polite to allow our visitors first chance. Remember that."

Vala said, "I'd love to see Orc in action. I'll be right behind you, nephew."

Jim was thinking, My God! They're callous enough about it! And cool, too! What kind of people are these? He knew, however, from reading the Tiersian books just how cruel the Lords could be. What had he expected?

Despite his repulsion, he was feeling Orc's emotions. The youthful Lord and, therefore, Jim, was excited and eager. At the same time, Orc, therefore Jim, was hoping that he would not make a fool of himself. It was possible that he would also be a dead fool.

Orc walked slowly into the denseness of the *shinthah* trees. Their branches, which began about six feet above the earth, merged with those of their neighbors. Vines crawled through the branches and let down loops close to the ground. Moreover, the *winshin* bush, a very leafy plant, grew among the trees. The tangle of tree, vine, and bush was ideal for hiding and ambushing.

Holding his spear in one hand, Vala about six feet behind him, Orc plunged into the thick growth. He moved slowly to avoid making noise. He was very tense and was sweating heavily. It suddenly came to him that the quarry had most of the advantages. He stopped when his foot struck something. He looked down. Half-buried in some kind of weedy growth was a spear. The hunted man had dropped it. Which must mean that he was badly wounded.

Despite this, Orc did not forget to be cautious. It was

possible that the man had placed the spear there to make the hunter think just what Orc had thought. He might be waiting close by, his hunting knife in his hand.

He gestured at Vala to indicate the spear. She nodded that she understood.

Though the cluster would usually be clamorous with the cries of birds and beasts, it was silent now. The tenants were watching the intruders, waiting to see if they were dangerous before resuming normal activity.

Orc parted a bush with his right hand and looked past it and down. There was the prey. He was a big man completely unclothed and lying on his back. By his open hand was a large knife. Blood flowed slowly from under the hand held to his shoulder. Sweat had washed all but traces of the blood from his torso and legs.

Orc said, "Har?"

Not until then had he known that the quarry was from a village near the palace-city or that he was his half brother. Los had many children by the native women; Har was one of perhaps a hundred. He was a superb tracker who had taught Orc everything he knew about jungle craft. He had been wounded by his own father, Los, who was separated from the group when he had thrown his spear on glimpsing the quarry. Later, Orc had come across Har's trail of blood.

The man was pale under his heavy tan. He stared at Orc, knowing that he was about to die. But he did not plead.

Vala came up to Orc. She said, "You must blood your knife, nephew. It is not correct to finish him off with your spear. Wait until I call the others. They must see you do it."

Jim felt Orc's sudden sickness. He knew what Orc was thinking. He would have to cut Har's throat and lick some of the blood off the knife. The coup de grace and the blood tasting were not new to him, nor did he find them distasteful. Far from it. But this . . . ! He knew and liked his half brother as much as he could like any *leblabbiy*, as the non-Lords were called. He told himself that he would sooner kill his father than he would Har.

But he had to do it. Not only that, he must not show any pity or kindness. By then, the others had arrived. Los said, "So, it was Har I wounded! And you get the credit for the kill! Well, that is the way things sometimes happen!"

"You wounded him, father," Orc said. "I couldn't have caught him if you hadn't. Why don't you lick his blood?"

Los frowned, and he said, "That isn't the Thoan way. Go ahead."

Orc went around the bush, scraping his skin against the abrasive leaves of that bush and the one beside it. The other Lords followed him. The natives stayed behind and would do so unless ordered to witness the killing.

Har's eyes were dulled. Yet, he was not so far gone that he did not recognize Orc. He croaked, "Greeting, brother!" He had never said that word to Orc during all their conversations. Though both knew that Los was their father, neither would ever say so. If Har had dared to do that, he would have been punished severely, perhaps with death. Now that he was to die, he did not care.

"You are immortal or nearly so," Har said. "Yet, you can be killed. That makes you my brother no matter who our father is."

A shiver of fire ran through Orc. He was struck, not with the audacity of Har but with the truth of his words. They were as frightening as lightning in the night when there was no cloud or thunder.

"Go ahead, Orc!" Los said.

Orc turned to face him. "I cannot do it," he said.

Los was not the only one who stepped back as if suddenly smelling a carcass long rotten.

Los shook his head, blinked, and said harshly, "I do not understand. Is something wrong?"

Orc took a deep breath before speaking. Only Jim knew

what courage Orc had to summon for what he was about to do.

"I cannot kill him. He is flesh of my flesh. He is your son and my brother."

Everything around Orc seemed to be fuzzy. The harsh edges of reality were blunted and soft. He felt as if he had stepped into another world that was not quite formed.

Los looked bewildered. He said, "What? What does that have to do with it?"

Vala turned and gestured at the head tracker, Sheon, to approach her. As all non-Lords did when called by a Thoan, he came swiftly.

"What is that man's crime?" Vala said, pointing at Har.

Sheon, looking at the ground, said, "Holy One, he slew a son of our chief after he caught him in bed with his wife. Har claimed that the chief's son attacked him with a knife, and he killed him in self-defense. But Har's wife witnessed otherwise. She said that Har meant to kill both of them. In any event, Har should have gone to the council and presented his complaint to it. It is against our law to slay a man or a woman caught in adultery. Har could have run away if he was attacked. There was nothing to stop him from running."

Vala turned to Orc. "See? He deserves to die by the law of his own people."

"Then let them execute him," Orc said.

"This is ridiculous!" Los shouted. "You're stupid! I do not understand you! He's not Thoan!"

"He's half-Thoan," Orc said calmly, though he was far from calm inside himself.

"Half is not the whole!" Los said. His face was very red, and his eyes were wild. "Kill him! At once!"

"Don't you feel anything for him?" Orc said. "He is your son. Or does that mean nothing to you?"

Luvah said, "Nephew, you're out of your mind! What

happened? Did you have an accident, strike your head against something?"

"Something struck me," Orc said. "It wasn't physical. It was like a great light . . . it's hard to explain."

"I'll strike you!" Los howled, and his fist caught the side of Orc's jaw. Orc was stunned for several seconds. When he was able to think clearly, he found himself down on his knees. The others, except for Los, looked as if they, too, had been struck. Orc's mother murmured, "Los! This is not necessary! There is something wrong with the boy!"

"Yes, there is, Enitharmon! He is not a true Lord! Did you lie with some native and allow yourself to get pregnant?"

Enithermon gasped, and Vala said, "That is a terrible thing to say!"

Orc was seized by something that was roaring. The sound was red. Colors did not have sounds, but many things happened in the mind that could not happen outside it. The insult to his mother had loosed all the desires to attack his father that had been caged since as far back as he could remember.

He was in a dream filled with a bright red light. He seemed to be standing outside of himself and watching himself. He saw Orc, the knife still in his hand despite having been half-conscious, come off the ground quickly. He saw Los step back, but not quickly enough to prevent the blade driving several inches into his left arm. He saw his uncle, Luvah, strike him on the side on his head with the butt of his spear. He saw himself drop the knife and fall onto his face but roll over so that he was faceup.

Then he was back inside himself. His father had raised the spear held in his right hand to drive it through him. His mother, screaming, grabbed the spear and struggled with Los. She wrested it from his grip and held it so that its point was close to her husband.

"Don't do it!" she screamed. It was evident that she would use the spear on him if he tried to kill her son.

Vala spoke in a high and tight voice. "Los! The *leblabbiy* are watching you!"

Los turned and glared. Sheon, the chief tracker, was walking back to his fellows. He did not want the Thoan to know that he had seen the fight, but it was too late for that.

Los pointed at Orc and said, "Bind him! He goes back to the palace!"

He pulled his beamer from his holster. "Vala! Come with me! We have to destroy them! I don't want them alive now they've seen us trying to kill each other!"

Vala said, "I think Sheon was the only one who saw us. He won't tell the others."

"I don't want to take the chance," Los said. "We don't want them to think we're no better than they, do we?"

He wanted to kill someone. If he was restrained from slaying his son, he would slaughter the *leblabbiy*. At another time, he might have listened to Vala. But not now.

Vala bit her lip, but she said, "Very well." She walked away with Los, her gun also drawn. As Orc discovered later, the natives had guessed what the Lords planned to do. The more passive and religious stayed to submit to their doom. Four *leblabbiy*, however, fled into the forest. They would be exiled forever from their tribe and would be men with a price on their head, prey for another hunt by the Thoan.

Orc was turned over, and his wrists were bound together with tape his mother brought out of a bag. While doing this, his mother bent close to him and whispered, "Do not anger your father again. I'll do my best to cool him down."

"He'll kill me," Orc said. "He hates me. He's always hated me. What did I do to make him hate me, Mother?"

CHAPTER

15

Orc had been stripped of his clothing and chained to a boulder near the main palace. One end of the ten-foot-long chain was attached to a steel plate secured to the giant quartzite rock. The other end was fixed to a steel band around his right ankle. For two days and nights, he had suffered this humiliation and discomfort. The sun burned him during most of the day. At night, Los allowed the clouds to come into the levels. Orc slept poorly because of the cold, wetness, and hard floor.

During the day, he ate one meal, brought by a servant. She left him a bucket of water to drink and to bathe. When he relieved bladder or bowels, he went around behind the boulder as far as he could. He had no toilet paper or wash rag. Once a day, a servant came to clean up the mess.

At high noon each day, his parents, aunt, and uncle had come down from the palace. Los had asked him if he was sorry that he had behaved so badly. Would he apologize and then promise that he would never do such again and would always obey his parents? Los added that even then his punishment would not be over.

"There are many Lords who would slay their son on the spot. But I do not wish to grieve your mother, and Luvah and Vala have pleaded for you."

"You should not have struck me," Orc said.

"I am your father! I have the right and the duty to do so when you deserve it!"

"You have struck me many times," Orc said. "I would think that a man who is so many thousands of years old would have some wisdom and love. You have learned nothing. Be that as it may, you have struck me for the last time. You may as well kill me."

Los turned and walked away, his long green robe flapping, the tall yellow feather on his wide-brimmed hat bobbing. His mother and his aunt stayed for a minute to beg him to bend to his father's will.

"You are so stubborn," Enitharmon said as tears ran down her cheek. "Your stubbornness will kill you. What will I do if I lose my firstborn?"

"Kill Los, and so avenge me," Orc said. "I think you'd like to do it, anyway. I do not know why you stay with him. Aren't there other worlds you could go to? How about Luvah's and Vala's?"

"You are determined to die," Enitharmon said. She kissed him on the cheek and left. Luvah, shaking his head, walked away. Vala lingered a moment.

"I'll sneak out tonight and bring you a sleeping bag and something good to eat."

"Don't endanger yourself for me, though I thank you. At least, you love me."

"Your mother does, too," Vala said. "You saw how she defended you when Los was going to spear you. But her character is such that she cannot stand up against Los unless she's driven to it, and then it doesn't last long."

"You'd think that she could have changed her character during the course of so many millenia. What good is the Lords' science if it can't change undesirable character traits?"

"There have been some who have changed themselves, though not always for the better. But most people cannot unfix their characters no matter how long they live. It's a matter of will, not of biological engineering. Would you allow yourself to be tampered with?"

She kissed him hard on his lips before leaving. Orc suspected that Vala lusted for him as he did for her. Or was she just a loving aunt, and had he, so young and inexperienced, misread her affection?

He looked at his father, still striding toward the major palace of the city of pylons. His son had seen more of the back of his father than his face, though that was most times the preferable side. Then he looked up at the third story of the glittering gold-block-and-much-gemmed wall of the palace. There, framed by a window, was his tutor, Noorosha. He was an intelligent and highly educated native who had been guiding Orc through programmed courses since the Lord was three years old. Now, he was looking down at his student, who should have been in class.

Orc waved at Noorosha, the person he loved most of all except for his mother and aunt. Why couldn't his father be like Noorosha?

The day passed, each minute like a whip stroke. While he paced back and forth, the chain dragging on his leg and clinking on the slightly roughened surface of the transparent floor, his mind was pacing. Back and forth, back and forth from thoughts of ways to escape to visions of killing his father.

Finally, night fell. The first moon rose. Two hours later, the second lumbered up. Jim, looking through Orc's eyes, estimated that it was half the size of Earth's moon. The first moon was half the size of the second one. Their markings, of course, were different from the one Jim knew.

After the clouds oozed over Orc, he lay down on the floor. It took him a long time to fall asleep. Jim also slept then. It seemed like a short time had passed when Vala's touch awoke Orc and, of course, Jim.

She was a dim figure crouching by him. "I've brought the bag and food," she said softly. "But I've brought more than that."

She held up an object that he could not see clearly.

"A beamer. Hold still. I'm going to cut your chain."

"You shouldn't do that!" Orc said. "I thank you, but I can't allow you to endanger yourself. My father will investigate thoroughly if I escape, and he'll find out you did it, and he'll kill you!"

"Not if you kill him first," she said.

She started to rise. Orc heard a thud. She grunted and pitched forward, falling heavily across his legs. Above Orc loomed a vague shape, but he knew that it was Los. Vala, groaning, rolled over Orc's legs, a hand pressing the back of her head. Then she started to rise.

"Stay down, you treacherous slut!" Los said.

Just beyond Orc's father was a vague and bulky figure. It looked to Orc like a vehicle of some sort.

"I should kill you, Vala!" Los shouted. "But I can understand why you felt sorry for him, believe it or not! After all, he is my son, though not much of one! I can remember how I loved him when he was a baby! But you have betrayed my hospitality! How do I know that you weren't planning on letting him help you kill me!"

He raved on, the gist being that, because he was merciful, he was permitting Vala and her husband to return to their universe. But they would do it at once and under guard. He would deal with his son, though they would never find out how he would do it. She would never see him again.

Vala started to protest. He screamed at her to shut up or he would shoot her on the spot. After that, she said nothing except to murmur, "I'm sorry, Orc." Los kept on ranting in the same manner for about five minutes. When he stopped, he bent over Vala and jammed the end of a cylinder into her arm. She collapsed immediately. Then he stuck the end against Orc's chest. He became unconscious and so did Jim.

Jim awoke at the same moment as Orc. Bright sunlight made Orc squint and, in a shadowy way, Jim also. The young Thoan was sitting on bare buttocks on a rock ledge. He was propped up against a vertical outcropping of stone. His hands were tied together behind him with rope. The ledge ended a foot beyond him. Below it was a precipitous slope of mountain, forested halfway down. At the bottom was a river snaking through an unbroken forest. Another mountain was on the other side of the river.

The sky was blue, which meant that he was not in his native world. Not unless he had been unconscious long enough to let two days pass.

Despite the blazing sun, he shivered from the cold air. There were patches of snow on the upper face of the mountain opposite him. He looked around then and saw that he was in a cave extending back from the ledge. Near him on the dirt floor was a square plastic sheet.

He walked to the sheet, lowered himself to his knees, and bent over to look at the plastic piece. As he had expected, it bore his father's handwriting.

> You are on Anthema, the unwanted world. If you are man enough to survive on it and find your way to the only other gate on this world, you may be able to get out of it. I give you a clue though you do not deserve it. The gate will be near a landmark resembling something you are wearing. But you will have to find the code allowing

you to open the gate. That gate leads back to your own world.

You only have to look for the gate on land, which cuts the territory of your search down to fifty million square miles. Though I should wish you bad luck, I do not. May you get what you deserve.

Orc groaned. Anthema, the Unwanted World! Made by those mysterious beings who had existed before the Lords, who had made the original universe of the Lords and then created the Lords to populate it. Anthema was so crudely constructed that the Lords theorized that it had been the pre-Thoan's first experiment in making artificial universes.

No Lord had chosen to live there. Indeed, very few knew how to gate to it.

Los must have put him in that vehicle and carried him to a gate in the palace or somewhere on his world. Then he had gated the vehicle with himself and Orc in it to this world. After arriving at Anthema via the interdimensional route, Los had used the vehicle to fly from the gate to this cave.

And what was that about the clue being provided by something his son was wearing? Orc was naked.

It was then that he felt the necklace and the object attached to it.

He heaved himself up onto his feet. Now he could bend his neck and see the object, which rested just below his breastbone. Though it was upside down from his viewpoint, he could recognize it. It was a round gold medallion, one of his father's, bearing a name, Shambarimem, and, below that, a raised relief of the Horn—a trumpet—of that legendary man. It was as close to a religious medal as a Thoan artifact could come.

What kind of a clue was that? A mountain that looked like the Horn? Orc, knowing his father's subtle nature, was sure that it was not as simple as that. In fact, the clue might not even be visual. Never mind. First, he had to get his hands free.

That was done, though not soon. He went to the tiny monolith he had been sitting against, turned around, and bent his knees. He raised his arms, squatted even more, and set the rope on the rather blunt edge of a small ridge on top of the rock and near its side. The position was both tiring and painful, but he kept sawing until the rope was halfway worn through. After resting, he resumed the sawing. When he felt the rope part, he brought his hands before him and untied each with the other hand, no easy task. After reconnoitering the cave and finding nothing to indicate a gate, he surveyed the valley. The only life he saw consisted of some strange-looking and awkward flying creatures.

He started climbing down the steep slope below the ledge. He had no reason to feel optimistic in this world certainly not made for him. His fury and desire for revenge would keep him going for a long time. But he could search the vast territory for a thousand years and still not find the landmark and the gate within or on or under or by it. He might even see the landmark and not know that it was what he was looking for.

He had troubles. Oh, Shambarimem, did he have troubles!

They came sooner than he expected. A loud shriek behind him froze him for a fraction of a second. A blow on his back knocked him forward. He heard giant wings beating. Pain as of very sharp and large claws stabbing his back made him scream.

Jim Grimson was also startled. He heard the shriek, felt the hard impact, and yelled from the agony.

The shock was too much for him. He was whisked out, up, and away far more swiftly than his previous journeys back to Earth. He awoke sitting on the chair in his room. He was shivering and sweating and somewhat numb. For a moment, the searing on his back from the terrible claws stayed with him. Then it faded.

Despite his fear, he would have tried to get back into Orc if his energy had not been completely dynamited out of him. It was a long time before he could rise from the chair.

CHAPTER

16

Today, the group session members were even more inclined to argue than usual. Their digs were sharper, and they took offense more quickly. Was there something in the air like itching powder? Or was it that they had reached a certain stage in their therapy where their anger and frustration were closer to the surface? These were burrowing upward toward the skin like worms chased out of the intestine by strong medicine.

Gillman Sherwood, the nineteen-year-old from Gold Hill, was getting more abuse than usual. Some of the group detested and distrusted him because his family was wealthy. Until now, he had responded with a slight smile and silence to the onslaught. That he would not defend himself made his attackers even more angry.

Foremost among them was Al Moober, a sixteen-year-old who had never had any money until he had started dealing in drugs. His career had lasted six months. Then the cops had caught him. But he had been accused of being under the influence and of possession, not of selling. He especially had it in for Sherwood, one of his former customers, because he suspected that Sherwood had turned him in to the narcs.

Sherwood's wrists were still bandaged from the deep slashes made when he had tried suicide. He had wanted to be a painter, but his parents had opposed that ambition. Both had agreed, when their son was only three years old, that he would go to Ohio State for his undergraduate education and then to Harvard for his law degree. After six months at Ohio, he had a "nervous breakdown." He came out of the sanitarium three months later, went home, and refused to consider going back to college. His parents had kept up their pressure despite their doctor's warnings. One night, Sherwood had used the blood from his wrist arteries to paint a nightmare vision on his palette. He had ended up in Porsena's Tiersian therapy group.

Moober had also told his fellow patients that Sherwood was bisexual and had added that Sherwood had made a pass at him. The girls thought that Sherwood was divinely handsome and looked much like a tall Paul Newman. Besides, he had made passes at several of them, and why would he go for a loathsome creature like Moober?

Moober had persisted in trying to invalidate Sherwood's descriptions of his adventures as Wolff, the hero Sherwood had chosen to emulate. Doctor Scaevola, today's group leader, had tried to stop Moober from doing this, but Moober would not quit. Then Scaevola had told Moober that he would obey the rules or be sent to his room to think about how he would like being kicked out of the therapy.

Moober had quit attacking Sherwood, though he was muttering to himself.

Jim Grimson was only half listening to the others. For one thing, he had been shocked when he had seen Sandy Melton this morning. She was sitting at the far end of the dining hall with the group of mild schizoaffectives. Until then, Jim had not known that Sandy was in the hospital. He had heard nothing about what had happened to her after that evening at Dumski's.

He had waved to her. She had smiled at him and resumed talking to the girl next to her. Jim planned to talk to her when he got the chance.

Another reason Jim had trouble concentrating was that he could not keep from wondering about what had happened to Orc after Jim had left him. His plight and his world seemed more real than this room and the people in it. These people did not know what real trouble was.

He became aware that Doctor Scaevola was speaking to him and that the others were looking at him.

"Your turn, Jim," Scaevola said. "We're all eager to hear what happened during your latest exploration."

Jim doubted they all were that eager. Most of them were too wrapped up in their own sojourns to care much about his. Or, at least, he thought that they were. He had learned something about himself in the short time he had been here. That was that he often attributed his own feelings to others, but there was often no match between the two. He must be more careful in the future not to assign to others his own thoughts and emotions.

Group therapy was supposed to be in some respects like a book club. The members would talk about various characters in the series and how they felt about them. They would then tell how they would have changed the situations or the endings in the books. Also, they commented on how each person's chosen character reflected the personality and the problems of the chooser. This interplay, however, was closely monitored by the group leader. It was not allowed to get to a point where the members were criticizing each other too harshly.

One of the difficulties the members had, at this stage in

therapy, was in giving full information about their experiences in the pocket universes. Jim shared this reluctance. Now, in answering Scaevola's invitation, he gave only the sketchiest outline of his adventures. He held back because it seemed to him that they should be very private. Somehow, if the others got too far into Orc's world, they would try to take over. His fellow patients would want his worlds just as the Lords desired the worlds of other Lords.

Moreover, Jim was convinced that the universes the other members entered into were purely imaginary. Though vivid and very detailed, they were nevertheless just fantasies. He did not reveal this to the group, of course. To do so would be to invalidate the worlds of his fellow patients.

Jim finished his somewhat halting and hesitant tale. Even as he spoke, he began to feel that it was made up. The others seemed to be looking doubtfully at him. Damn! They were invalidating him!

Monique Bragg, a black girl, said, "Your father, I mean Orc's father, struck you, Orc, a number of times. That sounds like your own father, Jim. He's unpredictable and confusing, too, just like Los, the way he treats you. Cruel and severe a lot of times but, sometimes, kind and tender, like a real father should be. That's bewildering to a kid."

"Which father you talking about?" Jim said. "My father in this world or the father in the other world?"

Monique smiled, revealing big white teeth. "Both, you dummy. Only this Los isn't like your real father in some ways. He's a very handsome and powerful person, lord and master of all he surveys, you might say, not a worthless drunken bum like your real father."

"Monique!" Doctor Scaevola said softly but firmly. "Please refrain from personal remarks."

"Sure, Doc," Monique said. "Only . . . I didn't say anything about his father he hasn't said. I was just pointing out certain things, how Los and this woman, Orc's mother—

Enitharmon?—resemble his own parents. They sort of reflect them, don't you think? That's what this is all about, anyway, isn't it? How this world and the Tiersian are mirror images, wasn't that what you said? Distorted mirrors."

"That's an aspect," Scaevola said, "but we don't want to dwell too much on parallelisms, especially those that're rather obvious. Unless you're leading up to another point?"

"Maybe it's the differences that're most important," Monique said. "Like Orc's mother seems to be under Los's thumb just as Jim's mother is. But she's beautiful and powerful, and she can stand up to him. To a point, anyway. Maybe she's going to rebel, even kill Los. That's something your mother'd never do, right, Jim? But maybe you're hoping she will some day. Is that so, Jim?"

"How would I know?" Jim said heatedly. "I'm not making this up, you know! Things'll go the way they go, not how I think they should go!"

There was silence for a moment except for Moober's brief snicker.

Then Scaevola said, "Of course! Remember, we're not writing stories. These things really do happen. Whether they exist inside your mind or outside your mind, they exist. A thought is as much an existent as a, uh . . ."

"A fart!" Moober said loudly and doubled up with laughter.

"Both evanescent but nevertheless existing in their own moment of glory or putridness," Scaevola said.

"Hey, there are millions of fathers and mothers more or less like mine on Earth," Jim said. "So, there are some in the Lords' worlds. Nothing strange about it. Quit the psychologizing, for Christ's sake."

Brooks Epstein spoke up for the first time during the session. He was a tall, dark, and lean youth who wore thick horn-rimmed glasses. Though he was from Gold Hill, he had escaped the insults and disdain cast at Sherwood. Epstein's father had been wealthy, but he had gone bankrupt and then killed himself. Epstein's mother had just enough insurance to place her son in therapy at Wellington Hospital.

"Quit psychologizing?" he said. "I thought we were here to do just that!"

"We're here to get therapy, get well, not sit around and analyze each other until we fall apart," Jim said. "Analyzing is like disassembling. We'll never put the pieces back together. Humpty Dumpty himself, you know."

"Thank you, Doctor Freud," Epstein said. "Anyway . . ."

The group broke up with almost everybody mad at everybody else. Doctor Scaevola tried to patch the rents and wounds and cool off their tempers before the session ended. This time, his soft words, reasonableness, and compromise had not worked. Some of the group were, so far, too timid to dare offend anybody. Others were inclined to be nasty, and the characters they had chosen to merge with were arrogant and ill-tempered. The staff members had to put the lid on these patients now and then. At the same time, they had to keep from suppressing the youths so much that they erupted out of control or were in danger of losing their Tiersian identities.

No matter how pugnaciously and offensively the members behaved, they were putting up a front. All had low self-esteem, a crippling part of their own personae. To gain a genuine self-esteem was one of the goals of the therapy but hard to achieve. To think of themselves as worthwhile, they had to become somebody else for a while.

A few minutes after the session, Jim was told that he had a visitor, Sam Wyzak. Doctor Scaevola was not available just then, so Doctor Tarchuna had to give permission for Jim to see Sam. He sent it through the phone in his office. Eager, Jim strode to the small lobby reserved for visitors. A male nurse, Dave Gurscom, stood in the doorway and watched them.

Sam rose from the chair when Jim entered the room. He smiled broadly and advanced toward his friend, his arms waving. They met in the middle of the room and embraced. Jim was very glad to see him, but he could not help wrinkling his nose at Sam's odor. Since Jim had been in the hospital, he had been showering daily and had sent out his dirty laundry to his mother. He said nothing to Sam about his unwashed body and clothes. After all, the clothes Jim was now wearing had been donated by Sam. Without them, he would have been clad only in hospital-provided pajamas, a robe, and slippers.

Sam lost his smile after they quit embracing. He sat down heavily on the chair.

"Jim, I got some things to say to you, got to get some things clear. There's a thing I got to do, and you won't like it. Or maybe you will, I don't know. But I've come to an impasse, as they say. Gotta go but don't really want to."

"Go where?"

"To California. Hollywood, to be exact. Gotta get the hell out of this cruddy place, the armpit of the universe. I'm in a bad fix. I'm in a rehab center for chemical dependents, for dope fiends, as my father says. The courts're on my neck. The judge says I gotta straighten out, he don't want me flunking, no way. He gets weekly reports from my folks and the school, and they just aren't good enough. I'm still flunking my ass though I am trying hard to bring my grades up."

He put his fingers over his eyes and looked at Jim through the spaces among his fingers as if they were prison bars. His voice got shaky.

"Jim, I can't take no more of this! I'm running off to California, gonna disappear, really drop out. I don't know what the hell I'll do there, become a street person, most likely. For a while, anyway. I'll be taking my guitar, though. I might get into a band. Maybe not. I ain't what you'd call a great musician, but that never stopped lots of rock stars. Anyway, I'm going to try for it. Anything'll be better than what I'm doing now."

Jim was silent for a minute. Sam had dropped his hands onto his lap, but his black eyes were zeroed in on Jim's face. He seemed to be hoping that . . . what? That his old buddy would utter wise words that would rescue him?

Jim waved his hand. It was a vague gesture that indicated nothing except possibly hopelessness. What could he, Jim Grimson, incarcerated in a mental ward, wearing borrowed clothes, estranged from just about everybody he could name except for Doctor Porsena and a few patients, the connections with them not really tight, what could he do for his old friend?

He could not help thinking about his own plans, too, though he felt like a big prick worrying about himself when Sam was in such a bad situation. Sam had told him on the phone several days ago that he could live at the Wyzaks' when he became an outpatient. He and Sam would share the bedroom and Sam's clothes and eat at Sam's table. Mrs. Wyzak, big-hearted as ever, had made the offer. She knew that Jim's parents were in a very small apartment and had no money to help support their son. Jim's eighteenth birthday was coming up soon. After that, the welfare money allotted for him would be cut off. Besides, Eric Grimson did not want Jim to live with him.

Now that Sam was taking off, would his parents still take his friend in?

Jim cleared his throat and said, "You're not talking to the wise old man on top of the mountain, the ancient guru who sees all, knows all, who can set you on the right path to health, wealth, and fame. I'm sorry, Sam, but I don't know what to say except to wish you luck. I could tell you to sign up for Doctor Porsena's therapy. But he's got a long waiting list. I was luckier than hell to be admitted so quickly."

Sam did not reply. His face was unreadable. But Jim thought that he detected reproach and fright in it.

"Jesus, Sam, I want to help you! But I just can't!"

Sam said, "I didn't expect nothing from you. You can't ask a drowning man to save you from drowning. I just thought I'd tell you what I'm going to do. I wasn't asking for your blessing."

"Damn, Sam! I feel like shit! I'm failing you!"

"What the hell," Sam said. He rose from the chair. "Mom won't refuse you even if I'm not there. In fact, she'll probably be gladder than ever to have you. Mothering's her big thing, you know. That and bossing people around."

His voice broke. Tears oozed out and slid down to the corners of his mouth. "Jesus, when we were kids together, pretty happy, you know, even though things were tough a lot of times, we couldn't have dreamed that we'd turn out like this."

Jim could think of nothing better to do than to enfold Sam in his arms and pat his back. That was all he could do, and maybe it was enough. Sam sobbed for a moment, then released himself and wiped the tears with a dirty handkerchief.

"Hey, Jim! We think we're grown up and don't need nobody, right! But when the chips are down, as the buffalo hunter said, we turn out to still be babies. I admit I'm a little scared. Why not? I'm just kidding myself when I pretend to be as tough as fried shoe leather. I wouldn't tell this to anyone but you, Jim. I don't really want to leave. Things've gotten too rough, though. It's adios, Belmont City! California, here I come! Mom's going to cry her heart out, but maybe, deep down, she'll be glad to get rid of me. She won't have to be on my neck all the time because I'm such a pain in the ass to her."

"Do you think you could keep in touch with me, write me a postcard now and then?"

"If I can steal a postcard and a pencil," Sam said. "I won't have much money."

He laughed, and he said, "Hey, it might be a lot better than I think! California's the golden state, ingots of gold laying around on the streets, ice cream cones growing from trees, starlets just aching to lay a skinny, penniless, dumb Polack. At least I won't freeze my ass off out on the street come winter. And even the garbage cans'll have food better than what I eat here."

"Maybe you should think more about it," Jim said. "Look before you leap, and all that."

Something came over Jim then. His words of caution suddenly seemed to be those of a coward. It was as if an electrical current running through him had reversed itself and was now running in the opposite direction.

He said, "What the hell, Sam! I don't mean that! It'll be a great adventure! It'll at least be different! Better to live like a lion for a day than like a dog forever! You know for sure you have no future here! Go to California! It'll be exciting, and it'll give you hope and endless opportunities! I wish I could go with you!"

Sam blinked as if Jim had disappeared in a blinding light. He said, "What happened to you?" Then, "Why don't you come with me?"

Jim shook his head. "I would . . . only . . ."

"Only what?"

"You'd have to be in my skin to know how I feel about this place, what I'm doing. This is my adventure, Sam, this ward. It's a world in itself, a world that . . ."

How could he explain to Sam about the universes of the Lords and his adventures as Red Orc? How could he make Sam understand that golden California was lead compared to the places he had been and to which he would return? No way would Sam comprehend it.

"You always were a little strange, Jim, even though we got

along great. What the hell could this puzzle farm have for you? For me, anyway. It'd be nothing."

He held out his hand. "So long, Jim. Hope we meet again some other place, a better place, too."

Jim shook his hand. That Sam had offered it instead of embracing him again meant that Sam had already distanced himself. He no longer felt as close to Jim. They were very good friends who had begun to be strangers.

Jim felt sick. That, however, was the way it had to be. Character determined destiny. His had sent him off on a different road from Sam's. It would have happened sooner or later, anyway. It had come sooner, that was all.

Nevertheless, he felt very sad. He also regretted that he had told Sam that he would be better off opting for adventure. Immediately after thinking this, he changed his mind, and much of the sadness and all of the regret vanished. It really was best for Sam, for anyone, to leave the familiar and to venture into strange country. That is, if the familiar was a place where hopeless hardship and unconquerable failure reigned.

Sam said, "Talk to my mother. She'll take you in when you need a home. You'll have to put up with a lot from her, but you won't starve to death. Just do what she tells you to do."

Sam turned and walked out without a backward look.

Jim called, "Good luck! I'll be with you in my thoughts, Sam!"

Sam did not reply.

CHAPTER

17

"**A**AAGH!"

The cry of the thing attacking Orc and Orc's cry mingled. Locked together, they were rolling and bouncing down the rocky face of the mountain. Orc had fallen onto his face, taking his attacker with him. Then he had rolled over. The creature had been under him for a moment. It had huge wings, a small body, a very long thin neck, and a head twice as large as his. Its beak was as hooked and as sharp as an eagle's. Its legs were exceedingly long for a flying creature. The claws were long, sharp, and curved, but they tore loose after their second rollover.

Despite its birdlike appearance, it had no feathers.

The two, three if Jim was counted, rolled and slid and soared down the slope. Both attacker and attacked were banged and bunged and gashed, and both cried out from pain. Then they slammed into the base of a boulder and stopped. Fortunately for Orc, the creature was between him and the rock when they crashed into it. Its body bones snapped; its wing bones had already cracked during the tumble.

Orc tried to get up so that he could seize the bird-animal around its skinny neck and break it. He was unable to do so. But the thing was also half-paralyzed. Its legs kicked, and it swayed its snakelike neck while its beak opened and shut, clack-clacking. After a minute or so, its enormous yellow eyes glazed, and it was dead.

Orc lay for a long time while the sun slid on its arc across the blue. He saw two creatures like his attacker above him. They were circling, their heads cocked to observe him. He hoped that he could get up before they decided that it was safe for them to land and dine on him. Meanwhile, as long as he was not in danger, he would take his ease. If ease could be called a state in which he hurt everywhere. He had lost skin from many parts of his body, including the private, and what was not scraped away was nearly so. Also, his head, knees, elbows, toe bones, ears, lips, nose, chin, and genitals had been battered many times. The pain in his head told him that he could have a concussion.

"Welcome to Anthema, the Unwanted World!" he muttered.

His father had certainly fixed him. But it would not be forever. If he, Orc, could do anything about it, and he would let nothing stop him, he would find his way to Los and kill him. Nevertheless, he groaned with pain. It was all right to groan and moan and even weep. No one was watching him.

Except me, Jim thought. I'm watching. But it's OK if he relieves himself with moans and groans. I'm hurting, too, every bit as much as he, and I wish I could moan and groan. I can't. But when he does it, he's doing it also for me, though he doesn't know that.

Jim thought intensely about loosing himself from Orc. He did not want to endure this pain a second longer than he had to. To return to his room in the ward would be to shed this tortured body immediately. But he hung on while telling himself that he would not desert Orc in the next few seconds. Something kept him from leaving. A sense of shame if he abandoned Orc? That was ridiculous. Orc would be neither hurt nor relieved if his invisible and intangible companion left him.

Yet, Jim felt that he would be a coward if he took the easy way out.

During Jim's battle with himself, Orc had risen and was walking slowly down the slope. Each movement of each limb was an odyssey of pain. Despite this, Orc did not stop. He left the pile of rock fragments at the bottom of the mountain and made his way through the forest. This was mainly trees resembling tall pines but with scarlet tufts at the ends of the branches. Their odor combined that of vanilla and peanuts. Large bushes with barrel trunks from the top of which sprouted twelve long fernlike fronds were in the spaces among the trees. Insects swarmed around the bushes. They seemed to be attracted by a yellow sticky fluid welling up from the base of the fronds. A stench like that of rotten potatoes with a dash of Limburger cheese rose from it.

The trees were populated with mouse-sized flying mammals. They swooped down, gulped insects, and flew back to rest on the branches. One fluttered by close to Orc. He snatched it out of the air, squeezed it until its thin hollow bones broke, ripped off its wings, tore off its head and legs, and drank its blood. Then, using his fingernails, he stripped off its skin and popped it onto his mouth. Chewing slowly so that he could separate the bones from the flesh with his tongue, Orc continued through the woods.

Jim was horrified. At the same time, he felt Orc's satisfaction at having something to eat. That feeling overcame Jim's disgust before long.

What Jim came to know quickly, because Orc was thinking

about it, was that young Lords were taught how to survive and even flourish in the wilderness. Orc had eaten raw flesh many times before. But when he was able to build a fire he would cook his meat.

There were plenty of flint in this area. He would work it into knives, spearheads, axes, and arrowheads. Then he would kill animals with the weapons he would make and from their skins make clothing and bags. After that, he would build a raft and float down the river.

Eighteen days after deciding this, he arrived on his raft at the broad mouth of the river. Beyond it was a sea.

CHAPTER

18

Someone else was in Orc's mind.

Jim had been frightened many times since entering the young Lord. That there might be another person or thing sharing Orc's mind terrified him. It was so . . . so . . . loathsome and . . . creepy-crawly. It made him so sick he would have thrown up if he'd had a stomach and a throat. The presence of a stranger—no doubt threatening—violated him.

Actually, he did not know the exact nature of the outsider who was now inside Orc. The first intimations that someone else—some Thing else—had moved in was two days after Orc had set up camp at the river's mouth. Jim felt the presence of the other. How could he put into words just how he sensed it? He could not. He just knew that it had not been there until the black moment when he became aware that it was present. It was like seeing the shadow of H. G. Wells's invisible man. Or like when, as a child, he had waked up in the middle of the night and known that a monster was in the closet and watching him from behind the half-open door. The difference now was there was indeed something in the closet of Orc's brain. Jim's imagination had not evoked it from his unconscious mind. It was truly there.

Just how did he know that the thing's purpose was sinister? The same way, he supposed, that a man dying of thirst in the desert knew why the vulture was circling above him.

When Orc had been within a day's travel on the raft to the sea, he had awakened that morning in a storm of blue stuff. It had been wind-blown from upriver, and it was composed of hand-sized azure pieces shaped like snowflakes. They gave off a strong walnutty odor. For a few minutes, the flakes were so numerous that Orc could not see more than ten feet away. Abruptly, the downfall thinned. A few flakes spun in, and the storm was over. They did not melt, but most of them were gone by evening. A horde of insects, birds, and animals spurted from the deep woods and devoured the flakes. Those that escaped the feeding frenzy turned brown many hours later and were ignored by the animals.

Orc, seeing this, decided he would share the banquet with them. The flakes felt like dried crystallized fungus. They tasted, however, like cooked and sugared asparagus. He stuffed himself with them though he had to drink a lot of water afterward. They dried out his tissues.

Jim theorized it might contain some sort of virus which infiltrated the eater's body. Then the virus would latch onto the host's nervous system and, somehow, change from a disorganized mass to a copy of the host's neural system. It became that being, or a copy thereof, because it was a ghostly reconstruction of the nerves and brain of the animal it occupied. It dispossessed the host as an identity, and it replaced the host's consciousness with its borrowed consciousness.

Jim had a figurative headache while thinking about this. He came to realize that he could not know where the thing came from or how it got into Orc's mind. It could be a coincidence that the thing appeared shortly after Orc had eaten the blue flakes.

Forget explanations, Jim told himself. Deal with the here and the now. Find a way to fight this unseen, handless, and faceless entity. Jim wondered how he could warn Orc about it? After a while, he realized that he could not. The battle, if there was to be a battle, was going to be between himself and the thing.

Since he was tired of just calling it a thing, he decided that he would name it. Everything had to have a name, a label. What could it be?

"Ghostbrain" came to him. As good a name as any. Ghostbrain it was.

Five days after arriving at the sea, Orc was hunting for fresh meat. After three hours, he glimpsed one of the forest-dwelling antelopes and began stalking it. An arrow was fitted to his bow, ready to leap forth and plunge into the brown-and-black dappled side of the cervine. Something spooked it before he could get within range. It leaped away, dodging around tall bushes and jumping over the shorter ones.

Cursing silently, he approached the area where it had been. He was cautious. Whatever had frightened it might be a large and dangerous beast. Then, peering through a bush, he saw the cause of the deer's alarm. It was about the size and shape of a skunk, its big bushy black tail waving. It was digging into the ground with its shovel-shaped and long-clawed paws. The food it sought was buried only an inch or two in the ground. It did not take long for the beast to uncover and to start eating it.

Orc would have been disgusted under different circumstances. The loathsome creature mostly ate carrion and excrement and anything edible that was dead or near-dead. This time, Orc was too astounded to feel repulsion. The meal the beast had unearthed was a pile of feces, which he had expected. What he had not expected was fresh human feces.

He was not the only person on this planet.

He whirled, scanning the woods behind him. His heart was beating hard, not because of joy but because that other person might be stalking him.

He glimpsed a dark face and a stone spearhead dropping behind a bush.

He got on the other side of the bush and looked intently all around him. The dark man could have companions. When he was fairly certain that there were none, he called out, "I am Orc, son of Los and Enitharmon! I am alone! There is no need for us to try to kill each other! I am looking for the gate out of this world! I have no quarrel with anyone but my father! Let us make peace! Each of us has a better chance of finding the gate if we pool our brains and resources!"

He waited. There was no response, and he was sure that the dark man had left the bush the moment he knew that he had been observed.

He repeated the speech.

Then a man spoke loudly, though from behind Orc. His Thoan differed somewhat from Orc's in pronunciation and pitch, but it was completely understandable.

"You say your only quarrel is with the accursed Los?"

"Right!"

"No one else was stranded here with you?"

"Not that I know," Orc said.

"Put the arrow back in the quiver," the man said. "Then stand up. I will come to you, though not very close, and I'll have my spear ready. But I would prefer that we be friends."

After some more talking, mostly to ensure that one did not

have any advantage over the other, the man walked out from behind a tree. He was shorter than Orc but broader. He wore a tight-fitting fur cap and a fur loincloth. A leather belt tied together with thongs was around his waist. It held leather containers in which were a stone knife and a stone ax. His quiver and bow had been left behind. His skin was deep brown, his nose was flat and broad, and his lips were fully everted. The hair that fell out from under the cap was gleaming black and slightly wavy.

When he was twenty feet from Orc, he stopped. The dark brown eyes looked wary, though he was showing large white teeth in a big grin.

"You are Orc, son of Los and Enitharmon," he said. "I am Ijim, son of Natho and Ocalythron."

"Ijim of the Dark Woods?" Orc said.

"Yes, I am—was—Lord of the World of Dark Woods."

"You are my great-great-granduncle," Orc said.

"Which does not necessarily mean that we are friends," Ijim said. "As they say in more than one world, you can choose your friends, but a cousin is a cousin, like it or not."

While they kept the distance between them unchanged, Orc outlined his story. During this, he kept glancing to both sides and looking swiftly behind him. What Ijim said about his being alone might be true. But an overtrusting Lord was soon a dead one, according to the ancient saw.

Ijim said, "So, you are the son of the extraordinarily beautiful Enitharmon and of Los, the Eternal Prophet, the Possessor of the Moon! Such was he titled when he lived in the world he ruled before moving into his present one, long before Enitharmon became his wife and long before you were born. Here, briefly, is my story."

A Lord, a woman named Ololon, had found a way to avoid the ingenious traps Ijim had set in the gate giving entrance to his world. Ololon had come close to slaying Ijim, but he had gotten away. However, while being pursued through a series of gates from one world to another, Ijim had been forced to take a gate which led he did not know where. It was one-way, and it opened, he soon found out, to Anthema. That was forty-four years ago. Since then, Ijim had been looking for the gate which would take him out of the Unwanted World.

Forty-four years! Jim Grimson thought. During that time, Ijim must surely have eaten the blue flakes. That meant a ghostbrain was now using his body and mind. So, it was not Ijim talking to Orc. It was a Thing.

Then he thought that that was not, in a sense, true. The ghostbrain had become Ijim, was thinking like Ijim, was, in effect, Ijim. The first Ijim was dead. The second Ijim was no different from the first. Thus, he was not one bit more sinister than the first one. That one had probably been sinister enough to satisfy anyone.

"As you said, nephew, neither of us has anything the other wants. Unless you desire Anthema!" He laughed wildly for some seconds, making Orc wonder if his long solitude had driven him crazy.

After wiping the tears of laughter with the back of his hand, Ijim said, "You can have it. I can't leave soon enough. So, what do you say, nephew Orc? Shall we drop this mutual suspicion and work together as a dedicated and loving team?"

"As much as two Thoan can."

"Good! Let us give each other the kiss of eternal friendship and not feel each other's back for a soft spot in which to thrust a dagger while doing so!"

Orc thought that his uncle's kiss was rather long, and he did not think that Ijim had to feel his buttocks for so long. Perhaps Ijim longed so for human contact that he did not want to let loose of human flesh without thoroughly warming himself with it. Also, Ijim may have lusted for only women while they had been easily available, but he was willing, after forty-four years of enforced abstinence, to take whatever came his way.

They walked back to the camp side by side. Ijim explained that he had seen Orc the day before. Instead of joyfully approaching Orc, however, he had stayed hidden. He had intended to study him for a while before announcing himself.

Orc said that it was quite a coincidence that the only two humans on a planet should cross paths.

"Not so much," Ijim said. "I came here out of the same gate you did, the cave. I explored the cave but the gate was too well hidden, must've needed a code word to be revealed. After forty-four years of searching vainly for another gate and living like a beast all that time, I came back here. It seemed to me that the outgoing gate might be located close to the ingoing. Of course, I thought that when I first got here. I looked the local area over so closely and so many times that, even now, I can remember its every detail. But I was going to make another try. It couldn't hurt. This time, though, since you have a clue on you, the Shambarimem medallion, we might have a good chance."

"Seen anything around here that could be connected, however remotely, to a horn?" Orc said. "Not just visually, perhaps verbally or analogically, whatever?"

"Nothing. But then I wasn't looking for a landmark which might be somehow linked to the image of a horn. Now, it's different."

After they got to the camp and talked some more, they went hunting together. Within twenty minutes, they had bagged a four-tusked piglike animal. Before eating it, Orc decided to swim in the river. Though he needed a bath, he also wished to find out if he could really trust Ijim. He left his weapons on the bank, but the dark man soon joined him. Satisfied that Ijim was, for the time being, anyway, a true partner, Orc got out of the water. Ijim stayed in. But he called out to Orc as Orc bent down to pick up his clothes. And Ijim laughed mightily. It seemed that he would never stop.

When he did, he said, "Don't dress yet."

"Why not?" Orc said. He was not sure what Ijim was up to.

"You can't see it!" Ijim shouted, and he laughed some more.

"See what?"

"Oh, that Los!" Ijim said. "He played a funny trick on you, but it's a sad one, too. Might have been sad for you, that is! Fortunately for both of us, Los did not foresee that you would find another Lord here."

"What are you talking about? Get to the point, man!"

"You can't see it!" the Lord of the Dark Woods cried out. "You might never have seen it, might've wandered forever over this terrible place and not seen it!"

"Are you going to hold me in suspense until I die from curiosity? Or will I have to choke it out of you?"

"There's a *map* on your back!" Ijim cried. "Between your shoulder blades and going down to a point almost even with your hipbones!"

Grinning, he waded out of the river. Orc kept his back to him so he could study the map, if it was indeed a map. Orc was not sure that Los had not played a savage joke on him that was a double joke. The map could be misleading and lead all over the planet and end up in a place that did not have a gate. However, why would he put a fake map where his son would probably never see it?

After Ijim had dried off his nephew's back with a piece of chamoislike skin, he turned him around to get the full light of the sun.

"What a sense of humor your father, may the silver arrows of Elynittria skewer his liver, has! Black, to be sure, blacker than Shambarimem's depression the first time his Horn was stolen, but it's worthy of evoking great laughter! On your back where you can't see it, ho, ho, ho, aauueeegh!"

"Choke to death from laughter for all I care," Orc snarled. "But first tell me what the map looks like. Better yet, draw it in the mud. I can transfer it to a parchment—after I make some."

Ijim had danced around, bent over and hoohawing and then almost strangling from the phlegm in his throat. When he recovered, he stood behind Orc again.

"There's a tiny black dot at the top of the map," he said. "A drawing of an arrow sticks out from it. I assume that's the beginning, the gate you and I came out of. There's a curvy blue line starting from the end of the arrow. On both sides of it are black broken lines in the shape of triangles. The mountains forming the river valley. So, the blue curvy line is the river we both took when we left the gate. It ends by spreading out into the crooked lines. The mouth of the river and the sea it empties into, I suppose. Where we are now. There are a few blue wavy lines beyond the river's end, but they're shorter and sharper. Must indicate the sea. Wait a minute."

After several seconds, he said, "I was looking for words to identify landmarks. There aren't any, and I doubt the map is anywhere near scale. It's a very rough and not at all satisfactory guide, but certainly better than none.

"Let's see. Here's a broken green line starting with a small arrow. It goes north of here since this estuary faces west, but there are no landmark signs along it. It then turns east, which should be inland. There is something where it turns! Let me look closely at it. It's very small."

Then he said, "Looks like the outline of an octopuslike animal. What in the name of Enion is that supposed to indicate?"

"We'll find out when we get there," Orc said sharply. His uncle, for some reason, was getting on his nerves. Yet, Orc should have been dizzy with happiness to have Ijim's companionship and to have him discover the map. Perhaps, Orc thought, it was because he felt like a fool and Ijim was laughing at him because he *was* a fool. But then Ijim seemed to find everything funny.

As the days went by and they walked northward along the coast, Ijim's too frequent and too easy laughter got on Orc's nerves. Finally, he could endure it no longer. He stopped his uncle in the middle of his hysterical and inappropriate heehawing.

"Why do you do that?" he said harshly.

Ijim blinked, and he said, "Do what?"

"Giggle and shriek all the time like an inexperienced and shy young girl who's nervous because she's with a boy."

Ijim looked sullen. "I didn't know I was doing that. If I am, and I don't admit I was, it's because I've been alone for forty-four years, no human being to talk to."

He began to whine. "You'd have some peculiar ways if you'd been as isolated as I was. Forty-four years! Think about that!"

"I suppose so," Orc said. "But if I was as silly and maddening as you, I'd surely want someone to straighten me out."

"Telling you that wouldn't be dangerous, would it? Oh, no! Speak up, and die, right? You're not the kind of person who'd take kindly to being insulted, right?"

Orc said nothing. After a few moments of silence, Ijim said, "Don't be angry with me. I just met you after forty-four years of absolute solitude and already you're yelling at me!"

"Just quit that insane laughing. Don't laugh except when there's something funny to laugh at."

Ijim shrugged his shoulders. "I'll try. But after forty-four years of suffering through every minute, every second . . ."

"And quit whining about 'forty-four years'!" Orc roared.

"I'm tired of hearing it! It's over now! Quit living in the past! You're not alone anymore!"

"I'd be better off," Ijim said. He looked hurt and comically dignified at the same time.

For a long while after that conversation, Ijim sulked. Only when Orc addressed him did he reply, and he did so in as few words as possible. That angered Orc almost as much as the laughter did. And, twice, when he suddenly turned around, he caught Ijim sticking his tongue out at him and gesturing obscenely.

"Manathu Vorcyon!" Orc said the first time he surprised his uncle in the act. "You're how many thousands of years old? Yet you behave like a spoiled child!"

"Can't help it," Ijim said. "Forty-four years of living . . ."

"Don't say it!" Orc shouted. "One more time, and I swear I'll leave you! You can be alone for forty-four more years! Forever, for all I care!"

For a long while, Ijim took care to avoid mentioning the length of his stay on Anthema. But he complained often and about the most trivial things. Such as stubbing his toe. He spent fifteen minutes talking about it and wondering bitterly why life had been so hard on him. Obstacles and injuries lay everywhere in his path.

At last, Orc said, "I've been treated unfairly, brutally, too, mostly by my father. You don't hear a word about that from me, do you? It's the way it is. Endure it. But try to do something about it. Try to change what you don't like. And quit yapping about it!"

"Yes, but . . ."

"No buts!"

"You're a hard man," Ijim said. His eyes became wet, and he snuffled. "Not all of us are made of stone. Some of us are genuine human beings, flesh and blood with a heart that feels, whereas yours . . ."

"Grow up! Or is it too late for that?"

Jim, listening to this, was struck with a thought. Struck was right, right on! Holy Mother! Orc could just as well be talking about him, Jim Grimson! He had been complaining about his lot and feeling sorry for himself a good part of his life. And, until recently, he had really done nothing to solve the problems he'd been whining about.

Then another idea hit him like a brass-knuckled fist. Ijim! Pronounced EE-jeem. But, in his mind, spelled Ijim. I . . . Jim. The Dark Lord of the Woods was named I (am) Jim.

Was Ijim—and, hence, all of this—just a fantasy?

Had his unconscious mind given him the name and the character of Ijim to show him, circuitously, himself?

For a moment, he came close to losing his faith that the Tiersian universes were real. He suddenly felt sick and, at the same time, weightless. The world, as seen through Orc's eyes, wavered and became cloudy. The light dimmed. He felt himself rising. He was headed back to Earth. But, though handless, he grabbed on to something—what, he did not know—and he held on. The light brightened; things became steady and clear again.

The Freudian significance of Ijim's name was too obvious. It was just a coincidence. He knew that this world and all in it were as real, as hard, and as sharp-edged as his native universe.

For a while there, though . . .

Thirty-two days after Jim's moment of dark doubt, Orc and Ijim came to the place indicated by the octopuslike mark on the map. They did not know they were there until they got to the end of a valley out of which a small river flowed into the sea.

Orc was trudging along the shore through water up to his

ankles. Behind was Ijim, silent (for once) except for the splash-splash of his feet in the rising tide. There were many large black boulders about ten feet high in this area. Orc was passing between two separated by about twelve feet when he stopped. Then he yelled.

Something under the water had gripped his right ankle. And then it yanked him hard toward the nearest boulder. Suddenly, he was on his back and being dragged, the green and stinking surface scum washing into his mouth and over his eyes.

Ijim shouted, "What is it?"

He snatched his stone ax from his belt and leaped toward Orc. The young Lord had stopped yelling and was futilely struggling to loosen the thing gripping his ankle. He yelled again when a section of the boulder toward which he was being hauled slid down. Inside the rock was an assembly of green serrations as sharp as sawteeth and larger than a lion's. Moreover, there were at least a hundred.

Then a brownish tentacle as thick as two fingers held together humped for a moment out of the water. Ijim, seeing that, screamed. He had also realized that the rock was really a plant or animal. And it meant to eat Orc.

Ijim screamed again. He jumped high. The clawed tip of another tentacle rose briefly from the spot he had just left. The Lord came down straddle-legged and hopped backward. The tentacle end thrashed around, groping for him.

Orc had by then gotten his flint ax from his belt and was chopping down on the tentacle pulling him. It was not easy to do since he had to sit up and lean far forward while being pulled along. He called, "Ijim! Help me!"

The Lord of the Dark Woods turned and ran away and did not stop until he was at a safe distance.

Orc shouted, "You coward!" After that, he was too busy. Especially since a second tentacle had coiled around the thigh of his other leg. But he kept hacking until he felt the grip on his ankle give way. When he was within a few feet of the gaping mouth, he hewed apart the other tentacle. But he came close to being snared by other tentacles as he ran ankle-deep through the water to where Ijim danced in a frenzy of despair.

Panting, Orc said, "I should kill you!"

He raised his ax, dripping with water and a thick green saplike fluid. Ijim ran and did not stop until he was fifty feet away. He turned, and he shouted in a high-pitched and quavering voice. "I couldn't help it! Forty-four years I've survived by running away! It's a conditioned reflex by now! But I'm not really a coward! I'll do better next time! You'll see!"

"Next time?" Orc yelled. "There won't be any next time!"

"Kill me then!" Ijim shrieked. "Find out what loneliness and no one to talk to mean! You'll end up being just like me! And the next time you need me, you'll be all alone! I won't let you down, I swear! If I do, I'll kill myself!"

He got down on his knees and lifted his hands toward Orc. "I'm begging you, don't leave me here!"

Orc spat toward Ijim. But he said, "All right! One more chance! But don't get near me for a long while!"

He went eastward, detouring the boulders by many yards. Ijim stayed behind him, and he did not come to Orc's camping place that night. Orc could see him in the light of the fire. He was a shadow sitting with his back against a tree trunk. In the morning, Ijim approached him. He was smiling as if nothing had happened. But the rest of that day, he did nothing to irritate Orc.

CHAPTER

19

Dawn brought with its light a darkness.

Orc opened his eyes and could not see. His nose seemed to be clogged. His mouth was held shut by something, and something was pressing on his tongue.

Jim had been aware of this some seconds before Orc was fully roused. Though he had screamed voicelessly with his no-tongue, he could not, of course, be heard.

Orc tried to tear off the thing covering his face. It felt fuzzy and sticky, and the tendrils enfolding the front part of his tongue tasted like prunes. He rolled around in the sleeping bag, which covered him to his waist. Then he scrambled out of it stood up, and then began whirling around and around as he struggled. He heard Ijim's half-strangled bellows just before he bumped into him. He fell backward from the impact and landed on his buttocks. Making no effort to get up, he dug his fingers into the meaty layer under the sticky and fuzzy top of the thing. He was unable to lift it. Then he felt along its edges, his fright now become mindless panic as his nose and mouth were entirely filled. When he found that the edges were near his ears, he got to his knees and groped around until he found his sleeping bag. If he could not tear off the thing choking him, he would die in a minute or so. Very soon, anyway.

Thrusting a hand into the bag, he located the scabbarded flint knife he kept by his side while sleeping. He slid its point under the edge of the choker. Though he cut his skin, he did not care. When he had half the length of the stone blade under the meaty layer, he lifted it. Then he turned the knife so that the cutting edge was up. Savagely, he pushed upward. The blade sliced through the fleshly stuff. He grabbed its edges and ripped them to one side. The stuff came out of his nose and mouth and from his eyes, though the violent removal hurt as if he were tearing tape from his skin. Now, he could see and breathe.

The thing in his hand looked like a bright-green piece of thick cloth with tendrils and thick growths on its underside. Drawing in deep breaths, he hurled it away and hastened to help Ijim. The Lord, who had also gotten out of his sleeping bag, was rolling back and forth on the ground while he vainly tried to rip the smotherer from his face. Orc used his knife to pry it loose and hurl it away. It fell among hundreds of similar things on the ground. The tree branches were festooned with them. Dozens more were slowly descending to the ground. Unlike those that had landed, they had swollen backs. Then he saw the humps of those that had just struck the earth. They were deflating. He supposed that they had been filled with gas.

He became aware that a half-dozen of the things were sticking to his body and that his sleeping bag was covered with them. These fell off shortly afterward. Apparently, if they did not land on an orifice in living flesh, they did not stay attached.

Everywhere he looked, up, down, around, on the trees and bushes, out in the river, were the bright-green plants. Or were they animals?

Ijim, blood streaming from his face, gasped for a while before speaking. His fingers, moving over his face, felt the liquid. He lifted his hand to stare at it.

"You cut me!" He laughed. "But you cut your own face, too! Only way to do it, heh?"

"Did you ever run across these things before?"

"Certainly not! I'd have never gone to sleep in the open without covering my face, you can bet on that! From now on . . . !"

"What about the stuff that also comes down from the sky, the things that look like blue flakes?"

"Sure," Ijim said as he rose. "At least a dozen times. It isn't bad eating."

Jim thought, Ijim's not Ijim. He's not human. If he ate the blue flakes, he's been taken over by the ghostbrain by now. The identityless nonentity had attained identity and entity-dom. But it would not know that. It would think that it has always been Ijim. It had no mind in its viral state. When it took over Ijim's mind, it began thinking. But it itself had no history of which it knew. So, it would always be Ijim to itself. Which, in a sense, was true.

Mister Lum had once said that humans had identity, but they had not yet succeeded in defining "identity." Jim tried to make his own definition now. The only result was confusion and a phantom headache. He abandoned the attempt and did not intend to resume it.

The thing that was called Ijim was to all intents and purposes the exact same as the original Ijim. Or so Jim thought. Somehow, that the Lord was occupied by a ghost-brain seemed to make him more sinister. That, Jim told himself, was because he had read too many science-fiction stories and seen too many horror movies. In these, the almost always evil alien meant to eat, enslave, or mind-possess humans. Yet, could anything be more sinister than a human being? Some human beings, anyway, like Hitler, Stalin, Mao, Idi Amin—the list was as long as a census report. So evil were they, they seemed to be nonhuman. But being evil was part of being human, just as being good was part of being human. And these demonstrably evil people, without exception, high or low, Albanian dictator or Chicago alderman, corrupt Senator or Washington pimp, thought of themselves as being good.

The two Lords broke camp and went east along the river. Late that afternoon, they set up camp again. Though they would normally have pushed on until close to dusk, they had to make sleeping masks to protect their mouths and noses from the green things. During the following two days, they saw a number of animals that had succumbed to the "chokers," as Orc called them.

Their tendrils were growing over the rotting carcasses. Those that had failed to kill were turning brown and brittle.

After that incident, Ijim began to fall into long silences broken by a low muttering. During these, he would stare wildly around. Orc would endure this behavior as long as he could. He would ask Ijim what he was thinking about. Always, Ijim would react as if he had suddenly been wakened from a very deep sleep. He would blink his eyes and shake his head and say, "What? What are you talking about?" Then he would deny that he was disturbed by anything.

Jim Grimson thought that the ghostbrain, not Ijim, was speaking during the fugues. Maybe it was having flashes of its life in a previous form before it became a virus or whatever drifting around on the blue things. Who knew what phases it had gone through? A person seeing a butterfly for the first time would not dream that it had been a caterpillar.

Thirty more days passed, though not without dangerous incidents. There were no more green chokers in their path, but they did see hundreds of thousands on the ground in another valley when they were going through a mountain pass. One afternoon, a sickening gas rolled down a hole in a mountainside, enveloped them, and left them vomiting for several hours and unwell for two days. The larger animals were similarly affected; all the small birds and animals died.

They thought that they were getting close to the place where the gate was if Los had not lied. Ijim checked the map on his nephew's back.

"The markings are almost at an end. Those wavy parentheses should mean the big lake just ahead of us."

They were standing at the top of a steep slope. Two miles or more away, at the foot of the slope, was the immense lake Ijim had expected. It was about two miles wide at the end nearest to them and broadened out until it melted into the horizon. The forest grew almost to the water. About two miles east, towering cliffs suddenly bordered the lake and ran as far as Orc could see.

"We'll have to build a boat or climb up and go along the edges of the cliffs," he said. "They're very rough and precipitous. I think we should make a canoe."

"Agreed."

Ijim continued his map reading.

"Apparently, when we come to near the end of the lake, we bear right. The last mark must point out the gate place. It's a circle with a cross in it and many horizontal thin lines over the cross. Maybe close, maybe not. But . . . one step at a time. As the Grandmother of All, Manathu Vorcyon said, 'Who gets ahead of himself sees his own backside.'"

Twenty days later, they had built an outrigger dugout with a mast and a woven-grass sail. It took them another ten days to kill enough animals, smoke and salt the meat, and collect nuts and berries for boatboard supplies.

"Los is making us work hard," Ijim said. "If I get a chance to capture him, I'll make him pay for that. How about skinning him alive, just to start off with?"

Orc smiled. If anyone was going to skin his father, he would be the one.

CHAPTER

20

The two Lords had traveled an estimated three hundred miles since leaving the lakeshore. Yet they had seen nothing resembling the symbol on Orc's back.

Ijim's fugues were becoming more frequent and longer-lasting. When he came out of them, he remembered nothing about them. In fact, he did not know that he had been in them. Orc, he said, was making up the whole business. He wanted to drive him crazy. Orc asked him why he would want to do that. Because, Ijim said, Orc was crazy, and the insane loved the company of their kind.

The young Lord realized that it was useless to continue arguing with his uncle. Ijim was the mad one in this twosome. Therefore, he would have to be watched carefully. Orc had thought that his uncle was going to refrain from violence until the gate was found. Now, he was not sure.

Jim Grimson was even more apprehensive than Orc. Ijim must die, and he must do it in Anthema. If he got to another world, he—the thing in him—might propagate its kind, and the next world and the next, all the worlds, might be taken over. Just how, Jim could not guess. The how no longer mattered. Ijim had to be killed here, and it would be best if his body and the thing possessing it were destroyed.

He knew that. Orc did not.

Ten days later, near high noon, the Lords were on top of a lofty ridge forming a wall along the right side of a river. They had been forced to climb up its slope and go along its back until they found more level ground. "For all we know," Orc told Ijim, "the landmark could be on the other side of the ridge."

And it was.

At the foot of the ridge was a plain stretching for perhaps forty miles. Another chain of mountains to the south bounded the plain. This contained scattered woods and rivers and creeks and some hilly country. A large, black, slowly moving object relatively near them was a herd of animals, grass-eaters.

"There it is!" Orc said. He pointed at a circular object about two miles from the foot of the ridge and close to a river so small it barely escaped being a creek. The structure glittered in the sun as if made of glass. Its outer walls, forming the circle, were high and thick. Enclosed by the circle was a cross-shaped structure. Its walls were as thick as the enclosing walls. Thinner walls ran parallel to the horizontal wall of the cross. The whole structure had to be that represented by the symbol on Orc's back.

"Great Mother of Us All!" Orc shouted, and he struck his hand against his forehead. "Mighty and wise Enion! How dumb can we be? We call ourselves Lords, and we're as mindless as worms! Why did we never connect the symbol on my back with that on the medallion! They both represent the grillwork in the end of Shambarimem's Horn! It was there right in front of us, and we never connected the two!"

Ijim was, at the moment, not in a fugue. He howled with delight and grabbed Orc's hands. They danced around and around, both grinning and yelling. Several times, they almost lost their footing on the narrow flat top of the ridge. Finally, panting, they stopped.

Orc frowned then. He said, "But it's a building, an artifact! I didn't know there were humans here!"

"Neither did I," Ijim said.

"Where's the gate? Inside that building?"

"Must be," Ijim said. Grimness had shouldered aside his joy. A few seconds later, he started to mutter. Knowing from experience that the Lord would follow him automatically, Orc started down the steep side of the ridge. Though he had to be careful because of loose stones here and there, he could stay on his feet. Ijim seemed to be enclosed on himself, but he did not fall. A part of him was still alert enough to handle simple situations.

Halfway down, Orc exclaimed, and he stopped. Ijim, still muttering, halted a few feet above him. The grassy ground around the herd of black long-horned animals had opened in scores of places. Orc was too far away to make out the details, but the openings were like the doors of trapdoor spiders. Where there had been grass were now round black holes with discs, grass-topped on the outer side, sticking straight up from the ground.

Out of the holes popped long lean gray creatures. They bounded toward the herd, which stampeded in the opposite direction. This was toward the woods fringing this part of the plain. Now, other gray killers were racing from the woods. The herd wheeled as one back toward the plain.

Directly in its path, more trapdoors swung up. Scores of hunters leaped out of the holes and, like the greyhounds they resembled, sped toward the antelopes. When they got to the edge of the milling herd, they shot long, thin, gray strands from their mouths. These arced up, shining in the sun, fell onto the prey, and stuck as if they were glue. Presently, many antelopes had fallen, their legs entangled in the strands. The hunters, whistling loudly, were on them within seconds and tore them apart with their teeth. The rest of the herd broke through the lines and galloped off.

Orc started down, saying, "Ijim! Those beasts must come from the glassy building through underground routes to the trapdoors. Now we know how to get inside it, if we have the courage!"

Ijim continued to mutter. When they were close to the beginning of the plain, they examined one of the trapdoors. Those in the woods had been closed. The gray beasts who had issued from them must intend to return via those on the plain. Orc pried up the round and partially grown-over lid with his spearhead. It rose up soundlessly. Around the neck of the hole was a rim into which the door fitted. The rim was a hard glassy substance, probably the same used to form the circular building.

The trapdoor was also made from the glassy stuff. Earth had been glued to its top and heaped and impregnated with the fixative. Grass grew from this earth.

The hinge was provided by a substance spread at the point where the lid would be raised. This was hard on the edges and semihard between them but flexible enough to permit the lid to be raised without breaking loose from the rim.

Orc suspected that all the grassy substance had been spewed from the gray beasts' mouths just as the entangling strands had been.

About three feet below the opening of the hole was a platform of dirt. The animals must have jumped out from this to the surface. Beyond that, the tunnel slanted down and probably became horizontal about ten feet below the ground. Its wall was enclosed with the gray glassy substance. This must line the tunnel all the way to the entrance inside the building and thus keep the tunnel from collapsing.

Orc lowered the door. They then watched the hairless beasts tear off chunks of flesh from the carcasses and take these into the holes on the plain. They were much more than the canines they resembled at a distance. A set of insectine pincers projected from the sides of their mouths. These moved independently of the heads' movements and cut and sliced the meat and then closed on large pieces. The beasts had long prehensile tails which curled around other pieces. Those animals with full burdens leaped into the holes carrying meat with their jaws, pincers, and tails.

Their ears were round, thick, and flat, and their pale-yellow eyes were large. After listening to their whistling for a few minutes, Orc decided that they were communicating in a limited form of code. He had counted seven variations of a series of long and short whistles.

"These are no dummies," he softly told Ijim. "Look at their foreheads. Plenty of room for brains in those skulls."

Ijim nodded. He had recovered from the fugue halfway through the woods.

"Fantastic creatures!" Orc said. "They're a combination of dog, termite, spider, and monkey! The Vanished Ones went all out when they made these! I'm telling you, Ijim, of all the sciences, biology is the most fascinating! Life and its multitudinous forms! However, the brain, the brain! That's the apex of life, the jewel!"

He told Ijim that *kamanbur*—"whistlers"—was as good a name as any for the beasts.

"Have to have a name for everything."

He and Ijim walked through the woods to the river. There Orc pointed out that the plain inclined downward to the *kamanbur* structure. "Dig a ditch from the river to the nearest trapdoor. Flood it. The water should fill the tunnel and drown the stories below the surface level. During the diversion, we enter the nest."

"Dig a ditch!" Ijim howled. "Are you crazy? It'll take us months to make the tools to dig with and then to do the digging! It's not a small project! Also, we'll be in full sight of the *kamanbur* while we're working. You think they're going to give us the time we need?"

"What else do we have beside time?" Orc said. "Or are you so busy with other matters?"

Ijim grumbled. He spoke of soft beds, soft sheets, and even softer women, and the delicious food and heady liquor and rapturing drugs and his triumphant assaults on the Lords of other worlds in the days before the accursed Los had chased him into this nightmare universe. Orc paid him no attention. He was thinking that antlers could be made into diggers to break up the earth. Shovels and spades could be made from strips of animal horns fixed to a hardwood base. Baskets to carry the dirt could be woven. Their tools would wear out soon, but they would just make replacements.

First, though, he had to check out the *kamanbur* nest. Ijim, expecting a ravening horde to burst from the trapdoors, followed him reluctantly. No *kamanbur* came out, though it was soon apparent that the men could be seen from the structure. There were thousands of holes, a half-inch in diameter, in the walls. These would pass through a certain amount of fresh air and of light and provide observation apertures for the *kamanbur*.

During the next few days, the Lords built a treehouse for sleeping and to thwart any arboreal predators. Then they intensively explored the neighborhood when they were not making tools for their project. And, to Orc's delight, he found a number of trapdoors on the other side of the river.

"Their tunnels go under the river!" he said. "Under! That

means we won't have to dig that tremendous ditch on the other side! We'll let the river flood the nest!"

"You mean we'll have to go down the tunnel under the river? And just how do you think we'll break the sheathing? And even if we can, the noise of hammering and pounding will bring the *kamanbur* running!"

"You've been a deep pain in my ass for some time now," Orc said. "You used to be so jolly I forgave you your irritating habits and your running off at the mouth. Not to mention your crazy fits. But I'm really tired of your pessimism."

"What crazy fits?"

Ijim was bristling.

Orc went down into the tunnel. The trapdoor was left propped open. The young Lord hoped that this would make some fresh air flow through the tunnel. Ijim did not come along with Orc.

"There's not enough space for two to work together," he said. "Anyway, this is just a reconnoiter. You don't need me."

"Fine!" Orc said. "You can work with your flint. We're going to need a couple of hundred awls before we're through."

Ijim had mentioned the night before Orc's descent into the tunnel that he should tell him that he tended to panic in closed small places. He would not like it if Orc told anyone about this. But there it was.

"That doesn't mean I won't be going with you when we try for the gate. I'll make it through with you. Somehow. I've done it before when it was absolutely necessary. And if it didn't take too long."

Thus, Orc was now alone as he crawled on hands and knees. He wore pads on his knees and gloves on his hands. He carried a lit torch and several extra torches. Attached to his belt was the end of a thin strip of rawhide. He had estimated the distance between the trapdoor and the point at which the tunnel would be deepest under the river. To make sure, he had probed the river in its middle to gauge its depth.

When the strip became tight, it would indicate that he should stop crawling. He hoped that the estimate was near the reality. He also hoped that the torch fumes would not overcome him. As it was, they made him cough and burned his eyes.

After a near unendurable length of time, the strip tautened. He took his gloves off, wet a finger, and held it up. There seemed to be a very slight flow of air, but he could just be imagining that. Wishful thinking or not, he had to go to work. He got down onto his back. After removing from his bag the wooden support he had built, he set it by his side. Having placed the torch upright in the support, he incised a square on the top of the tunnel with one of the sharp flint scrapers from the bag.

Ijim was right. Hammering or pounding would bring the *kamanbur*. Eventually, he would have to use a stone hammer. But that could wait until the last moment. The scraper made a screeching noise which he hoped would die out before it reached the other end of the tunnel.

He was taking a chance that some lone *kamanbur* or a pack of *kamanbur* would come along this tunnel. If that happened, it would happen.

Though the glassy substance was hard, it was softer than iron. It could be cut as easily as bronze, though "easily" was only a relative term. Tiny flakes shining in the torchlight fell down onto his chest. Stopping now and then to wipe the sweat from his face or to drink water from his leather bottle, he moved the edge of the scraper across the lines of the square. After an indeterminate time, he stopped. The torch fumes seemed to be stronger, and he felt somewhat faint. His moistened finger could detect no movement of air. Alarmed, he took the torch from its support and crawled back toward the entrance trapdoor.

He and Ijim had arranged signals for emergencies. The Lord of the Dark Woods would tug the strip twice, pause, then tug it twice again to call Orc out of the tunnel. Orc would do the same if something happened to him that required that Ijim drag him out by the leather strip. Orc crawled back to the platform. The trapdoor was closed. The end of the strip which Ijim was to hold was lying on the platform. Something must be wrong if Ijim had shut the door.

He rolled the torch down the slope so that its light would not be seen when he raised the door. Slowly, he moved the door up about an inch. He saw several *kamanbur* moving around at the base of the tree which held the little hut he and Ijim had built. The lower branches were festooned with the shiny gray strands spat from the creatures' mouths. When he raised the door another inch, he saw that the treehouse was beyond the reach of these. Ijim's dark face was in a window.

An hour later, the beasts had left. Orc crawled out of the tunnel and went to the tree. He called up softly, "What happened?"

Ijim, while climbing down, said, "They came to investigate. I think they came through a tunnel upriver and then circled around through the woods. I saw them before they got close, and I ran to the tree. I'm sorry I didn't have time to signal you. The only thing I could do was to close the trapdoor and hope they hadn't seen me doing it. I guess they didn't."

"Maybe, now they've satisfied their curiosity, they'll leave us alone," Orc said.

He went down the tunnel after a while and resumed work. The next day, he crawled to the other end of the tunnel before he began his scraping. He had to determine that that exit-entrance was open. Or, if it were closed, that it could be opened from the tunnel side. A pale light in a round frame and loud whistling sounds showed that there was no trapdoor on this end. Since he might be smelled by the tenants, he went no closer.

Six days later, while he was incising, a drop of water fell on his face. That was soon followed by a steady drip. He continued scraping away in the narrow trenches forming the square. Water was soon oozing out from all four of the lines. Then, in one corner, it spurted out. He got out of the tunnel.

"I don't think it's going to give way until it's hammered at," he told Ijim. "The *kamanbur* will hear me. But if I can loosen it enough so the water breaks through entirely, it won't matter."

"You don't want to wait until tomorrow?" Ijim said. He was pale under his dark pigment.

"Let's get everything ready now," Orc said. "That won't take more than a few minutes. Then I go back. Be ready."

The sun was three-quarters of the way across the sky. Big black clouds were building up to the west, and the faint sound of thunder reached them.

The trees on the north side of the bank partly obscured the vision of the watchers in the nest. Orc and Ijim had also transplanted several large bushes to conceal their activities. Orc was not worried about being seen. But a party of *kamanbur*, reinvestigating the men, could show up at any time.

When he got back to the square, he drove several flint awls into its corners. His stone hammer struck again and again against a leather pad placed on the blunt end of the awl. He did not want to make much noise until he was ready to begin hammering on the square itself. The awls punched through the corners easily enough, though he had to use a different tool for each corner. The ends became quickly blunted or broken off.

Water had formed in a pool below the square. He was half-sunk in it. Suddenly, water spurted out of the tiny hole just made in a corner of the incised square. Its high-pressure jet half-blinded him, and he had to stop several times to blow water out of his nose. Despite the difficulties, he finished with the awls. Then he used a heavy stone hammer. The force of the blows was decreased by lack of space to swing the hammer and by his position on his back. Also, he had moved back so that his face was not directly below the square. That changed the angle of attack. He persisted, knowing that many lesser blows would equal a few strong ones.

Between the impacts of the stone on the square, he could hear whistlings. The *kamanbur* would soon be on him.

Then, as he had expected—no way to avoid it—the shiny gray square shot down and against his chest. It struck hard enough to hurt him. The water spouted through and hit him with a force harder than that of the square. He rolled over, though the water pressed him to the tunnel floor for a moment. He began crawling away as swiftly as he could. Water rose until he was swimming, though its advance bore him upward at a slight angle toward the trapdoor. The tunnel had become black as soon as the water had doused the torch flame. His tools were left behind. It was his life that concerned him now.

Ijim was supposed to be hauling in the line as hard and as swiftly as he could. If his efforts were doing any good, they were not apparent. Orc could feel no tug on the line.

He saw daylight ahead. The trapdoor had been left open. Then he could see nothing. The water had filled the tunnel and was rising faster then he could swim. A few seconds later, he burst into the nearly vertical part of the tunnel just below the trapdoor. Ijim grabbed Orc's outstretched hand and yanked him on out. The water surged up above the hole and fell back. Thereafter, it stayed level with the surface of the river.

The thunderheads were closer, larger, and blacker. Orc hoped that the lightning, thunder, and possibly rain would come soon. For some reason, he thought that all that would aid the Lords' invasion of the nest. It would certainly make it more dramatic.

Some weapons, including bows and arrows and short spears, were in watertight cases. Ijim helped strap one on Orc; Orc helped Ijim with his case. With other weapons inserted in containers in their belts, they plunged, Orc first, into the dark tunnel. Ijim was still pale, and his teeth were chattering. But he looked determined. Orc, however, was not sure that his uncle would have the courage to follow him. The claustrophobia would be made worse by having to swim all the way into the nest. As it was, Orc was not sure that they would not drown before reaching their goal.

Just as he believed that he could no longer hold his breath, he saw a glimmer above him. He thrust upward desperately, and his head broke the surface. A few seconds later, Ijim's dark face was beside him.

Ijim drew in several long breaths, then gasped, "That was the most terrible thing I've ever endured! I thought . . . ."

"Quiet!" Orc said softly. While dog-paddling and sucking in air, he looked around. There was just enough space between the water and the ceiling for their heads. The pale light from an opening in the floor of the story above shone on a ramp ascending from the water to the opening. Around them floated the bodies of many *kamanbur*, adults and puppies. No sound came from above.

He swam to the ramp and went up it on his hands and knees. When he got to the room above, he took his ax from its container. Ijim, still gasping, was close behind him. A faint breeze moved over Orc's wet skin and brought him an unidentifiable stench. The room was empty of *kamanbur* but not of other living creatures. Some were in large cages constructed of the dried gray strands and set along the bases of the walls and halfway up them. The grasshopper-sized insects therein glowed intermittently but made a steady light. The off phases of half of them were balanced by the on phases of the other half.

"Fascinating," Orc said. "A very unusual symbiosis between insects and mammals."

In larger cages attached to the walls were two other types of insects. One had scarlet-and-yellow-striped wings which beat as swiftly as a hummingbird's. Their combined noise made a low roar. These obviously kept the air moving. There were also spidery things the size of Orc's head. He had no time to determine their function.

He undid the waterproof case. From it, he took a short flint-tipped spear, a quiverful of arrows, and a bow. The spear was in a slender case within the larger case. After fitting the quiver strap over his shoulder, he strung the bow. Then he fitted an arrow to the bow. Having done all this very quickly, he trotted off along the curving wall. He passed a number of hallways. Not until he came to one with a larger entrance did he halt. This should lead to the room at the intersection of the two buildings that formed the horizontal and vertical arms of the cross within the circle, as seen from the top of the ridge. His guess was that Los had placed the gate at the intersection. But he had no idea on what floor it would be.

"Hurry!" Ijim said behind him. "They'll be coming down as soon as they get over their scare!"

Orc did not reply. He ran down the hallway past the insects in the walls. The light was not strong, though that coming through the thousands of holes in the walls added to the illumination. Abruptly, he was in the room in the central part of the cross.

He stopped. He was in luck. There, in the center of the round-walled room, was the gate. It was made of the shimmering more-than-diamond-hard metal called *tenyuralwa*.

Around it were piled *kamanbur* bones. These were a warning to the nest tenants to stay away from the upright square. Some time ago, the gate had been erected by Los, who had by some means kept the *kamanbur* from attacking him. After he had left, the creatures had investigated the gate. Some had gone through the side, which was set with a trap, and had perished. The parts of the bodies that had been in this world when the foreparts were burned or cut off had been arranged around the gate by the *kamanbur*. All the skeletons were of the hind parts only.

"If the *kamanbur* come down now," Ijim said, "we won't have much time to figure out how to get through!"

The gate was a metal square seven feet high. Its base had been secured to the floor with a hard black stuff, Thoan glue that no acid could dissolve or any fire burn away. Orc put his bow and arrow down, removed his spear from its case, and put it by the bow. After picking up a bone, he went to the other side of the gate and threw the bone through the square. It passed through unhindered and landed on the floor. That meant that the opposite side of the gate was the entrance to the other world.

Ijim had untied and unrolled a leather bundle and removed from it two torches and the ignition materials. They were a box containing wood shavings, splinters, dried grass, twigs, and two roughened flints set into wooden handlers. He arranged the inflammable material in a pile and began striking the flints together.

Orc walked around the square, kicking bones out of the way. Then he cast one through the opposite side of the square. As he expected, it disappeared. Another bone thrust a few inches into the square and quickly withdrawn was unsheared. A second later, he repeated the same action. This time, all the bone extended past the middle of the gate had been sheared off. That part was not visible because it was in the other world.

Ijim was cursing. The sparks struck from the flints had not set fire to the pile. He said, "Sometimes, it takes a lot of time! But we may not have that!"

Orc was too intent on his tests to reply. He put a legbone in again and again, counting seconds, *rlentawon, rlenshiwon, rlenkawon, rlenshonwon, rlengushwon.* Translated, one thousand one, one thousand two, one thousand three, one thousand four, one thousand five. When he had used up that bone, he began testing with another.

Ijim said, "Ah! Finally! Success!"

Orc turned to face him. The Lord of the Dark Woods was holding the end of a pine brand just above the fiery pile. The smoke from the flames was drifting slowly toward the nearest exit, which was the square of the gate.

"Listen carefully, Ijim. The trap seems to be a time-interval shears. I don't think the timing is random. We have approximately a second and a half to get through. The field goes off just that long. We have to stand close and jump through. But we must raise our hands up and hold our elbows close to our body. Our legs must be in the same vertical plane as our bodies. Anything sticking out too far ahead of our bodies or too far behind will be cut off."

Ijim nodded, and he said, "One hop does it. It'll be awkward to do that and go through without bending our knees."

Ijim understood as well as Orc—after all, he was many thousands of years older—that each man would have to use a bone first to test and thus to estimate the time base on which to start counting before taking the hop. There would be nothing accurate or guaranteed about the counting. Mostly, it would be luck that would get them through safely.

"One chance only," Orc said. He started, then stared past Ijim.

"We won't have time to practice jumping before we make the real one. Give me a torch."

Ijim, who had been bent over while lighting the second torch, straightened up and whirled around. By then, the room near the archway was filled with forty or so *kamanbur*. They spread out, their heads hanging low, jaws open, teeth gleaming, saliva dripping, pincers clacking together, prehensile tails straight up but curling at the ends. Their yellow eyes were fixed on the men.

Orc saw directly down the mouth of one. Inside it were two hornlike projections. These would be the guns, as it were, out of which were shot the thin quick-drying strands. Ijim advanced to the pile of bones encircling the gate, shouted, and waved the torch at them. They shrank away from him. Then one of them, a large female, emitted a series of long and short whistles. The gray beasts formed a circle around the bone enclosure.

Orc said, "They may have figured out that they can come through the gate on the other side without being harmed. They could attack us from two sides."

He ran around the gate and swung the torch back and forth at the *kamanbur*. They moved back but not as far as when they had first been threatened.

Ijim screamed, "Let's do it now! I'll go first! You watch my back!"

Orc could not help wondering if Ijim was planning to shove him back through the gate when he jumped after him. The idea of doing that to Ijim had occurred to him, though he had rejected it. Why should Ijim do that? He would still need Orc. But the Lords, like the *leblabbiy*, did not always act logically.

Orc ran back to the other side. He waved his torch as he did so. Gray strands shot out from the mouths of those in the front rank. They fell short by a few inches. After the range-finding tests, the *kamanbur* moved about a foot closer to the Lords. By the time he reached Ijim, the Lord was burning off several strands wrapped around his legs. The quickly flaming strands stank like a mixture of garlic and rotten potatoes.

The leader whistled some more messages, and they retreated. Then a dozen advanced a few feet from the pack and crouched. They looked so much like runners at the blocks that Orc understood what they meant to do. They would dash forward in a body and, when very close, jump. While still in the air, they would expel the entangling strands. Their prey would not be able to burn them all away before the *kamanbur* fell upon them.

"Now!" Orc yelled.

Ijim turned around slowly. His eyes were as unmoving as glass balls set in cement. His lips, however, were writhing as he articulated very swiftly but not very clearly.

Orc groaned. Of all the times that the fugue had overcome Ijim, this was the worst.

There was nothing that Orc could do for him—except one thing. It would give his uncle little chance to live, but it was better than nothing.

Orc snatched the torch from Ijim's hand and sent it whirling toward the crouched beasts. Whistling in alarm, they scattered as the torch fell near them. Orc grabbed Ijim and swung him around, then seized him by the waist and ran him forward. Ijim was still muttering when he was lifted and thrown through the gate.

There had been no time to stick a bone through the gate and withdraw it while counting. Orc had, however, lifted him up and cast him in as vertical an angle as he could manage.

Blood spurted from the empty air. Though the back portion of Ijim was severed, it had fallen on through. But not quickly enough to prevent some blood, driven by arterial pressure, from shooting back through. The leader whistled. The beasts rallied and formed ranks again. Another series of whistles launched them. Those on the other side of the gate were coming as swiftly as those on this side. If he did not act fast, he would be knocked down or entangled before he could leap through the square. They would pass through that side of the gate unharmed and prevent him from coming through on his side.

He threw the torch over the square. It spun in an arc and struck the lead *kamanbur*. It shied away, and others ran into it. The whistling was deafening.

Orc did not look behind him. A delay of a second might be fatal. Then again, it might be just the time he needed for success.

Yelling, he ran up to the gate, then stopped. He lifted his arms and held his legs as straight as he could. He was hoping that the *kamanbur* behind him would not get to him in time to knock him through the gate. Without pausing or taking enough time to check that his body attitude was as vertical as possible, he rose up on his toes.

He gave another yell as he hopped forward.

That was too much for Jim Grimson.

He had been striving to tear himself loose from Orc. Orc might make it; he might not. Jim did not want to chance it. If Orc died, he might die, too. Though he had risked all the dangers up to now, he could not face this one.

Abruptly, he was flashing through a lightless space. He

could feel nothing except a vague sensation of speed. But he could hear whistles.

Then he was back in his room. The clock indicated that he—rather, his astral soul or whatever it was—had been gone for two hours and three minutes.

CHAPTER

21

Though Jim's life as Orc had been exhausting and perilous, it was surrounded by a light different from the light of Belmont City. The suns of the other universes shed a soft and golden light. Earth's was still gritty and harsh.

If only he were not so tired, he would have returned at once to Orc. Should he fail to get into him, he would know that Orc was dead. That meant that he would have to choose another character with whom to integrate and to become. If, that is, he then chose to continue therapy. With Orc gone, what was there left for Jim Grimson?

It did not matter that other patients were now using Red Orc as their personae. Their Orc was the fictional Orc. He had been in the brain of the real Orc, son of the real Los and Enitharmon.

What most delayed his return was his fear that Orc had been cut in two.

Would Orc have allowed that to stop him from going back if he were in Jim Grimson's skin? No!

Jim's birthday came. The only ones who celebrated were Jim and his fellow patients, with Doctor Porsena showing up briefly during the muted festivities. His mother and Mrs. Wyzak sent cards and phoned him. His mother could not get away from her job to visit him. The cake that Mrs. Wyzak said she had left in the lobby got lost somewhere along the delivery route. Just his luck, Jim thought. And he was still too depressed and still too fearful to attempt reentry into Orc.

Two days after his birthday, he was called out from lunch in the dining hall. Gillman Sherwood, officer of the day, said, "It's your mother."

"Now?" Jim said. "She's supposed to be working."

Sherwood raised his eyebrows as if the thought of a mother who had to work was surprising.

Jim's heart was beating hard when he entered the visitors' room. Only very bad news would bring her here at this time. It had to be a death in the family. His sister? His father? If it was his father, his son was feeling far worse about Eric's death than he had imagined he would. He should not have such distress, a pang of terrible loss. But, after all, whatever had happened between them, Eric was his father.

By the time he had reached the entry, he was convinced that Eric Grimson had died. Booze? Accident? Suicide? Murder? Any of those was possible.

Eva Grimson rose from a chair as Jim strode through the doorway. She was in a print dress which fitted far too loosely and was too thin for cold weather. Her face had become more gaunt and lined. The darkness around the eyes was blacker. Though her worn brown cloth coat hid the thinness of her body, her birdlike legs showed that she must have lost weight everywhere. But she smiled when she saw her son.

Jim took her in his arms as he cried, "Mom! What's wrong?"

Eva began weeping. Jim felt even worse. He had seen his mother weep only a few times. "Is Dad all right?" he said.

She pushed herself away and sat down in the chair. "I'm sorry, Jim," she said. "So sorry. But your father . . ."

She began sobbing. He got down on his knees by her and put his arm around her heaving shoulders. "For God's sake! What is it?"

"Your father . . ."

"He's dead!" Jim said.

She looked surprised. Instead of answering immediately, she took a handkerchief from her handbag and dabbed at her eyes. Jim had the irrelevant thought that her tears would not destroy her makeup since she never used it.

After sniffling, she shook her head. "No. Is that what you thought? In a way, it might be . . ."

"Be what?"

She must have meant to say "better." But she would not allow herself to continue to have such thoughts, let alone voice them.

"Nothing. Your father . . . he insists that we move to Dallas! You know, in Texas!"

It took Jim several breaths before he could think clearly. His chest still felt tight. Then he said harshly, "He might as well be dead then! You, too! You . . . you . . . you're deserting me!"

She took his hand and pressed it against her wet cheek. She wailed, "I have to go with him! He's my husband! I have to go where he goes!"

"No, you don't!" Jim said. He jerked his hand away from hers. "Damn you and damn him! All the way to hell!"

Not until later, when he reran the scene in his mind, did he realize that he had almost never before spoken to his mother like that. No matter how angry he had been with her, he had almost always been gentle. She had been hurt enough by his father.

"For the sake of blessed Mary, mother of God, don't say that, Jim!"

She reached out to take his hand again, but he moved it away.

"He can't get a decent job here. It's killing him, you know that. He's heard . . . a friend told him—you remember Joe Vatka?—there's plenty of work in Dallas. It's a booming town, and . . ."

"What about me?" Jim said. He began pacing back and forth, his hands clenching and unclenching. "Don't I count? And who's going to pay for the insurance, for my therapy? Where am I going to live when I'm an outpatient? I don't want to give up therapy! This is my only chance to make it! I won't, I won't!"

"Please understand, son. I'm torn, I'm being pulled apart. But I can't let him go without me, and he says he will if I don't go, too. He *is* my husband. It's my duty!"

"And I'm your son!" Jim shouted.

Kazim Grasser, a black nurse, put his head in the room. "Everything OK? Any problem?"

"This is a family matter," Jim said. "I'm not going to get violent. Beat it!"

Grasser said, "OK, man, just take it easy," and he withdrew his head.

"And why doesn't he come here and tell me instead of sending you?" Jim bellowed at his mother. "Is he afraid to face me? Does he hate me so much he doesn't give a shit about me?"

"Please, Jim, no bad language," she said. "No, he doesn't hate you, Jim. Not really. But he is afraid to face you. He feels like he's a failure . . ."

"Which he is!"

". . . as a husband and a father and a provider . . ."

"Which he is!"

". . . and he thinks you would attack him. He says . . . he says . . ."

"Say it! That I'm crazy!"

Eva put out her hand. "Please, Jim. I can't stand much more of this. If it wasn't such a sin, unforgivable, I'd kill myself!"

"You do whatever you think is best for you," he said, and he walked out of the room. Her voice shrieked through the doorway, "Jim! Don't do that!" Though he hesitated, he did not turn back. When he got to his room, he sat down and cried. Loneliness was a tide that swept him away over the horizon, far from all human beings, to an island also called Loneliness.

Even in his grief, he thought that that phrase would make a great title for a song. "The Island Also Called Loneliness."

The brain was a funny thing. In the midst of deep-purple grief, it sent strange messages. Always working, working, working simultaneously on many different subjects, and why it semaphored reports about certain workings when the timing was wrong, no one knew.

Or was the timing wrong? Maybe the brain was trying to soften the grief by distracting itself from itself.

If so, the ruse worked only for a minute. Jim dived deep into black and cold waters and would not come up for some time. His fellow patients did their best for him. Doctor Scaevola, who had taken over for Doctor Porsena while he was gone to a three-day conference, tried to bring light to Jim. He failed.

That very evening, just after the group session, Jim was again called to the visitors' room. "Mr. and Mrs. Wyzak," the O.D. told him. "They aren't the bearer of good news, Jim. Not the way they look."

The Wyzaks stood up as he came in. Mrs. Wyzak burst into tears, ran to him, and enfolded him in her big strong arms. His face was crushed against her big breasts. He smelled a cheap perfume.

Mrs. Wyzak wailed, "Sam is dead!"

Jim reeled inside himself. He felt numb. Her voice became distant, and he seemed to be drowning in soft cotton candy. Everything was floating away except for the breath-stealing cottony stuff. He could see through it as through many strips of gauze.

Nor could he cry. The tears that had flowed that afternoon were all he had. The spring had run dry, and only the stone from which the water had issued was left. It was cold, hard, and dry.

He sat down while Mrs. Wyzak told him about Sam. Mr. Wyzak sat voiceless, his head bent, his body sagging. Her story was brief. Sam had run away. He had hitchhiked several rides. The last one was with the driver of a semi-trailer. No one knew why it had happened, but the rig had jackknifed, gone over the edge of a steep hill, and rolled many times to the bottom. The driver had been badly injured and was now in a coma. Sam had been thrown clear of the cab but was crushed by the trailer. The funeral would be in three days.

"I didn't want to just phone you," Mrs. Wyzak said, dabbing at her eyes with a handkerchief. "I wanted to be here when you got the news. You and Sam . . . you've been best friends since you started walking."

She began sobbing. Jim did all he could to console her though he did not share her heartache and grief. Nothing was getting through to him. Sam's death seemed to have taken place long ago.

When Doctor Porsena, after his return from the conference, had his first private session with Jim, he worked on Jim's nonfeelings. Near the end of the hour, the doctor said, "It's possible that you're suffering from doubly intensified grief. You have a very vivid and visual-tactile-olfactory-auditory imagination. Your journeys in the World of Tiers are usually realistic and intense. There, you live as fully as you do here.

"What I'm saying is . . ."

He paused, waiting for Jim to supply the explanations, if he had any. Self-revelation was superior to that given by another. The light should come from within.

Jim could see the white fingers groping around in the blackness of his brain. What the hell did The Shaman expect from him? Did he think an eighteen-year-old screwup was Doctor Freud himself?

What was Porsena's key word? He gave such words to his patients, though they were embedded in the various strata of his sentences. If the patient could dig up the key and then figure out how to use it, he could open the door to another blaze of light.

Grief was a heavy liquid supposed to dilute memory. But being Orc had improved his memory considerably. It was as if some of the young Lord's near-photographic memory had rubbed off on Jim. He could recall almost verbatim everything Porsena had said during the session. So, run a scan. Let the cursor stop at the key word or phrase and highlight it.

"Ah!" Jim said. "Double!"

The Shaman smiled.

"'Doubly intensified grief,'" Jim said. "You think I have an extra burden of grief. I got one load as Jim Grimson, and I got another as Orc. Both of us were rejected—that's a mild word—by our fathers. Both of us are in a bad fix. I don't know about both of us having just lost our best friend. I doubt Orc'll feel bad about Ijim dying."

Jim twisted his lips from one side to another. It was as if he thought that moving the mouth would activate his brain. Then the psychiatrist said, "Ijim is dead, as far as you know. Is he the only loss?"

"Uh, well . . . let's see. There's, there's . . . how about Orc himself?"

Porsena did not reply. He was leaving it up to his patient.

"I mean I don't know if Orc's dead, too!" Jim said. "If he is, then I've really lost! The whole ball of wax! That's more grief than I can handle!"

"Others?" the doctor said.

"Grief . . . grief? Well, as Orc, and he's really me, and I'm really him, I explained all that, there's my mother . . . I mean Enitharmon. Lost her. And I love Aunt Vala, too. Lost her, also. I suppose their loss would be strong. I know Orc certainly went through some grief about maybe never seeing them again. But his grief got turned into hate for his father. He . . ."

After a long silence, Doctor Porsena said, "He . . . ?"

"He did something about it. Just didn't sit down and cry about it."

"Was that the right or wrong way to behave?"

"That's a . . ."

Jim had been about to say that it was a stupid question. But he would not say that to The Shaman. Anyway, The Shaman always had a reason for voicing anything, even if it might seem irrelevant or dumb.

"Right, of course. Except . . ."

"Except?"

"It was the right way in that it was action taken to solve the problem. Only, Orc was taking the most violent course. I mean he was going to kill his father and anybody else who got in his way! Maybe he should have figured out a better way. I don't know. It could be the only way there is."

Jim blushed. That did not escape Porsena's eye. The doctor said, "You're embarrassed."

Jim struggled with himself, then said, "OK. After all, it's not like I'm having the incestuous thoughts Orc has. I sure never had them about my own mother. Orc means to marry his mother after he kills his father—after some torture, that is. He's also got the hots for his aunt. In fact, Orc's hornier than a pack of minks in heat. I told you he's screwed twenty of his sisters, half-sisters, his father's children. All of them beautiful even if they are . . . oh, jeez, what am I saying?"

"Natives? Non-Lords? What the Lords call *leblabbiy*?"

"Yeah. I'm sorry. It's like the *leblabbiy* are ni . . . I mean, blacks. I didn't mean to use that word, you know. I don't really think blacks are subhumans. But I grew up hearing it everywhere."

"I know," the doctor said. "What're your thoughts about the Lords' acceptance of incest?"

"Well, look, Doc . . . I mean, Doctor. I've read a lot about the ancient Egyptians, been doing it since I saw *Caesar and Cleopatra* on TV. You know, the movie version of G. B. Shaw's play. With Claude Rains and Vivien Leigh. I know that brothers and sisters of ancient Egypt's ruling class married each other and had children. So did the Incan rulers. Anyway, I think Farmer had something in the Tiers books about brother-sister marriages. So, what with reading about that and reading the books on Egypt and seeing the movie, I didn't have much trouble accepting that. Anyway, when I'm Orc, I tend to accept what he accepts. It's a culture thing. The Lords don't have genetic defects, so there's no problem passing bad genes on to their children. So why shouldn't a mother marry her son?"

When the session ended, Jim felt only a very slight lessening of the numbness and depression. Oh, well, it didn't matter. Nothing mattered.

CHAPTER

22

Jim had sunk into the very center of his own pocket universe of depression. This was composed only of melancholy and self-despising, two elements that were not going to make a sun to light up his world. He did what was required of him—except to dive through the tragil—but slowly and tiredly. Even then, he was counting the numerals in the arithmetic of the night. He listed his flaws and failures and did not stop until he got to number thirty-seven. He could recall all of them. Why not? He had spent much time after the age of twelve contemplating them. Though there had to be more flaws, these were enough to satisfy the most self-pitying.

He did not get any sympathy from Doctor Porsena.

"You cannot continue to drag your chains around and whine, 'Woe is me!' like some castle-haunting phantom. You were making excellent progress—in fact, phenomenal. Now, you've regressed. It's as if you've not only gone back to the lowest previous point of lack of self-esteem in your life, you've plunged below that. Reached that personal nadir, as it were."

Jim summoned up enough spirit to say, "As opposed to the Zenith, right? Well, I was never one for TV."

That took the psychiatrist aback for a moment. Then he smiled, and he said, "If you've got enough fire to make a pun, rotten as it is, there's still hope for you."

Jim did not think so. That remark was the last flicker of a dying flame.

"What if Orc is dead?" Jim said. That question caught him by surprise. It had shot out of his mouth as if something had exploded in him.

Porsena's lips formed the ghost of a smile. He was, Jim thought, not only The Shaman. He was The Sphinx. That expression was exactly like the smile on the stone face of the Great Sphinx of Giza. Jim could see the pyramids and the palm trees beyond him. The wisdom of the ages was behind that age-cut face and behind the doctor's, too.

"What if Orc *is* dead?" Porsena said. "You select someone else to become."

At least Porsena had not argued with him that Orc was only a fictional character. He must think that Orc was, but he was going to play by Jim's rules. Never invalidate. That was the Golden Rule, and Porsena was the Golden Ruler.

"I don't want to be someone else," Jim said.

"Then find out if Orc is dead or alive."

"I'll do it," Jim said. "I'll do it for you."

"No. You'll do it for yourself. You'll do it because it's the thing to do for you and you only."

He leaned forward over his desk, his bright blue eyes locked onto Jim's. "Listen up, Jim. I'm aware that I'm an authority figure to you, perhaps a father/mother substitute. That's good in one sense because you've reacted differently to me than you have with other authority figures. You've done your best to please me, though that is not necessarily desirable. But I am here only to guide you through your therapy. Perhaps that's too cold a way to put it. I like you, and I think we might eventually become friends after your therapy is complete. I do have authority, and I'm not your peer. At the moment, I'm your superior, though I won't take advantage of that—unless it's for your good.

"But we may have to work a bit to temper your attitude toward me. I'm not God, I'm not your parents. I expect you to hear my advice and then to use your judgment concerning its value. Nevertheless, there'll be times when I'll override your judgment. I am older and wiser, and I am a thoroughly trained professional. However, I am human. I can make mistakes and errors.

"On the other hand, I'll be far less likely than you to do so. Keep all this in mind. We'll do some work on your attitude, as I said. But your therapy is the big thing here. So, I insist that you reenter Orc or pick another character to enter. If you don't, your therapy will be ended. Do I make myself clear?"

Jim nodded.

"What would Orc do if he were in your shoes just now?"

"Huh? Oh, I see what you mean! Sorry, I was thinking of something else. If he was me, he'd've jumped right back through the tragil. But I'm not him, not yet, anyway. Orc never would've been in a depression. Not for long, anyway. I know him, and . . ."

"Do what he'd do, even if it seems to be against your nature, no matter how hard it is to do. This isn't easy work, you know."

"I'll try. Hard," Jim said.

He did not think he could do it, not in his state of mind. But there were ways to alter those states. Porsena would not approve those ways. In fact, taking any drugs except those prescribed was forbidden on pain of immediate expulsion. But desperate situations demanded desperate means. Before the group session that afternoon, Jim got Gillman Sherwood to one side in the main hallway.

"I hear you're dealing, Gill."

"Not at all," Sherwood said. "I wouldn't do that. Hell, I'm here to get rid of the monkey, among other things."

"Let me put it this way," Jim said. "I understand you may have access to certain cures for what ails me. I'd like to get hold of one, preferably one of the *speedy* kind."

"It could be," Sherwood said. "But there are a lot of rumors, mostly false, running around this place."

"Speed's the word," Jim said.

"Might be what the doctor ordered. However, nothing's free in this harsh world."

"I know the price," Jim said. "I got the wherewithal."

That morning, the mail had brought him a ten-dollar bill along with a note from his mother. At first, he was tempted to send both back. Yet, he needed money badly, so he had put the bill in his pocket after tearing up the note. And here he was, spending half of the ten on amphetamine when every cent he had should go for absolute necessities. He despised himself. At the same time he was looking forward to the rush through his body and mind.

Gillman Sherwood put his hand on Jim's shoulder. "There are other ways to pay debts than with money."

"Forget it!" Jim said. "I told you last time, no way!"

Gillman's smile was aloof and haughty, so superior. Jim hated it, and he hated having to deal through this big prick.

Gillman said, "Don't knock it until you try it."

"Jesus Christ!" Jim said. "You've hit on every boy and girl in the place! Do you love being turned down? Is that part of your problem?"

"Hey, there's more than one here knows an offer they can't refuse! I don't need you, Grimson, any more than I need a wart on my ass! I'll slip you what you need when we're alone next time. Bring the wherewithal. Otherwise, no tickee, no shirtee."

What would Red Orc do? Probably kill Sherwood and take his entire supply. Couldn't do that.

Though Sherwood's parents were wealthy, they sent him little money. Thus, if he wanted extra cash, he had to deal in nickel-and-dime stuff. His father had been a steel magnate. Despite the shutting down of the industry in the Youngstown area, he had interests in other businesses and was said to own half of Belmont City. His only son had seemed destined to be one of those tall, athletic, blond, and handsome scions who would sweep through life untroubled by the anxieties and dire straits of the great unwashed, the rabble, the seething masses.

Not so. Even the extremely rich had problems they shared with the lowly poor. Gillman was bisexual, with a leaning toward males. If his gay-hating father had known that, he would not have been so eager to make him into a businessman. Gillman was passionate about becoming a painter. The senior Sherwood was appalled by this. He insisted that Gillman go to Harvard to get an M.B.A. and then become his partner. If he wanted to paint as a recreation, fine, though he should not brag about it to anyone who might think only a pansy would be an artist. If he wanted to be a patron, that was different.

Gillman, like so many now in therapy, had gone berserk. He had slashed his wrists and painted a self-portrait with blood. Then his drug-addiction had been revealed, and here he was in the mental ward of Wellington Medical Center.

Jim would have empathized with Gillman if he did not act as if he were the Duke of Kingdom Come. Jim also thought that Gillman's choice of Kickaha as his persona was a hoot. Kickaha would spit in the son of a bitch's face.

A few minutes later, he was talking to Sandy Melton. She had not been able to get into a long conversation with him since she had entered the project. She was classified as schizoaffective and was now taking lithium carbonate. She adored her Caucasian father though she did not see him enough to satisfy her. He was a traveling salesman for a large pharmaceutical company with headquarters in Belmont City. Sandy detested her mother, who was Korean. From early childhood, Sandy had suffered because so many of her grade-school classmates had called her "slant-eyes," "Chink," "Jap," "gook," and "Mongolian idiot." Her high-school friends had refrained from this, but her acquaintances were not so discreet.

Yet, her long glossy black hair, uptilted eyes, and high cheekbones made a beautiful whole. And, though only five feet two inches tall, she had relatively long legs and a petite but full-busted figure. Despite this, she thought that she was ugly. Though shy, she had been a very energetic, sometimes overzealous and near-frenzied business manager and agent for the Hot Water Eskimos. But when she suddenly became depressed, she was very withdrawn and lethargic. She would then let her duties slide.

From an early age, Sandy had not liked her mother, mostly because her mother had not seemed to like her. Kuo Melton was surly, untalkative, and a bad housekeeper who spent most of her time watching TV soap operas and game shows. Though she had been in the United States for twenty years, she spoke English very poorly.

Sometimes Sandy was in a forgiving mood, and she would explain to her friends that her mother had had a hell of a childhood and youth. She had been sexually abused and half-starved and homeless for years before Abe Melton married her. At that time, she was beautiful and looking for a way out of her country. Sandy's father had told her that Kuo was genuinely fond of him and he of her during the early years of their marriage. That was certainly no longer true.

Sandy's method of entering the World of Tiers was unique. She would take all of her clothes off while chanting the first four lines of the Buddhist Lotus Sutra over and over. Then she would press her palms against the full-length mirror on the wall of her room. While doing this, she would use Jim's ATA MATUMA M'MATA chant. Two chants were better than one. After about seven minutes (seven was a magical and mystical number), and while she concentrated on the entry point five inches inside the mirror (five was another mystical number), the glass would turn soft and rubbery.

As soon as she felt the mirror become just a Jell-O, she would begin muttering swiftly the words of the song "Over the Rainbow." What was good enough for Dorothy of Oz was good enough for her. And three chants were better than one.

Her ectoplasm, as she called it, would travel through the palms of her hands. It would fall forward through the ever-thinning substance into the universe she had chosen. When she had passed completely through, she (as ectoplasm) was in a male body. She had long wanted to be a male because her father was, though she also felt that this desire was morally wrong.

The universe beyond the mirror was like nothing described in the Tiers series. It was flat, and she could fall off its edge if she got too close to it. Its human inhabitants were all Caucasian males, except for one gigantic female kept under guard in a huge castle. She was like the queen termite in a nest and was force-fed with a honey that made her so large and so fat that she became larger than the kitchen in a mansion. The queen was the mother of the entire human population and bore five male babies in a single birth every three months.

Once a year, a tournament was held—Sandy was a great reader of medieval romances—and the champion became the queen's lover and the begetter of that year's babies. After he retired, he had to help other ex-champions take care of the babies, dust the castle, wash dishes, and do other household tasks. Being permitted to do this service was a great honor.

Sandy, in her persona as Sir Sandagrain, roamed the world in quest of the man who held the secret to everlasting happiness. While wandering, she had to joust with innumerable knights, bad or good, and invade the many castles of evil warlocks and robber barons. Like all males in this world, they wore masks. So far, Sir Sandagrain had not found The Man with the Golden Mask, he who had the secret.

These adventures as the questing knight, though bloody and perilous, helped to protect her against the sometimes overwhelming stresses of Earth. When she felt she had had enough relief from her terrestrial life, she pressed her palms against the mirror. She repeated the same three chants in reverse order. The Jell-O-like softness crystallized. At the moment of complete hardness, it was ready to admit her ectoplasm back to her female body.

Sandy was making some progress in her quest for a stronger persona and lack of confusion about her sexual identity. She was beginning to come out somewhat from the wild swings of mood and her withdrawal tendencies. Like Jim and most of the others, she was slowly surrendering her own private and uncontrolled delusions to the controlled delusions of the World of Tiers.

"Jim, I've talked to my dad twice," she said excitedly. "He's always talked about divorcing Kuo, but it was just talk. He's very resistant to the idea of divorce. But now, I don't know, he may be coming around to it. He knows how much I hate leaving the hospital and going back to that house. It's terrible. But only because Kuo's there!"

Sandy never referred to Kuo as her mother.

"Aren't you thinking about adapting yourself to Kuo?" Jim said.

"No. I couldn't do that unless she went into therapy, too, and did some changing herself. Takes two to tango, you know. She would never do that."

The dining hall was noisy, though it had quiet spots occupied by withdrawn juveniles. Jim and Sandy sat down across the table from a lovely, gentle, and fragile girl, Elizabeth Lavenza. Her stepfather had been sodomizing her since she was ten years old. Several months ago, the monster, as Elizabeth always called him, had tried to kill her when he had caught her phoning the police. She had managed to fight him off by jamming the receiver into his mouth and then hitting him over the head with a poker. These were the only violent acts she had ever committed, and she was suffering from guilt because of them. (This reaction was totally incomprehensible to Jim.) She had then run out of the house and down the street. Despite her stepfather's injuries, he had lurched after her swiftly enough to catch her. He was strangling her when the squad car arrived.

Elizabeth used what she called her "powerpack" to enter the Lords' universes. This was the five books of the series taped together, forming her battery to energize the opening of the way. Several others in the therapy did the same.

Near Jim was another table at which sat the members of a group in which he was particularly interested. These were whispering, their heads as close together as they could get them. Their universe was one they had made up with the help of Doctor Porsena. Though it was nominally in the World of Tiers, it was not one that its author would have been likely to create. This was ruled by a Lord called Kephalor. He was a brain the size of a pocket universe because he was also the universe. Its inhabitants were electrical entities whose forms were the neural impulses of

Kephalor's brain. In fact, the group called itself The Neural Impulses. (Jim thought that this would be a great name for a rock band.)

It had been agreed among the members that, when Kephalor forgot something, an impulse would die. That meant that the member embodying that impulse would also die. But he or she could return as a new thought, though his identity would be different.

Jim had heard that the harmony in the group had turned a little sour. One member was claiming that she and she only was Kephalor's subconscious mind. Since the subconscious ruled the conscious, the other neural impulses would have to do as she commanded. This demand was to be expected. One of the behavior characteristics that had brought the girl to Wellington was her irrepressible desire to control others.

After lunch, Gillman Sherwood and Jim stepped around a hall corner. No one else was in sight. Gillman held out five black beauties, uppers, in the palm of his hand.

"Normal price is two dollars each. But my first customers get a discount. Only a dollar each."

Jim handed him the ten-dollar bill at the same time that he took the capsules. Gillman opened his wallet, which was packed with paper currency, and made change for Jim.

"Welcome back to the real world," Sherwood said.

"This is just temporary," Jim muttered. "I need it to get over a hump. After that . . ."

Sherwood smiled. "Sure. But if the temporary becomes permanent, I'm your man."

Jim, hating Sherwood and himself, turned and walked away. That evening, he sat for a long time while looking at the black beauties, which did not seem so beautiful now. What would Orc do? Jim really did not know. Now and then, Orc had remembered, briefly, the ecstasy gotten from certain drugs. But Jim had also received the impression that these had no bad side effects and were not chemically addictive.

In any event, Orc needed no drugs to give him courage.

And then there was Doctor Porsena. No doubt at all, he would be very disappointed if his patient went back over the edge. Not that, Jim told himself, he had ever been really hooked. He was not a "dope fiend," as his father called drug-takers. He just used the stuff now and then. Though, to be honest to himself, he had been using uppers and downers and smoking marijuana more than he had last year. Still, he was a long way from jumping onto the bandwagon called Hooked.

Or was he?

After a half hour, he sighed, and he rose from the chair. He flushed the capsules down the toilet, though not without regret.

Ten minutes later, he shot through the circle in the center of the tragil.

CHAPTER

23

Orc was writhing in agony on a glittering and hard floor. Since there was no one else there, he did not have to play the stoic. He screamed.

Jim suffered as much as Orc, which did not seem fair since he had no body. He should go back to Earth at once until Orc's pains were gone. Unfortunately, he could not concentrate on the techniques needed to effect the return. By the time he could do that, he would be able to endure the pain.

Though half-blinded by the fire in the backs of his heels and in his buttocks, Orc could see that he was in a vast tunnel. Its walls shone with the light from a multitude of six-angled, vaguely insectoid creatures hanging on the walls. Additional illumination came from round knobs on the ceiling, walls, and floor. Intermingled with them were thick patches of green stuff that looked like lichen.

In the middle of the tunnel was a deep trough through which clear water ran. Orc, standing on his toes, walked stiffly to the stream, lay down in it, and immersed himself up to his neck. The water was very cold and shocked him. It also gave relief as it chilled his blood and somewhat soothed his pain.

Sitting there, Orc could see the bloody footprints he had made on the crystalline floor. As he had hopped through the gate, the extreme tips of his heels and buttocks had been sheared off by the ray. They would heal in time, but was he going to get that time?

That depended, just now, on how much blood he was going to lose. Also, if he survived that, how far he could walk while looking for food and then the gate. Unless, that is, the gate was nearby. He doubted that it would be.

Los had said that the gate in Anthema would lead back to Orc's native world. He had lied. There was no such place as this on or in that planet.

Orc crawled out onto the tunnel floor, which was a few inches above the surface of the stream. The agony would come back when he got warm again, but he could no longer stand the cold. He wished he had cloths, anything, to bandage his wounds.

He saw the front half of Ijim's body. It was lying face-down. Orc, when coming through the gate, had landed on it and skidded on the organs and blood.

Orc was wearing a skin loincloth and a belt with a sheath and a flint knife therein. All the other weapons and the food supply bag had been left behind. He walked on his toes, wincing at every step, and stripped the half-corpse of its severed loincloth and belt and a knife. This was now a half-knife, since the ray had cut it longitudinally, but it might be useful.

With his own knife, he pried off pieces of the green stuff growing on the wall. Beneath them were small tubes projecting from the crystal. It seemed to him that these might be conduits which fed the plants. When he saw some yellow liquid starting to ooze from the tips of the tubes, he thought that his idea could be correct.

He wrung the fluid out of the plants, which felt like thick wet moss. He decided to call it *omuthid*, Thoan for moss, and placed pieces of it on the wounds. That made him wince, but they stuck to his skin as if they contained glue. The flow of blood was stanched. Then he ate a small bite of another piece of *omuthid* stripped from the wall. It was rich with fluid, easily chewed, and tasted like caramel mixed with raw broccoli. Though it might be poisonous, he did not care. Not at this moment, anyway. If he did not get sick from this piece, he would eat more of it later.

What was left of Ijim's body could be a protein supply, for a while, anyway. If Orc had not known the Lord so well, he might have eaten him. But, though he felt that he might regret doing it, he shoved the half-corpse into the stream, which carried it away.

He would be stuck in this area until his wounds healed enough for him to walk easily. Normally, three days would do it. Meanwhile, he would eat, sleep, drink water, and hope that no predator came along. He had no way to estimate the time except by his sleeping requirements. It seemed to him that roughly three days had passed since he had been here. During this period, he explored, mostly on tiptoes, a quarter mile each way. He found nothing that he had not seen near the gate. He also investigated this. The square of metal looked the same on this side as it did on the other. He made a rope of the *omuthid* and threw one end through the gate. The part that went through the gate was cut off.

Because of the wounds, he had to sleep on his face on the hard crystalline floor. Unfortunately, he rolled and turned then, and he awoke often and painfully. The only good thing about his situation was that the temperature remained comfortable. Also, the air did not become stale but moved slowly through the tunnel.

Each "day," after awakening, he removed the *omuthid* patches from the wounds and replaced them with fresh pads. They came off as if they were indeed glued. The wounds were healing, but the areas of skin covered by the patches were pricked with many red dots. They looked as if the *omuthid* had applied tiny suckers to the skin, and the green stuff had a distinct reddish underlay. At the end of the three days, he concluded that the *omuthid* was sucking his blood, though not in large quantities. He was not as strong as when he had entered this world. Of course, his diet might be lacking in vitamins and minerals.

Nevertheless, he could walk without too much pain, and he could sit down for several minutes before he had to remove his buttocks from pressure. After another sleep, he set out upstream as instinctively as a salmon seeking its hatching place. The tunnel ran straight for an estimated twenty miles, which he traversed after sleeping only once. The light stayed steady, as it had done since he had been here. The tunnel was silent except for the drumming of his blood in his ears. To get rid of that, he began talking to himself and also sang often.

The feeling of loneliness and the thought that he might be here until he died kept him company. It was not the sort of company he cared for.

Finally, he came to a fork in the tunnel. At the base of the wall between the two tunnels was a bubbling pool. Along one side of each of the forks was a shallow trough through which water ran. These emptied into the pool, but the bubbling and the swirling in it indicated that it was also fed by a spring.

Orc took the tunnel to his right. After a while, it widened and became as big as that which he had left. He trudged on, singing a song his mother had taught him when he was a child. Suddenly, he stopped, and he turned to face the left-side wall. Something flickering along the wall, halfway down its height, had caught his eye.

Whatever it was had ceased, but he kept his head turned toward the wall while he walked on. Then, he stopped again. His brain had not been playing tricks on him, not unless he had gone crazy from solitude. A series of large black figures, symbols, perhaps, moved in a rather speedy parade along the wall. They came from behind him and traveled ahead of him until he could no longer see them.

They ceased for a few minutes. Or perhaps it was for an hour. Orc had lost his sense of time. Only when he counted the seconds and the minutes could he be sure of its passage.

Suddenly, the first of a series of the symbols, many of them repeated in different combinations, sped along on the wall. Parts of them were obscured when they passed beneath the *omuthid* and knobs. After several hundreds had sped by, they stopped. Orc resumed walking. Some time later, another series began. Orc counted the seconds then. The train took thirty-one to pass him.

If they made a message, its transmission was slow. But he was quickened by it. No natural process could produce such distinct and differentiated figures in an obviously artificial order.

Some minutes later, another string of the same symbols, repeated in the same arrangement, shot by. After that, the wall was blank.

Orc hastened onward. The tunnel curved gradually to the right until it seemed to be going at right angles to its original direction. When he got very tired, he stopped and ate. By now, he was sick of the taste of caramel-cum-broccoli.

Jim Grimson was as fed up as Orc with the *omuthid*. When the Lord ate it, Jim ate it. Orc's problems were also Jim's. But Jim had others, too. The ghostbrain, his shadowy cotenant, seemed to be getting larger. Now that Orc was just sitting and chewing, no emotions raging in him, though his mind was active, he was in a relatively quiescent state. Thus, Jim was able to concentrate on his own thoughts and act as he wished. But he was still half Orc and likely, when his host was aroused or irate, to be slammed back into a near-Orc persona.

Jim "moved" closer to the ghostbrain. It "retreated." There could be no movement in the physical sense, just as there could be no "seeing" or "hearing" or "touching" by beings without limbs or sensory organs. Jim "knew," however, that he had advanced and that the ghostbrain had backed away.

He continued to go toward the thing. It kept on moving away. Was it afraid of him? Perhaps Jim was dangerous to it. If that was so, he would have to find out how it could be attacked. Easy to say; hard to do.

Orc slept, ate with little appetite, and started walking again. Presently, the tunnel opened into a vast glittering cavern. The growths furnishing the light were far more numerous per square foot and larger than those in the tunnels. Also—what a delight—there was sound! Many small birds or animals lived among various plants and twittered, squealed, trumpeted, and cawed.

The creatures looked as if Tenniel had been on LSD when he had illustrated *Alice in Wonderland*. Or as if they had been designed by a deity whose own god was Euclid. They were many-angled, some of them long-legged cubes or nonahedrons on wheels, their skins spotted with triangles, circles, squares, and crosses.

The plants looked as if they were part crystal, part vegetable. Some of them bore berries or hexagonal fruit. The green mosslike *omuthid* was everywhere, on the floors, walls, and ceiling. At least a hundred feet above him was the ceiling, and the cavern itself extended beyond his eye's reach.

Standing on a ledge about twenty feet above the cavern's floor, Orc could see several creeks. They did not run straight, as in the tunnels, but meandered as proper creeks should.

He had been taken with the ecstasy of the sounds of living creatures. Shortly thereafter, he was seized with a rapture caused by sight of a human being. He was naked and walking slowly through the forest toward Orc. But he did not seem to be aware that an intruder was in his exotic Garden of Eden.

Orc had to fight against rushing down and greeting the man. He crouched down close to a boulder and studied the person as he made his way through the plants. There was something peculiar about him. He did not seem to have a quite human construction. His gait was unhurried and stately as if he owned this world, which, indeed, he might. When the man was closer, the details of his face and body became clearer.

He walked slowly and dignifiedly because he could not walk otherwise. The joints of his shoulders, hips, elbows, knees, and wrists were bulbous and somewhat shiny. And the head, neck, and trunk were larger than they would be in a normally proportioned man.

Orc shook his head. He had been momentarily under an illusion. His imagination had supplied what the man did not have because Orc expected him to have it. Where Orc had seen male genitals was now a smooth place, skin dotted with gleaming crystals. The he was an it.

It had no weapons, though. Orc stood up and shouted through cupped hands at the being. It stopped, though it did not look startled. Then the mouth opened. It could have been a smile, but its teeth shone like jewels.

Orc climbed down and walked to the creature, which had resumed its slow pace. When they were ten feet apart, they halted. Orc greeted it in Thoan. *"Koowar!"*

It said, *"Koowar-su shemanithoon!"*

"Greetings and come in peace!"

The teeth were white diamonds and obviously had been

made in a biofactory. They had been fashioned so that they resembled human canines, incisors, and molars.

"*Neth Orc,*" the young Lord said. "I am Orc."

"*Neth Dingsteth.*"

The being's name was Dingsteth, one Orc had never heard before. It spoke with a slight impediment. No doubt the diamond teeth caused that.

To Orc's rapid-fire questions, Dingsteth responded slowly. In due time, Orc learned that this world had been made by the Lord called Zazel. Zazel of the Caverned World. He was also the maker of Dingsteth, who was now the only sentient being in an entire universe. The world consisted of rock perforated with tunnels and caves, some of which had floor areas a thousand miles square. But it was, in a sense, a living being. It did not seem to have a consciousness. Or, if it did, it had given no sign of one to Dingsteth.

"It's a vast semimineral-semiprotein computer in which many different forms of life exist. Half of the fauna and flora herein are symbiotes of the world of Zazel. I'll explain all that later. It detected your presence and notified me. I am, in reality, the Lord of this world even if I did not make it. Perhaps you saw the message traveling along the wall? It's a very slow computer."

"I saw the message. What happened to Zazel?"

"He killed himself. He went mad. Or madder. I think he was crazy from the beginning. Who else but an insane person would create this kind of world? But he had an easy death. He let the computer suck his blood, drain him dry. Then, as he had ordered me to do, I cremated him."

Dingsteth looked at Orc from head to toe, then said, "Turn around, please."

"What?" Orc said. "Why should I?"

"Tell you later. Please do as I requested."

Frowning, Orc rotated. He had never obeyed anybody's orders except his parents', and, for some years, he had disliked doing that. He was a Lord, and Lords commanded, not non-Lords.

Dingsteth did not nod because the swollen ring which was its neck prevented that. It said, "Good! So far! There are no indications of crystallization!"

At Orc's somewhat alarmed question, Dingsteth said, "If you're active enough, your metabolism is able to stave off the crystallization of your flesh. But you have to sleep, and it is then that the cells slowly begin to turn into stone."

"What kind of a world is this?" Orc said. At the same time, he decided that he was going to get out of it as quickly as possible. "And how have you kept from being crystallized?" he added.

"Zazel made me so that I have an innate resistance, a biological defense."

"Is there a gate out of the Caverned World?"

"There could be. I may be able to find out for you. I have access to all the tremendous amount of data that Zazel stored in the world."

Orc was not accustomed to being humble, but this situations demanded that he be. He was not going to risk his survival just because of his pride. He would bend, though not break it, if he had to.

"Would you find out for me?"

"Why not?" Dingsteth said. "I will unless some reason for not doing so occurs to me or I find the reason in the computer."

"Thank you. One immediate question, though. How did Los manage to penetrate this world and set up the gate I used to get here?"

"Los?"

Orc told his story.

Dingsteth said, "The fatal flaw in Thoan culture is that the children of the Lords of a particular world want to be its sole ruler. That desire was understandable and feasible in ancient days when the Lords had the means to create new worlds. Then the children, when they became adult, could move out of their parents' universes into their own. Now, they are restricted to those worlds already made. If they knew that the means for making new worlds still existed, they could abandon their bloody conflict. That has kept their population down considerably, as you know, and is responsible for your present plight. If the Thoan were logical, they would get rid of that cultural trait."

"Hold it!" Orc said excitedly. "You said that the means for making new worlds still exists! Where?"

"Here. I did not mean that the creation engines are still around. I meant that this world has the data for making new ones. Not only the instructions for operation but how to make the materials needed and how to construct them and to supply them with power. Et cetera."

"You can access all this?"

"Of course."

Orc shook his head, then rolled his eyes. "All this time! The knowledge has been thought lost for thousands of years! And it's here! In this desolate and undesired world!"

"It's not such a bad place," Dingsteth said.

"I apologize if I hurt your feelings," Orc said. "I've only been here a short time, so I shouldn't judge the place with the little data I have of it. But you must understand that it's not my kind of place. Anyway, I'm eager to get back to my own world, for reasons I've explained."

"I don't understand revenge," Dingsteth said. "The capability for that was left out of me when I was made. A good thing, too, I think. By the way, the video data of your father setting up that gate you came through are stored in the world's memory. Would you care to see them?"

"I was wondering how he managed to gate into and out of this world."

"I let him in. I am always curious, and I wanted to talk to

him and find out all about him. He was the first in centuries to try to get in. Zazel did not play the game you Lords play. He set up codeless gates, though they can be opened from this side. I permitted Los to come in, but I was disappointed in him. He was in a hurry, so he said, but he promised to come back later. He never did, and that was over five hundred years ago. Evidently, he's not to be trusted. When you first mentioned his name, it didn't register. But, as we've been talking, I recalled him. I . . ."

Orc said, "You didn't tell him about the creation engine data, did you?"

"No. The subject didn't come up during our brief conversations. I would have, but . . ."

"Dingsteth," Orc said, "Listen to me! Hear my words of advice and caution! Do not ever tell anybody else about the engines! If you do, you might be killed—after you've shared that knowledge! There are many Thoan who would like to get the secret and keep it for themselves! They would torture you, then slay you."

"How about you?" Dingsteth said.

"I would be very grateful if you would show me that data, then open the gate long enough for me to pass on to Los's world."

"You did not answer my question," Dingsteth said. "Which means, I'm afraid, that you are concealing from me some of your intents and purposes. I don't know you well enough to understand your personality. But, if it's like most of the other Lords, Manathu Vorcyon is a notable exception, you'd be thinking about killing me after you learn all you can about the creation engines."

Orc had to laugh. Then he said, "Zazel certainly made you an open and exceedingly frank person!"

"If I told you how to operate, rather, cooperate, with this world, you would have to give some of your blood to get the data you desire. You have to apply your face to a monitor-input and let it suck your blood before it'll give you what you want. But it wouldn't let you go unless you knew certain codes, which I am not going to tell you. You'd be sucked dry."

"Just tell me how to gate out," Orc said. "That's all I want."

He was thinking—Jim was aware of this—that he would return some day in a small armed vehicle and get the information. Dingsteth was the only one who could let him in, but Orc would find a way to cajole it into doing that. Or he would come back through the *kamanbur* gate.

He said, "Why did you admit my father? Also, why did you let him set up a gate which kills others when they try to get through it?"

"Why not? What do I care? As it stands, you're the first Lord to get through. Your uncle, Ijim, did not make it through, and the chances are that the next one to try it will fail. It'll be interesting to observe those who follow you, if any ever do."

Orc did not want to dwell on the gate. Dingsteth might get the idea that it would be a good thing to remove it because of the possible danger for itself. Another possibility was that Dingsteth might lack the means to dismantle it. Also, Los would have set up the gate so that anybody trying to dismantle it would be killed.

Dingsteth looked as if it had been encoiled in thought, too. Suddenly, it said, "I'll go with you!"

Orc was surprised. After a long silence, he said, "Why?"

"I know everything about this world. I am bored with it. Zazel did not set me up to be invulnerable against that. As for loneliness, I do not know what that means. Zazel made me so that that feeling, which afflicts all humans, is absent from me. I only know that because the world told me, and I've no idea what loneliness feels like.

"I do have an intense curiosity. I need other worlds to feed that. Therefore, I will go with you. You can be my guide and instructor until I am able to proceed on my own. In return for your services, I will let you pass through the gate and I'll go with you and provide you with much data."

How naive it was! Orc thought. No matter how much knowledge the being had, it was, in many respects, ignorant. It did not know that, once Orc got to his native world, it would be a burden. He could not afford to have it wandering around and perhaps telling the natives that Los's son was back and seeking revenge. Also, Dingsteth should, for Orc's purposes, remain in the Caverned World. It could open the gate for him when he returned to get a creation engine. Which, Orc now remembered, could be reversed to become an engine of destruction. Or so the historians said.

He would have to string Dingsteth along until the moment of departure. Perhaps he could get it to stay here but also promise to let him back in when next he showed up.

Dingsteth said, "Wait here."

It returned ten minutes later. Orc had thought of following it to watch it, but he decided against that. From the little information he had gotten, he thought that the walls were in league with the being. Their monitors would see him following Dingsteth and report that to it.

"I gave some blood, and the world agreed to open the gate for us," it said. Its upper lip bore a small wound. "Let us go now."

Orc walked with it to the other end of the cavern and down a tunnel. At the end of approximately thirty minutes, the being stopped. Orc looked around. There was nothing to differentiate this area from any other. Dingsteth placed its hand on the near wall. The wall here was free of the *omuthid*. After several seconds, it said, "The gate is now open."

There still seemed to be nothing except glittering crystalline stone before them. Orc was about to say something when Dingsteth plunged its hand through the stone up to his ring-shaped wrist. "See?"

"You may go first," Orc said. His politeness was actually caution. He still did not trust the being; it might be asking him to step into a fatal trap.

"Very well," Dingsteth said. Its voice seemed very tight, and its face was set in an unreadable expression.

It walked forward but stopped just before its nose encountered the wall. For a long time, while Orc, puzzled, watched it, it stood still. Then it stepped back, hesitated, and advanced again. Only to halt a half-inch from the wall.

Finally, Dingsteth turned toward Orc. "I can't do it!" it said, and it groaned.

"Why?" Orc said. His distrust might be well-founded. A trap could be, probably was, on the other side.

"For the first time in my life," it said, "I am afraid. Until now, I've never known what apprehension and fear meant, though I've read those words in the records. Zazel must have put those states in me because a being without fear and caution eventually perishes.

"The moment we started out toward the gate, I began feeling very strange emotions. My heart began pounding, my stomach seemed to grab itself and try to fold itself into itself, and I began shaking. The closer we got, the worse the symptoms were. At this moment . . ."

Its teeth began chattering. The sound of diamonds clicking against diamonds was one which Orc would never forget. Finally, Dingsteth mastered itself enough to stop shivering.

"I can't!" it wailed. "I feel as if something on the other side will destroy me if I go there! I feel . . . I feel as if a great void will be waiting for me! I'll step through the gate and fall into an immense space and fall and fall! Then I'll hit the bottom and be broken, smashed, into a thousand pieces! And that's very peculiar, you know! I don't even know what a vast space would look like! I've lived in this enclosed and straitened world all my life and have no idea what a really large space would be!"

"You're suffering from intense cases of agoraphobia and acrophobia," Orc said. He was, however, wondering if Dingsteth was putting on an act to get him to go through the gate first.

"I know those words, but, until now, I never knew what their true meaning was! What it is, it's fear of the unknown! I am unable to leave this world! I just can't, I just can't!"

Orc was not going to coax it through the gate. And he might as well take advantage of it while its wits whirled around as if in a centrifuge.

"Listen, Dingsteth! Your curiosity and desire for new knowledge drive you to leave this place. These are valuable factors. Your excessive fear of the unknown is a crippling aspect of your persona. It's a mental sickness, and I know you cannot conquer it by yourself. I'll tell you what I'm going to do. When I return, I promise I will, I'll bring a drug that will suppress that fear. Then you'll be able to venture forth and do what you want to do."

"That would be thoughtful of you," Dingsteth said. "Only . . . I'm not sure that any drug could overcome this great fear."

"I promise you it will."

"But I'm not sure that I want to take any such drug. It could make me do something that would kill me!"

"I'll bring it, and you can take it or not, depending on how you feel about it."

Orc did not care whether or not Dingsteth used the drug. All he wanted was for the being to let him back through the gate. He would have to test its existence himself. To throw Dingsteth through the gate to activate a trap was to put Orc in a losing position, whatever happened. If the being died, it could not admit him when he returned. If there was no trap,

Dingsteth would be horrified and forever offended. It would never allow him in after that.

"I will bring back the drug," Orc said.

"I'll admit you so I can try it," the being said. "At least, I think I will. Good concatenation of events for you, Orc, son of Los and Enitharmon!"

"For you, too," Orc said.

He stepped through the gate that was also a crystalline wall.

CHAPTER

24

Orc was not in Los's world. His father had not told him the truth about the gate on Anthema leading back to his native universe. Or had Los lied or just been misleading?

Orc had gone from Zazel's Caverned World to one which the local natives called Lakter. After a while, Orc realized that the Thoan knew it as Jakadawin Tar. That is, Jadawin's World. It had once been Thulloh's World, that is, Thulkaloh Tar. But Jadawin had gotten through the gate-traps, and Thulloh had been forced to gate out to save his life.

Lakter was a planet where the stars "seemed" to swarm through the night sky like fireflies. Orc thought "seemed" because so many things in the pocket universes were illusions. The gate was in a cave at the foot of a mountain on a large tropical island. Orc had gone down through the jungle to the seashore. After watching the natives for some days, he had revealed himself to them. They were peaceful and friendly, though they had some customs that Orc thought were bizarre and sometimes brutal.

The Poashenk language was not derived from Thoan. He learned it quickly enough despite encountering some sounds unknown to him until then. He lived in a hut made of bamboolike wood and grass with a good-looking woman, hunted and fished, ate well, slept much, and healed his body. His soul was not so quickly repaired. Despite his seeming patience, he burned to find the next gate. After he became fluent in Poashenk, he questioned all who claimed to know something about the world outside the island. That was little and was mostly half-legend.

Meanwhile, his brown-skinned hosts gave him a drug, *aflatuk*, made from the juices of three plants. Orc drank it and also smoked the shredded bark of the *somakatin* plant. Both put him in a pleasant and dreamy state where he moved and thought in slow motion. The taste of a fruit or of roasted meat lasted for hours, or seemed to. Orgasms seemed to span both ends of eternity. Eternity, of course, in reality had no beginning or end—unless you had taken in *aflatuk* juice and *somakatin* smoke. Then you saw the start and the finish of what could not be begun or finished.

Orc might have tried the drugs just once or perhaps several times and then quit. But these two had no bad aftereffects, and he was told that they did not hook the user.

It was some time before he observed that the tribe's adults did not have good memories. Then Orc's wife had a miscarriage, and he found out that miscarriages were rather frequent. Though he noted these facts, he was not disturbed much by them. However, when he began missing his aim while hunting—he had always been a superb archer—he did get alarmed. And when he began to forget significant items, he was even more perturbed. But these mental upsets passed with time.

On certain days, the Poashenks traveled to other villages

of the supertribe of Skwamapenk for ritual festivals or just to have a good time. Orc saw that the five tribes meeting for these occasions were equally hooked on *aflatuk* and *somakatin*.

It was not until the fifth festival that he felt a vague alarm. The revelation was slow in coming, but, when it did, it jolted him, though not strongly. Hooked. All the users of the drugs were hooked, and that included himself!

That night, despite the painful urgings to drink the juice and smoke the bark, he resisted. Without saying good-bye to anybody, he put out to sea in his dugout. Though he had food and water, he did not take any of the drugs.

The next day, he regretted leaving the *aflatuk* and *somakatin* behind. Why had he been so stupid? Before nightfall, the craving was twisting his body with agony, and his cries were swept away by the wind, heard only by himself and a few seabirds. He was being carried away from the island, and he had no idea where other land was. Willingly or not, he was taking the cold turkey cure.

Jim Grimson also suffered, agonized, and, figuratively, bit his own wrists and tore at his flesh with his fingers. He, with Orc, screamed, saw demons rising from the sea and vast menacing ghostly figures looking down from the clouds, and felt as if his flesh was gnawing into his bones and spitting pieces out and the bones were trying to eat their way through the flesh to his skin while being eaten by the flesh.

Between these tortures, Orc, hence Jim, plunged into abysmal depressions. Orc saw himself sitting on the dugout bow and grinning at him. The strange thing about this vision was that it told him that, in some perverted way, he was enjoying his depressions.

He came close to leaping into the sea to end it all.

Then, suddenly, he suffered no more. The drugs had fled his body. He was weak, gaunt, and thirsty from not eating and drinking, but he had won one battle. No. He had won the war. He swore that never again would he take any drugs.

Unfortunately, during his deliriums, he had thrown the food and water supplies overboard. He now had a war against thirst and starvation to wage. He would have lost this if a ship had not rescued him. This, however, was manned by slavers. He was shoved into the hold and manacled along with several hundred other unfortunates.

His captors were very tall men from the far east of the large landmass reported by the Poashenks. They were lighter-skinned than the islanders and armed with steel weapons. Their vessel was equipped with sails and with oars to be used when the wind was light or nonexistent.

The slaver-pirates made two raids on a large island. With the ship packed to overcapacity with slaves, they sailed for three weeks northward. Orc survived the horrors of the hold. He was not sure that he would live through the slavehood itself. He was sold to a grower of a hemplike plant and put to work in the fields. The labor from dawn to dusk under the killer sun, the bad food, the unremitting humiliation, and the busy whips of the overseers put a heavy strain on his patience and toleration.

He knew what the penalty was for not obeying orders completely and industriously. He realized what talking back to the overseers or even being slightly surly would bring on him. He still had to control himself with great effort. He observed everything carefully, and he looked for ways and means to escape.

Jim Grimson not only shared Orc's sufferings, he had his own. He had stuck to Orc no matter what ordeals and dangers the Lord went through. When the agonies of withdrawal came, they were too much for Jim. He chanted the release phrase. He remained in Orc's mind. Horrified, he tried again and again. He could not get loose. Then he was swallowed up in the self-rending and the brain-fever nightmare visions and deliriums. He was too much Orc to be Jim Grimson.

After the withdrawal agonies were gone, Jim thought that he could now spring himself and return to Earth. But he decided that he could hang on and in a little longer. He endured the slave ship because Orc did not find the ordeal unendurable. For the same reason, Jim stayed while Orc was a plantation slave.

One day, he concluded that he had had too much too long. He would leave. When enough time had passed for the situation to change, he would return.

Again, he was horrified because he could not tear himself away. Now, though, the ghostbrain was holding him. It had moved closer and had "seized" Jim with phantom pincers. Somehow, Jim knew that it had put forth something similar to a crab's claws and clamped them down on him.

After that, the ghostbrain did nothing. It seemed content, for a while, anyway, just to hold on to him. Jim was anything but content. He struggled. He chanted. He cried aloud, figuratively, to a God he did not believe in. All was in vain.

Shortly after this, Orc rebelled. He had not planned to do so; he just stepped over, or was forced to step over, his limit of endurance. His overseer, Nager, did not like any slave in his gang, and he particularly disliked Orc. He made fun of Orc's white skin, spat on him, lashed him more than he did the other slaves and for lesser offenses, and always put Orc on double duty when that was needed.

That late afternoon, just after Nager had told the water bearer not to give Orc a drink because he did not look thirsty, Orc reached out and lifted the whole bucket to his mouth. The next second, he was knocked down. Nager's foot drove into his stomach. Then he brought the whip down on Orc's back. The young Lord took six lashes before he saw red. He jumped up through the scarlet cloud that seemed to envelope everything, and he kicked Nager in the crotch.

Before the other overseers and some guards could get to him, Orc snapped Nager's neck.

Despite his struggles, during which he killed a guard and crippled an overseer, he was brought down to the ground. The chief overseer, pale under his dark pigment, almost frothing at the mouth, ordered that Orc be beheaded at once.

The slaves, having abandoned their duties to watch, had formed a ring around Orc and the men who held him. They were a silent group, but their faces revealed their hatred. There was not one among them who would not have done what Orc did if they had been able to do it.

Orc was on his knees, his trunk bent forward, his hands gripped behind him, his head pushed forward. The chief overseer had unsheathed his long sword and was approaching Orc. He was saying, "Hold him steady! One cut, and I'll take his head to the master!"

Jim was more than just terrified. If Orc died, he would die. He was convinced of that. He screamed out the releasing phrase and made the most violent mental effort of his life, which lately had been filled with such.

He had the sensation of passing through a colorless void. Not black. Colorless. Cold burned him. And he was back in his room.

Its lights were on. He was on his feet but bent over. His hands were squeezing the neck of Bill Cranam, a security guard. Bill was on his knees, and he was bent backwards. His eyes were popping; his face was turning blue; his own hands were clamped on Jim's wrists.

Someone was screaming at Jim to let loose of Cranam.

CHAPTER

25

Two blows of a billy club on the backs of his elbows paralyzed Jim's arms. His hands fell away from Cranam's neck. An arm clamped down on his neck from behind. Choking, he was dragged from Cranam and thrown down onto the floor. The other guard, Dick McDonrach, stood over him, holding his billy club high.

"Don't move, damn you, don't move!" McDonrach said hoarsely.

Despite this warning, Jim sat up. He was naked. Before the last two entries, he had removed his clothes. He had had the idea, probably wrong, that they interfered with the ease of transition.

"What's going on?" Jim said hoarsely, looking up at McDonrach. He felt his neck.

"We made a surprise drug sweep," the guard said. "We found you sitting in that chair; you didn't seem to hear us. We searched your room. We found this!"

He reached into his pocket and brought out a plastic bag containing some black capsules. Triumphantly, he said, "Uppers!"

Jim felt dazed and stupid. He said, "They're not mine! I swear they're not mine!"

At the same time, he saw out of the corner of his eye faces in the doorway. He turned his head. The doorway was packed with patients in their pajamas and dressing gowns. Sandy Melton looked very sad. Gillman Sherwood was grinning.

Bill Cranam, tenderly feeling his neck, staggered over to McDonrach's side. His voice was hoarse and squeaky.

"Jesus Christ, Grimson! What got into you? I had a hell of a time waking you up, and then you attacked me! Why? Haven't we always been good buddies?"

"I'm sorry, Bill," Jim said. "I was still in . . . that other world. I mean, I wasn't all here. I didn't even know what I was doing."

"Godamighty!" McDonrach said. "I got blood all over my shirt!"

Jim had seen the stains, but they had not registered. He was numb. He would have sworn that he had flushed the black beauties that Sherwood had given him down the toilet.

"You got it when you grabbed Jim from behind," Bill said. He went around Jim and stopped behind him.

"Jesus, Mary, and Joseph! Your back's bleeding like a stuck pig! How'd you get those deep cuts? We never touched your back, I'll swear on a pile of Bibles!"

Jim could feel now the agony of the whiplashes and the wetness and salty sting of the flowing blood.

He said, "I got them . . ."

He fell silent. How could he explain? For the moment, he did not have to do that. What was really important was clearing up how the drugs got in his room. That son of a bitch Sherwood! He had to have something to do with it! But why would he try to frame anybody? How had he done it, if he had?

McDonrach, a big, burly, and huge-paunched middle-aged man, led Jim into the bathroom. He stood Jim before the mirror with his back to it. Jim, twisting his neck around as far as he was able, could see his back in the glass. There were at least six long and deep cuts. These had been inflicted on Orc by the overseer's whip. Yet they were also on his back. The blood was starting to cake.

"I'll clean you up," McDonrach said. "But don't make any sudden moves. I don't trust you."

"I'm not crazy," Jim said. "I was just, well, immersed, really into it. I didn't know what I was doing. But those capsules, Mac, they're not mine. Somebody's trying to frame me."

"That's what they all say."

Mac used a towel to wipe the blood off, then washed the cuts with soap and water and patted them dry with a paper towel. After that, he applied rubbing alcohol to the wounds. Jim clamped his teeth together hard but made no sound.

"You'll have to go to the emergency room for professional care," McDonrach said. He was grinning as if he enjoyed hurting Jim. "But I don't think those're going to get infected. Get your robe and slippers on."

"OK," Jim said. "But I didn't buy those uppers or bring them here. I'm innocent."

"Nobody your age is innocent."

"A fucking philosopher!" Jim said, snarling.

The red haze that had surrounded Orc was now around him. He had thought that he could be cool and play it cautiously and wisely. But McDonrach's last remark triggered the rage that Orc—that he—bore always within himself like a low-grade fever. Add to that the injustice of being accused of using drugs, and the fever boiled up into a very high grade, indeed.

He did not know what he had done to McDonrach. It may not have been he, it may have been Orc. Whatever he did do, it was Orc's fighting skill that he had used. McDonrach was lying on his back on the green and white tile floor, now touched with red splotches. He was unconscious, and blood was flowing from his ear.

Jim screamed, and he lunged out through the bathroom door. He saw Cranam bringing the billy down against his skull. After that, blackness.

When he came to his senses, he was on his back on a table in the emergency room on the first floor of the hospital. His back pained him, but his head hurt worse. Doctor Porsena, dressed in a checked woolen shirt and Levi's, was talking to the intern on duty. Two uniformed policemen stood just inside the door. A few minutes later, they were joined by a plainclothes cop. She talked to the two fuzz, then held a low-voiced conference with Doctor Porsena.

Jim had rolled onto his side but facing them to watch them. After a lot of hand waving and head shaking by the doctor and the cop, the doctor came over to Jim. He said, "How are you, Jim?"

"*Excelsior!*" Jim said. "And I don't mean the stuffing for couches."

Porsena smiled thinly. "*Ever upwards!* No need for me to tell you you're in a hell of a mess. But I think we can work things out, though that won't be just to make it easy for you. Roll over. I want to look at your back."

Jim did so. Porsena whistled. "How'd you get those? They can't be self-inflicted?"

"They are . . . in a way. They're Orc's wounds. He got them from a slave driver he was uppity to."

"You have had stigmata, Jim."

Jim wished that he could see Porsena's face. He said, "Yeah, but I only had the bleeding, Doctor. Never had the wounds. My flesh was unbroken. The blood just sort of oozed out from the skin. Those are real cuts, deep. They hurt, too. They're not psychologically induced, as you shrinks say. You're not trying to invalidate me, are you?"

"We'll talk about them later. There's also the matter of the drugs to investigate. I understand you claim they were planted. Meanwhile, you'll be kept down here overnight for observation of a possible concussion. I'll be up and around for some time trying to find out what happened. Good night, Jim."

Next afternoon, Jim was back in his room. His cuts were covered with taped-down gauze, and they pained him far less than he had expected. Maybe, just maybe, he had absorbed Orc's ability to heal wounds quickly. It did not seem likely, but anything was possible.

Jim did some detective work of his own, though he was restricted to his room except for meals and the therapy sessions. The Thorazine Doctor Porsena had prescribed for him made him too complaisant and fuzzy-minded. Despite this, he had little trouble figuring out what had happened while he was in the Tiersian worlds. Or, as everybody else believed, in a trance.

Sherwood's connection was an attendant, Nate Rogers. The patients knew this, but their "code" forbade them to inform the staff. Jim had seen Rogers pass drugs to Sherwood only once, which was enough. What must have happened the night before was that the drug sweep had surprised Rogers. Panicked, he had ditched the drugs in Jim's room. He could have done it easily, right in front of the patient. Jim was out of this world—literally. Of course, it was possible that Sherwood had done it out of spite.

Never mind the speculations. Get to the heart; bite down on the jugular. Orc would do that. Hence, Jim Grimson would do that.

It was not yet lunchtime. Jim walked down the hallway, greeting the few patients. No staff or nurses or attendants were present to send him back to his room. Nate Rogers, a tall and well-muscled but ugly man in his late thirties, was leaning against the door of the linen closet. He was contemplating a cigarette in his hand as if wondering if he should light up here or do it in the smoking lounge. When he became aware that Jim was approaching, he smiled. "How's the boy, Jim?"

"Not in a good mood, you sneaky son of a bitch!"

Jim grabbed Rogers, spun him around, and pushed him through the door. Rogers stumbled ahead, trying to keep from falling. Jim switched on the light. The attendant caught himself on the far wall and spun around. He was red-faced, and he looked menacing.

"What the hell is this, shithead?"

Jim told him what it was all about, though Rogers must have already guessed.

"You'll tell Porsena what you did or I'll beat you into doing it."

"What? Are you crazy? Yeah, of course, you are! You're all crazy as bedbugs!"

"Don't forget that," Jim said. "We'll cut your throat if you turn your back on us. I will, anyway. You coming with me to Porsena's office?"

"Shit!" Rogers said. "You got nothing, absolutely nothing, on me! Get lost, punk, or I'll wipe the floor with you!"

"Your clichés could do that."

"What? What's that?"

"Listen," Jim said. "You won't believe me, maybe, but I know how to kill you in two seconds with my bare hands."

"Bullshit!" Rogers said, and he sneered. "Even if you could, you wouldn't! You wanna go to prison for life?"

"I've seen you give Sherwood drugs," Jim said. "So've a lot of other kids. If they think I've been framed, they'll forget about this stupid code of silence. They'll stand up for me."

"Sure they will! In a pig's ass! You think they want their supply cut off?"

"There's only a few buying illegal drugs from Sherwood," Jim said. "They'll be outnumbered. OK. What about it? You got five seconds. One, two, three, four, five!"

Rogers, swinging his fists, ran straight at Jim. A second later, he was flat on his back, his eyes glazed and his mouth open. Jim waited until Rogers had recovered his wits.

"I just clipped you on the chin," Jim said. "That didn't do my hand any good. Next time, I kick you in the belly or ram three fingers just under your heart and squeeze it until stops. I don't like to do this, Rogers. No, that's wrong. I'm really enjoying this."

He was lying. It had suddenly occurred to him that he should be doing something tricky but nonviolent to get Rogers to confess. Wasn't that what Orc would do? Maybe he had, after all, done the wrong thing. He might be making this mess worse.

Too late now. His course was set. No turning back.

"So you can do all that?" Rogers said. "I'm just staying here on the floor until you leave. I might start yelling, too. You think you're in trouble now? Wait and see what deep shit you'll be in!"

The door swung open, its edge barely missing Jim. He stepped to one side and saw that Sherwood was standing there, the door swinging shut behind him. The big blond youth was blinking with surprise and alarm.

Jim stepped in behind him with his back to the door, now closed. He said, "Going to make a deal here, Sherwood? I got one for you!"

Rogers had to have in his pockets the drugs that Sherwood was going to buy. Without thinking about what he intended to do, Jim shoved the youth forward. Immediately, he opened the door, stepped into the hallway, slammed the door shut, and leaned hard against it. Sandy Melton was coming down the hall. He called to her to bring the security guards.

"Tell them I caught Sherwood and Rogers in a drug deal!"

Sandy was confused.

"What? You're turning them in? But . . . !"

"It's my ass or theirs," he said. "Get going!"

She came back a minute later, followed by two day guards, Elissa Radowski and Ike Vamas. Jim had to strain against the door to keep Sherwood from ramming it open.

He said, "Quick! Rogers and Sherwood were dealing in there! I caught them! You better get in fast before Rogers ditches the stuff!"

He stepped back, unlocking and swinging the door open. Sherwood fell through it onto his hands and knees. The guards charged into the room. Jim saw Rogers with a plastic bag in his hand. Evidently, he had just swallowed its contents. Only a person in a mindless panic would do that. And it did him no good. The guards pulled six other bags from the inner pocket of his white attendant's jacket. Then he was taken to emergency, where his stomach was pumped before the downers killed him.

Sherwood made a bad mistake while the guards were taking Rogers away. He came up off the floor and grabbed Jim's testicles. Before he could squeeze them, he was knocked backward by the heel of a palm slammed against his forehead. His neck and back bent backward; he screamed with pain. Some minutes later, strapped down on a gurney, he followed Rogers to the emergency room.

Jim stood against the wall, shaking his head and blowing out air. Again, the red cloud had settled over his mind, and he would have kicked Sherwood in the ribs if Sandy Melton had not clung to him while she screamed at him to be cool, for God's sake.

Doctors Porsena, Tarchuna, and Scaevola came then, pushing through the crowd of patients and attendants. It took some time for them to quiet down and disperse all but Sandy and Jim and more time to get their story.

After the questioning, Porsena ordered that Jim be locked in his room. "Mainly to keep you out of trouble and to allow you to settle down," he said. "I'll be seeing you when this mess is cleared up. I don't want you making still another."

The usually unflappable psychiatrist was angry. His set face and his tone of voice made that obvious. Jim went unprotesting to his room. That even Doctor Porsena was upset with him impressed him very deeply. But Porsena did not, as Jim had expected, summon him to his office later that day. He did give Jim another Thorazine after ascertaining when he had taken the previous one.

The tranquilizer did not soothe Jim. He became furious, then agonized with repentance, then furious again. Instead of going to bed after lights-out, he paced back and forth in his room, freezing with misery, burning with rage.

CHAPTER

26

Jim was in the psychiatrist's office for his private session. A new framed paper with big fancy printed letters was hanging on the wall. Jim could not read it from his position, but he supposed that it was a recent honor. The doctor had more diplomas and citations than a Hollywood magnate had yes-men.

A new bust was on the top shelf in a corner. Below it were the white, stony-eyed, and bushy-bearded busts of some ancient Greek and Roman philosophers and statues of a sitting Buddha and St. Francis of Assissi. Curious about the addition, Jim got out of his chair to look at it while Porsena was still scribbling on a paper.

The face, except for the mustache, closely resembled Julius Caesar's bust. It was Doctor Porsena's. Below it was inscribed: TO THE UNKNOWN PSYCHIATRIST.

Though Jim was in no mood to laugh, he broke up. The

doctor had a hell of a sense of humor, though it was usually rather restrained and quiet.

At the beginning of the session, Porsena had outlined the "mess" Jim was still in. His words were very rapid but clearly articulated and lacking pauses, almost as fast as an auctioneer's. He always spoke thus when he was dealing with a subject that had to be disposed of before the real business, therapy, was gotten to.

Rogers had been allowed to quit his position without being charged with drug dealing. To get that, he had had to make a full confession and to drop the charges of assault and battery he had threatened to make against Jim. Gillman Sherwood had also not charged Jim with assault and battery and intent to kill. The doctor had made it clear that, if he did, he would be accused of dealing, too. Moreover, he would be kicked out of the project.

Sherwood was back in his room but under strict probation. He walked with a stiff back, his neck hurt when he turned it, and he kept out of Jim's way.

Cranam and McDonrach had also not pressed charges against Jim. They were in trouble because Doctor Porsena claimed that they had mishandled the situation with Jim. Though they could continue to work as security guards, they would not be attached to the mental ward.

"I believe firmly in giving a person a second chance," the doctor had said. "In this case, you're getting one, too. You're as much on probation as the others. Now, I spoke of your unusually vivid imagination. It has helped you progress faster in your therapy than your fellow patients. I don't want you to get a swelled head just because of that. You were just lucky to have been born with it."

The doctor paused. His blue eyes invoked images of the Vikings of whom Jim's grandfather had told him. The eyes were those of Leif the Lucky, staring across the sullen and dangerous sea which seemed to go on forever. Somewhere, beyond some distant horizon, was undiscovered land. Was it too far away? Should he turn back to Greenland?

Doctor Porsena's expression changed subtly. He had made up his mind. He said, "It's time to begin shedding Red Orc's undesirable characteristics."

Jim said nothing. He sat in the chair as rigidly, except for the blinking of his eyelids, as if Porsena had dipped him in a cryogenic cylinder.

Finally, the doctor said, "How do you feel about this?"

Jim shifted his buttocks, looked at the ceiling for a moment, and then licked his lips.

"I . . . I'll admit I'm scared. I feel . . . I feel as if I've had a . . . a great loss. I don't know . . ."

"You know," Porsena said.

"Is it really necessary? Aren't you rushing things? I've just gotten into Orc. Jesus, how many days has it been since it started? Not many!"

"The number of days in therapy is not significant. We're not a penal institution. What counts is the rate of progress in your therapy. And you need not be ashamed because you're frightened. At this stage, every patient is panicked. I'd be very suspicious if your reaction was casual. I'd wonder if you were genuinely and deeply in Orc's persona. But I've not the slightest doubt that you are."

"Too deeply?" Jim said.

"That remains to be seen."

"What are his bad features?" Jim said loudly.

"You tell me."

"I'd rather go over his good features first."

"Whatever order you desire. Before you do that, what are your feelings, emotional and physical, just now? Besides being scared."

"I feel better when I'm talking about what's good about Orc. My heart is still hammering hard, though. And my bowels, they feel kind of greasy. I have to urinate, too."

"Can you hold it? Or would you be too uncomfortable?"

"I don't know," Jim said. "I guess so. It isn't as bad as I thought a moment ago."

"Orc's desirable characteristics? Those you felt you lacked or were too weak?"

"Listen!" Jim burst out. "I can't quit going into him! He needs me! There's the ghostbrain! I got to get him rid of that! If it takes over, he won't be Orc anymore! Not really! I wouldn't want to enter that body if its mind was no longer Orc's! I'd hate that! Besides, what would be the point?"

He paused to swallow. His lips and mouth were very dry.

"Besides, you aren't going to let me enter again!"

"I didn't say that," the doctor said. "That's something you assumed, and I want you to look into that assumption. When you know why, tell me why you think I'll make you abandon Orc. That's what you think, isn't it? That you'll have to give up Orc? But I haven't said you'll have to do that. I don't want you to enter him for some time, which time will be determined by your progress. Later, you will continue the entries. Now, what are his good traits?"

"Ah . . . undaunted courage. Determination that won't stop. Ingenuity, using the materials at hand to attain his goal. A burning desire to learn all sorts of things. Curiosity. A great self-esteem. Boy, do I wish I had it! Ability to adapt to any situation, to get along with people, high or low, if it's to his advantage. Patience of a turtle. But he's rabbit-fast when he has to be."

"Anything else?"

"Well, there's his relations with his family. Not all good, but he really loves his mother, though he gets mad at her because she doesn't stand up strongly enough or often enough to his father. Still, she is strong. Also, Orc is crazy about his Aunt Vala. As for his relations with the natives, especially his half sisters, he's never been cruel to them. I suppose you could say his seducing them, knocking them up, was not exactly Christian behavior. But he never forced them, and the natives think bearing a Lord's child is a great honor. It sure makes life in general better for them."

"What is your estimate of your success in absorbing, as it were, Orc's good characteristics? Have you been able to raise your own self-esteem, for instance?"

"You're the one's supposed to judge things like that!"

"I'm asking you."

"Well, I think I've got a lot more sense of my own worth, which is good. I mean . . . my self-esteem is much bigger than it was. Better. Only . . ."

"Only what?"

"Is that self-esteem mine? Or is it borrowed from Orc? Am I still playing Orc when I'm on Earth, and is it going to stick?"

"A person with genuine self-esteem does not care what people think of him," the doctor said. "He or she is his own judge of self-worth. I'd say that a true indicator of your genuine self-esteem is your behavior when you're presented with a problem. You seem to take matters in your own hands now. You don't mope around. You don't just wish you could do something about a situation but don't do it. Is my observation correct?"

Jim nodded, and he said, "Seems to be on the mark. I'm not as cowardly as I used to be. I don't think so, anyway."

"Perhaps you were never as cowardly as you thought you were? You fought the bully, Freehoffer, when you could have walked away from him."

"Sure!" Jim said. "And have everybody thinking I had a yellow streak a mile wide down my back?"

"If that happened now, would you fight because you were more afraid of social condemnation than of physical violence or because you just were not afraid of him? And you thought that to continue to give in to his bullying was wrong?"

"The latter, I suppose. How would I know unless it happened again?"

"It did happen again, in a sense. You did not have to be pushed into a corner until you got so desperate you tackled Sherwood and Rogers. As soon as you knew what the situation was, you charged on in and solved it. You could have done it differently and better. The point is that you did it at once.

"Now let's discuss Orc's undesirable characteristics."

"That's easy. He's arrogant. But he can't help that. He's been raised as a Lord. They think they're God's chosen people, even though they don't believe in God. In fact, they're the only people, so they think. Other humans aren't real people."

"You're excusing him. Do you think that arrogance is an undesirable characteristic? For you?"

"Yeah, sure. I don't want to be a big prick."

"Is Orc, as you say, a big prick? In the sense you mean, that is?"

"Yeah."

"What else?"

"Well, there's his cruelty. That seems to go along with being a Lord. But in the beginning, when I was first in him, he did have some compassion. He got into trouble with his father because he refused to kill his half-brother, even if he was a *leblabbiy*. I don't think he's got any compassion or empathy left. Not much, anyway.

"Then there's his continual rage. Most of the time, anyway. He's always mad. But it's because of the way his father treated him and his mother's failure to stop his father from gating him out to Anthema. Why did they do that to their son? He was just not going to bow and scrape to his father and kiss his ass all the time and put up with Los's uncalled-for blows and kicks and insults, that's all. Of course he was in a rage. You can't blame him for that. I'd be madder than hell, too. So, is that bad?"

"We've discussed appropriate anger and inappropriate anger," Doctor Porsena said. "You told me that Orc was considering using the destruction engine in Zazel's world to destroy his own world. That would not only kill his father. His mother, brothers, and sisters and several million natives and, in fact, all living creatures in that world would die. Is that appropriate revenge?"

"It was just a fantasy!" Jim said. "Hell, everybody has fantasies like that! But they don't act them out! Besides, he was going to rescue his mother and brother first!"

"And let everybody else die. As for these common fantasies of revenge, those who have them usually don't act them out. But Orc does. That is, he will if he goes back to get the destruction engine. If he does get it, will he use it?"

"I hope not. That'd be horrible. But I won't know if he will do that unless I reenter, will I?"

"You probably do know now," the doctor said. "But you won't admit that you do. However, what would Orc have done if he had been framed as you were?"

"The same thing," Jim said proudly. "I did what I thought he'd do."

"Would he have assaulted the two guards? Not if he was thinking as coolly as you say he does in most situations. I admit you were provoked. Not enough, in my judgment, to react so violently. And do you think it was necessary to assault Sherwood and Rogers? Couldn't there have been another way to expose them?"

"Yeah, sure. If I snitched on them. But I couldn't prove anything just by telling the guards or you. I had to catch them in the act. There was no other way. Anyway, I'd never snitch!"

"You had exposed them. But you hurt Sherwood."

"He attacked me!"

"Your defense was more like offense. A very violent offense."

"That's what Orc would have done!"

"Exactly. Was it appropriate for you?"

Jim frowned and bit his lower lip. Then he said, "You're telling me that acting like Orc then was wrong behavior for my situation."

"I didn't tell you that. You told me. And . . . ?"

"OK. I see now. I hadn't sorted out what was appropriate in Orc's behavior and what was inappropriate."

"And for you."

The psychiatrist pursued the subject. Jim realized that Doctor Porsena was being a guide who let his client make his own map as they traveled. But he could not anticipate the direction in which the guide was taking him.

At the end of the session, the doctor told Jim to get, each day, the prescribed amount of Thorazine from the pharmacy.

"You'll be on it for a while. Not very long, perhaps. Meanwhile, you are not to reenter. I'll tell you when you can do that. I want you to have time to evaluate your experiences and your feelings about them. Then we'll talk about reentery. I stress strongly, and I know what I'm doing, that you do not use your tragil until I say you can. No launch until the mental weather is good, right?"

"OK. I hear you loud and clear."

When Jim stepped out into the hallway, he was suddenly in a bright light. He could not tell Doctor Porsena what the light had revealed to him. He would be very alarmed and would take measures that Jim would not like. Maybe, though, the doctor already suspected the truth.

Jim was addicted to being Orc.

CHAPTER

27

There were several items that neither the doctor nor Jim had mentioned. One was that Jim did not have to worry about Orc having been beheaded by the slavedriver. After all, had not Farmer written that the young Lord, now known as Red Orc, was alive in the middle twentieth century A.D.? Thus, Jim's worry that Orc might be killed was unfounded. Knowing this, why was he so concerned?

Another item was the discrepancy between Farmer's account of the Lords and Jim's direct knowledge of them. In the World of Tiers series, Vala was sister to Rintrah and Jadawin. In the real worlds of the Lords, Vala was sister to Enitharmon, Orc's mother. Rintrah was the second child of Los and Enitharmon and was Orc's younger brother.

After some thought about this, Jim had concluded that Farmer's knowledge was fragmentary or received through a filter which let some but not all information through.

Doctor Porsena and his staff believed, though they had

never said so to the patients, that the World of Tiers series was pure fiction. Jim knew better. Farmer was said to have had some genuine mystic experiences, and he must have been or maybe still was a receiver of a sort. Somehow, impressions of the Lords' worlds had been transmitted to him. Their light had come to him through a glass darkly by interuniversal psychic vibrations or other means. But he did not always have their exact frequencies, and "static" interfered with his reception. Thus, he could be expected to receive not quite accurate messages. Also, since he was writing what most people thought was fiction, he could make up stuff to fill in the cracks, as it were.

Nevertheless, despite some errors in chronology and identification, Farmer's WOT arrows were usually in or near the bull's eye. Also, some Lords whom Jim knew or knew about were not necessarily those of whom Farmer wrote. They could be descendants of the originals or their relatives. How many Robert Smiths and John Browns living in the fifteenth century had numerous descendants in the twentieth century? Los, Tharmas, Orc, Vala, Luvah, and other names could be, though not common, not rare.

Jim had more urgent problems than these. Since he was on probation, he had to control his "antisocial" behavior. That became increasingly difficult because of his mounting grouchiness and quick-to-ignite temper. He was hooked on Orc, and, since he could not enter him, he was suffering withdrawal symptoms. If his brain could have teeth, they would ache. If it had a nose, it would drip and sniffle. If it had a voice, it would be pleading, between screams, for a fix.

However, he was able to temper his temper somewhat with a technique Orc used. It seemed to Jim to be similar to some Yogic mental techniques he had read about. But it could be learned much more quickly. After all, the Lords had had many thousands of years to perfect it. Though it was not able to dissipate the withdrawal effects, it did dilute the pain and irritability. The technique was like lifting now and then the cover on a boiling pot to let out some steam. Meanwhile, Jim managed to keep from snarling at and insulting people.

He did feel a little better when Mrs. Wyzak phoned to reaffirm her invitation for him to live at her house while he was an outpatient. At Sam's funeral, Mrs. Wyzak, sobbing, had enfolded Jim in her arms and promised him that he would have a place he could call home. Despite her grief, she had also told him that he would have to obey her rules. No drugs, no smoking in the house, no foul or blasphemous language, strict attention to his schoolwork, daily bathing, punctuality at mealtimes, no loud music, and so on.

Jim had promised that he would do as she wanted. He did not think that he would have much trouble. He had progressed greatly in outward behavior—except for the present withdrawal symptoms—and he could keep his "antisocial" thoughts to himself while around her.

His elation about Mrs. Wyzak's offer was quenched the next day. His mother phoned that she was visiting him that evening. He expected her to tell him exactly what she did tell him. His parents were leaving for Texas in five days.

He felt tears rising; his heart seemed to fall in on itself. Though he had toughened himself for this moment, or thought he had, he was badly hurt. But he succeeded in closing the valves on the tears. He was not going to let her see him cry. He did not want her to tell his father that he was so deeply affected. Eric Grimson would rejoice at the thought that his son was a sissy.

Jim did not ask why his father was not there to face him. He knew why. The coward!

Eva Grimson, sobbing, left him. She promised that she would send money for his hospital insurance. Also, she was sure that she could send money for clothing, schoolbooks, and other necessities. His father would find a good job, but Jim would have to be patient.

"I'll be patient forever," he called to her as she stumbled to the elevator. "It'll be forever before I come to Texas! Maybe I'll come before then if my father dies!"

That was cruel. Not cruel enough for him in his present mood.

A few minutes later, as he walked down the hallway toward his room, he was stopped by Sandy Melton. She was very happy though not superexcited. Her manic phases had been toned down by her therapy. Besides, this time, there was a reason for her happiness. She had gotten a letter from her father which she wanted to read to Jim.

Ordinarily, he would have been glad to share her joy. It angered him just now to see someone else happy.

Nevertheless, he mastered his impatience.

"Daddy's going to get a job here at his headquarters company! Listen! 'Dear Sandy, my favorite daughter.' He's only got one child, me, you know. 'As I've told you far too many times, I'm tired of traveling-salesman jokes, and I'm fed up with being one.' He means with being a salesman, not a joke. 'I wouldn't mind so much if I was a great traveling salesman. But I just can't hope to ever be in the same class with St. Paul of Tarsus, who's maybe the greatest of all, Genghis Khan, who sold death to millions of slaughtered people, the man who sold refrigerators to Eskimos, and Willie What's His Name, Arthur Miller's salesman, great only in his struggle against failure. Anyway, I've been offered the position of sales supervisor at my favorite cold heartless corporation, Acme Textiles. Do you think I'm going to turn it down for any ethical, moral, philosophical, or monetary reasons? Think again! So, my darling daughter, I'll be crossing the Rubicon, burning my bridges behind me, and storming the breach once again, the latter being, namely, your mother, poor wretch. Whether or not it's high noon or midnight dreary, she and I are having a showdown. I'll be in a position to support her on separate maintenance or a divorce, whatever God and her evil temper decide.'"

Sandy jumped up and down, the letter fluttering in her hand like a flag of victory.

"Isn't he great? Isn't he marvelous? I know what he has in mind. Divorce! He must've got over his guilt about her, wish I could but I will, and he's going to be home nights, and I'll be there!"

Jim hugged Sandy, then said, "I just have to go."

"But I want to celebrate!"

"Damn it, Sandy! I don't want to hurt your feelings, but I can't stand it! I'm sorry. I'll see you later!"

He strode away. His tears were going to stream before he got to his room. Sandy called after him, "If there's anything I can do to help, Jim?"

Her sympathy and care touched the lachrymic button. He began to weep and sob. He ran to his room, slammed the door shut behind him, and sat down to let his grief flow. He would have liked to throw himself on the bed and press his face into the cover. He did not do that because that was what a woman would do.

In the midst of the outpouring of tears, that thought came to him. And that set up a domino effect somewhere in his brain. The last thought to be bumped out—the others toppled in the dark—was the advice his grandfather, Ragnar Grimsson, had once given him.

"It's a peculiarity of the Norwegian culture and of the English and American, too, that men are not supposed to cry. Stiff upper lip and all that. But the Vikings, your ancestors, Jim, cried like women in public or privately. They soaked their beards with tears and were not one bit ashamed about it. Yet, they were as quick to draw their swords as they were to shed tears. So, what's all this crap about men having to hold in their sorrow and grief and disappointment?

They get ulcers and heart damage and strokes because of the stiff upper lip, don't you know, old bean, old chum, old chap?"

Orc, like most Thoan males, was a stoic in certain situations and a weeper and groaner in others. If he was in physical pain, he did not show it. But when joyous or grief-stricken, he could howl, weep, and carry on as much as he wished.

The latter behavior seemed to Jim to be a desirable character element. However, in this Earthly time and place, he would be regarded as a weak sister if he incorporated that part of Orc's persona. Whatever strength of character he had absorbed from the young Lord, he was not strong enough— as yet, anyway—to ignore others' opinion about this trait.

By the time for group session, he had gotten over much of his grief and anger. At least he felt as if he had, but he knew that strong emotions were sneaky things. They hid, and then they popped out when something opened the gate for them. At the moment, he was thinking that, if his parents had deserted him, they had done so under duress. They should get away from here so that they could climb out of the poverty pit. It was really not their fault that he was unable to come with them. Well, it was partly their fault. But what else could they do? And he was strong enough to take care of himself—after the therapy was complete.

It would be hard to tackle his studies now and hope to graduate from high school with at least a B-minus or C-plus average. Going to college and supporting himself while striving to get good grades would be even more difficult. But he could do it. Others less equipped with will and intelligence had done it.

That thought surprised him. Jesus, Mary, and Joseph! What had happened to him? Not so long ago, he had believed that he was too dumb to earn, really earn, graduation from high school. Suddenly, he was going to go to college and do well at it. He was even eager to plunge into his studies.

Strange sea-change, he thought. Metamorphosis. The cockroach had turned, seemingly overnight, into a human being. Maybe not a high-class human but a better class than he had been. He owed that change to Orc. No. Ultimately, he owed it to Doctor Porsena, The Shaman, The Sphinx. But the psychiatrist would tell him that Jim Grimson owed the change to himself. Though he had gotten help, he had done what no one could do for himself.

Feeling high, he went to the session to tell the thirteen other members just how good he felt and why he was on the Yellow Brick Road and the rainbow was just around its bend. Today, though, most of the Tiersian Musketeers, as they called themselves, were also in a mild manic phase. Mild was a relative word. Compared to their gloomy and hopeless mood when entering therapy, mild was wild.

They were so eager to talk that Doctor Scaevola, the group leader, had a hard time keeping order. Part of his difficulty sprang from their attitude toward him. Though he was enthusiastic about Tiersian therapy as an "as-if" or fantasy-using technique, he obviously did not believe that their trips were real. His tone of voice and facial and body language betrayed his incredulity.

According to one patient, Monique Bragg, who had been filling in as an office clerk now and then, she had overheard Porsena and Scaevola arguing about the concept of parallel worlds. Porsena had not said that there were such things. But he had maintained that recent speculation in theoretical physics indicated that parallel worlds were possible. Scaevola had been outright scornful of this.

Scaevola also had some trouble relating to juveniles, or anyone else, addicted to rock music. He liked only Italian opera and classical composers.

Scaevola finally quieted the group down. Brooks Epstein, eighteen years old, spoke first. He was tall and rangy and had a Lincolnesque face. His voice embarrassed him because it was so thin and shrill. It was not fitting for a lawyer or surgeon. Despite this, his parents wanted him to be one or the other. Brooks admitted that these professions were reasonable and desirable—if you cared for them. But he passionately desired to be a baseball player. He had told his parents that he would go to college and then Harvard if he failed to become a major league player. That had not satisfied them. But he had held out against them and also against his fiancée, who was wholly on their side.

While the argument was raging and Brooks was becoming more despondent but increasingly stubborn, his father had killed himself. Though the cause seemed to be the failure of his hardware store chain and an inevitably fatal case of myeloma cancer, Brooks was devastated with guilt. His abandonment of the Jewish faith had enraged and hurt his parents and deeply shaken his fiancée. His mother had never said openly that his father's worry about this had brought on his bankruptcy and cancer, but it was evident that she believed it.

Attending Harvard had then become an impossibility. Brooks was happy about this, though at the same time he felt guiltier. Then a rich uncle in Chicago had offered to finance his studies in whatever university Brooks selected. The catch was that he return to his faith and get either a legal or medical degree. His mother and fiancée had pressed him hard to accept the offer. They were as relentless as hungry wolves circling an elk floundering in deep snow.

One night, Brooks went ape, as he put it. Using his baseball bats, he had broken furniture, expensive art objects, and windows. Worse, he had threatened to bash in the skulls of his mother and fiancée. The police had hauled him away.

After failure with Freudian, Jungian, and Sullivanian therapists and a stint at Est in California, he had ended up in the care of Doctor Porsena.

The persona he had chosen was that of the Yidshe knight, Baron funem Laksfalk. The baron was a character in the first book of the series. He lived in the Dracheland tier of the tower-of-Babel-shaped planet ruled by Lord Jadawin. Though this was inhabited by creatures Jadawin had made, it was also populated by the descendants of people from Earth. Jadawin, as conscienceless as any Thoan, had abducted some groups of medieval Germans and German Jews and gated them to his world. These had two separate feudal societies which Jadawin had encouraged to resemble those found in the Arthurian tales. In the first book of the series, the wandering knight, funem Laksfalk, had fallen in with Kickaha and Wolff after a joust. He had died fighting bravely by Wolff's side against a band of savages. But Brooks chose to enact his adventures during the years before funem Laksfalk's last stand.

Brooks Epstein reported that, as of today, his heavy burden of guilt and anger seemed to be lighter. This was because he knew that the baron, should his father die, would not suffer guilt if he was not responsible for it. He, Brooks, had not caused his father's bankruptcy, cancer, or suicide. Therefore, he should not suffer from guilt. Despite his rationalizing, he was still suffering. But he felt that he would get over that.

As for his profession, he still intended to become a baseball pitcher. It was not a criminal line of work, which was more than you could say for that engaged in by many lawyers and doctors.

After Brooks had narrated the previous night's adventure, the group talked about how they felt about the Yidshe baron and how they would have altered his situation. Jim was aware that Doctor Porsena and his assistants were interpreting the remarks as they applied generally to the group. He guessed that, later in therapy, they would interpret these as they applied to the individuals uttering them.

It seemed to him that the World of Tiers was being used as a sort of communion. The patients had very personal— idiosyncratic?—and uncontrollable delusions, unrealistic desires, and hallucinations of various degrees. But all now shared in this communion, the Tiers series. They were heading toward each other, converging, drawn together like flies scenting honey. And they were unconsciously modifying their views of the Lords' worlds, shaping them into a dimly seen common world. Its shape would be realized when they were well advanced in therapy. They would know then that they had torn apart their own little boats and put the pieces together as a large ship.

Maybe he was just allowing his imagination, not to mention his metaphors, to run away with him. In any event, he sensed that the therapy was working well for most of them. However, the world he entered, Orc's world, was not fantasy. It was as real as this one. More real, in some respects.

The next to speak was fourteen-year-old Ben Ligel. He had had some hallucinations when he was on drugs and just as many as when off. The primal loner, his main problem was his close-to-panic unease in unfamiliar situations or when with anybody but a few close friends. Now, he was not, most of the time, unbearably uncomfortable when with his fellows. But when the times came that he could not stand being too close to others, he escaped to the other worlds.

To do this, he put a Tiers book on his head and used it as a "gravity gate." Headfirst, he was pressed down into the pocket universe he had chosen. Simultaneously, gravity pulled the book downward on that part of his body still on Earth. When the cover of the book reached the floor, he would find himself in the other world.

Ben stayed there until the "latent tug of gravity" pulled him back to Earth. He was always refreshed by the voyage, and he was able to endure the "social pressures" for some time.

Third to speak was seventeen-year-old Kathy Maidanoff. She was not backward in telling the group that she had been diagnosed as having a borderline personality disorder, gender confusion, and nymphomania. Though she had, so far, been chaste while in the hospital, she did get sexual relief through erotic dreams. She would put a Tiers book close to her head and another on her crotch. Then, almost always, she would dream of sex with a male or female character. She had just entered a phase of therapy in which she was being taught how to control her dreams. Jim was astute enough to guess that the staff was not doing this just to enable her to enjoy the dreams better. The process had something to do with getting her to control her delusions. Then, these would gradually be stripped from her through other techniques.

Jim had not mentioned that he was master of the controlled dream technique. He did not, however, require book aids. While in Orc, he had learned through him how to prefabricate dreams. Now, when Jim slept, he used these controlled wet dreams to relieve himself. They were much more satisfactory than masturbation. "Look, Ma, no hands!" Their danger was that the dreamer could become addicted to them. In time, he or she would regard flesh-and-blood lovers as cumbersome, time-wasting, and unnecessary.

Jim had noted that Orc's partners in the dreams were usually his aunt, Vala, and his mother, Enitharmon.

Quite often, Jim also put the women, lovelier than Helen

of Troy or Vivien Leigh, in his programmed night visions, sometimes at the same time. That it was incest, though secondhand, was the dressing on the salad.

Early that night, Jim made a decision that he knew might ruin everything for him. He could not help it. His own arguments against the idea did not help him resist it. He would be disobeying Porsena's orders. He did not want to do that. Yet, he would.

At ten minutes to eight, he passed through the black hole in the center of the tragil. Despite Porsena's forbidding it, he planned to enter Orc. Not just once but many times during this night. And, since he dare not journey every night—too much danger of being caught—he would compress the many into a single night.

From ten minutes to eight in the evening to six in the morning would give him time to hurl himself over spans of many years.

What had he read when in Mr. Lum's class? It was from the poet, William Blake.

"Hold infinity in the palm of your hand/And eternity in an hour."

He would not go so far as to say that he would time-hop, via Orc, through eternity in one night. But he would try to squeeze into ten hours as many slices of eternity as he could.

Just before he started chanting, he saw Porsena's face. It was disapproving and sad. The chanting faltered and almost faded away into silence. But Jim felt a stronger pull. Orc and the exotic worlds behind the walls of Earth punched through the black hole and shattered Porsena's face. Its fragments flew away and Jim flew through the fragments into the tragil like a World War II bomber through flak.

Suddenly, he was in intense pain. He screamed voicelessly. Orc, however, was grinding his teeth together and was not even moaning softly. He would not give his father any satisfaction from hearing him cry out.

Orc was stretched out against a cross. His feet rested on the ground, but his hands were nailed to the horizontal arms. He did not think he could endure the agony for another second. Yet, he did.

CHAPTER

28

Not so Jim. He had suffered enough with and through Orc. Enough was enough and more than enough. Despite this, he managed to hang on for a minute. Orc was high on the side of a mountain. Far far below, at the foot of the mountain, was a broad lake fed by a river. On the lakefront was Golgonooza, the new palace of Los, the City of Art. A river ran on its far side. The buildings were of varicolored metal, soft looking and all rising from the ground at a gentle angle and then becoming steeper, but never entirely vertical, until they got to perhaps a thousand feet. After that, they went straight up for many hundreds of feet, then leaned outward. They seemed to melt into each other at various levels. Green, scarlet, orange, and lemon-colored vegetation grew on many of these. Much of this consisted of trees, some of which grew at right angles to the vertical surfaces of the buildings.

Los had been working on the city-palace, on and off, for

several centuries. He planned it to be the most magnificent of Thoan structures, greater than Urizen's Insubstantial Palace.

Los had caught Orc just after he had entered a gate into this world. Yesterday, he had crucified his son despite Enitharmon's desperate pleas. Los was about to drive in the second nail himself when he was attacked by her. Before she had been knocked out, she had clawed his face bloody. Now, Orc's mother was imprisoned somewhere in Golgonooza.

Unable to withstand the pain any longer, Jim changed the mantra, and he was back in his room. The time was still ten minutes to eight. The minor hand had moved an almost imperceptible degree. Shaking from the ordeal, he got a drink of water in the bathroom and rested in the chair for a while. Then, sharply aware that he was losing time and he had many trips to go, he began droning, "ATA MATUMA M'MATA!" This time, the chant did not have to go on so long. Seven repetitions hurled him through the black hole. The next time, he was sure, it would only take five. The trip after that would need only three. The remaining trips would continue to take three. He did not know why. It just was that way.

His time target was a year later. He landed in Orc in a situation which would once have embarrassed him. But he had been in the young Lord in too many similar circumstances to be taken aback. Orc was making violent love to his aunt Vala. That, apparently, was how she desired it. A gentle lover was not for her. Jim was caught up in the raging maelstrom of lust and had no time or inclination to think about the surroundings. Not until both were spent was Jim able to do anything on his own. Though also suffering the effects of the "little death," as some called postcoital lassitude, he was lively enough to note the immediate environment.

The two Lords were in a magnificently furnished bedroom

as large as a mansion. The walls and the pillars crawled with changing colors. The windows were twice the size of a football field. They, too, bore shifting colors, tints, and hues. Now and then, they became transparent. Then, Jim could see a black sky with many stars. Later, the top of a planet came into view. As Jim discovered after a while from Orc's and Vala's conversation, they were in a satellite with a figure-eight orbit.

They had fled through various universes after Vala had rescued Orc from the cross. They did not go to the world of Luvah, Vala's husband, because Luvah and Vala had split up. Unlike most Lords, Luvah had not killed his spouse but had allowed her to try her luck at dispossessing another Lord of another world.

Los, like a hound of heaven, had dogged his son and sister-in-law as they passed through gate after gate. Then they had been separated—they did not say why—and Orc had gone on. But they had found each other after many adventures. This world was—had been—Ellayol's. After getting through several gates set with many traps, Orc and Vala had killed Ellayol, his wife, and his children.

This news deeply disturbed Jim. The Lords were so murderous, and Orc seemed to have lost whatever humane feelings he had once had.

Vala and Orc had gated to this satellite to enjoy a lovers' vacation. Shortly after learning this, Jim was on fire with the same flames burning in the two. There was another rest, and then they were at it again. This went on and on with not much talk between the bouts nor many thoughts about the past. When they started to gash each other with their fingernails and to lick each other's blood, Jim loosed himself. Not, though, before "touching" the ghostbrain. Jim still did not know if the thing had distenanted Orc's intelligence or was taking it over as slowly as some cancers ate up a body. What made him "shudder" when he touched it was that it touched him back. Something had definitely though briefly put its "finger" on him. Jim had been shot with loathing then. Yet, he had had the feeling that there was something vaguely familiar about it.

After returning to his room, Jim rested a few minutes. Faintly through the wall on one side came the sound of a girl sobbing. Through the other wall Jim Morrison shrieked the words of "Horse Latitudes" while The Doors banged, twanged, and pounded. The lyric was one of Jim's favorites, true poetry, he thought. He had not heard this 1967 hit for a long time, but Monique Bragg liked to tune in the "Golden Oldies" program.

Jim sighed. He did not want to put off reentry. For the moment, he was too wrung out by the sexual frenzies to start chanting again. Though he had not exerted himself physically in a direct sense, his role as a not so innocent bystander had worn him out. He now knew all there was to know about tender love, learned while Orc was making love to the native woman. He also knew too much of violent love, as demonstrated by Vala and Orc. Though his erotic adventures had been few on Earth, he, as Orc, had had enough to make Casanova and Henry Miller look like bumbling lovers.

More minutes passed. Finally, he shot himself through the black center. His target was six years later. Surely, this time, Orc would be in a relatively happy situation. Statistically, there were bound to be such.

By Shambarimem's Horn! Orc was back in a suite in his father's original city-palace. No one else was in it, and no sound came through the heavily barred and open window. He had been captured again while trying to make his way through the city of Golgonooza, the killing of Los his goal. Vala had gated out to somewhere. That was seven months ago. And he, Orc, had been taken to his childhood home, the palace of the clouds, and imprisoned there.

Jim was shocked to find out that that was not all Los had

done to his son. Orc's body felt peculiar. It had muscles it had never possessed, and its legs and feet were numbed past feeling, and it moved in a frightening and strange manner.

Then Jim saw Orc's reflection in a towering mirror. His surprise and horror were so intense that he came close to tearing loose and returning to Earth. The naked body of the Lord was, from the genitals upward, just as it had been. But the lower part was a serpent's. Orc had no legs. He was joined to a gigantic snake's body fifty feet long, its scales a bright green. At regular intervals, the green bore five-angled scarlet patches. Orc's torso was held upright by the powerful forward part of the reptilian body. He moved across the floor as a python moved.

He had become an ophidian centaur, half-man, half-snake.

Jim knew enough of Thoan science and history to know who had brought about this metamorphosis. Los, instead of killing his son, was torturing him again. He had used the biological knowledge and means still available to the Lords to make this monster. His son's legs had been lopped off, and he had been fleshily welded to a headless snake.

Sometimes, Los came to this now-deserted palace to mock and to jeer at Orc. He had told his son that Enitharmon was back with him. After their reconciliation, they had had three more children. These were Vala, named after the aunt because Enitharmon desired it, Palamabron, and Theotormon. All had been borne by surrogate mothers. Orc had been the only one Enitharmon had carried. She had wanted to experience natural childbirth at least once. That one time had been enough to discourage her from having more.

"However, I have learned my lesson," Los had said. "From now on, as soon as the children become adults, I will send them on to other worlds. Some of these will be unoccupied by Lords, their masters or mistresses having been slain. On others, my children will have to test their wits and agility against the rulers."

Enitharmon did not know that her son was being held prisoner or that he had become a monster. Los had told her that he had learned that Orc was safe in the world of Manathu Vorcyon. That ancient woman had adopted him, and he was continuing his education in her peaceful universe. Someday, Los would permit Enitharmon to visit Orc. That would have to be a long time from now, though. It would happen when the passionate hatred of Los and Orc had cooled down.

Meanwhile, Los was keeping Enitharmon busy with raising children—with the help of many servants.

Orc did not know if his father was telling the truth or not. It was possible that his mother was still imprisoned or had been murdered.

Jim touched the ghostbrain again and was touched back.

It definitely had become larger.

He decided to stay with Orc for a while. He was fascinated with the study of the conjunction of man and snake. The first thing he noted was the connection of the circulatory systems of the two bodies. The reptile was warm-blooded, which meant that it was not really a reptile. Its body had been made in Los's laboratory to meld with Orc's, which required that the same kind of blood run through it. The serpent body had its own heart since the human heart alone could not have pumped nearly enough blood for the immense bulk.

The front end merged with the human part just below Orc's anus and his genitals. But he was spared the humiliation of having to excrete on the back of the serpent and befouling himself. The food he ate went through intestines in his stomach and then was shunted to the ophidian's stomach. Part of his urine had to go through his own urinary canal; most of it went through the serpent part.

To stay alive and healthy, he was forced to eat and drink huge quantities. If he tried to starve himself to death, he would suffer not only his own hunger pangs but the serpent's.

"Metaphorically, you've always been a snake," Los had said. "Now, you're metaphor and reality combined."

"A snake who can bite!" Orc had howled. "A serpent who can crush you!"

His father had laughed. Then he had said, "When I catch Vala, I'll make her into a fit mate for you. I look forward to watching you two coiled together while making snakish love. Trying to do it, anyway. That'll be a sight never seen before!"

Orc did not reply. He did not wish Los to know how much he longed for companionship, especially female, especially Vala's.

Escape seemed to be impossible. Trap-beset gates were just beyond the single door and the four windows. Los never entered the room, though he sometimes opened the door to jeer at his son. Usually, he talked to Orc from a TV wall-screen. He liked waking Orc up in the middle of the night. Orc did not become angry about this. The time of day or night meant little to him, and he welcomed the sound or sight of a human being, even of his father. Of course, he would not let Los know that.

Three months after capture, Orc's two bodies broke out in jewels.

CHAPTER

29

At first, Orc thought that he was suffering from a carbuncular infection. Hard nodes sprang up mushroom-swift on both bodies, though his face and neck were free of them. They itched intensely, and the thin skin over the hard swellings broke at the slightest scratch. A little blood but no pus flowed from the ruptures. The broken skin revealed a many-faceted substance that was rubbery in its initial stages. Then it became as hard as a gem. The growths could be of any color or shade.

Orc realized that he was not infected with any ordinary disease. The Thoan were immune to pimples and boils or, in fact, any skin infection. Los must be responsible for the outbreak.

In a week's time, the swellings had grown larger. They were the size of a walnut and much harder than the shell. The skin over them stretched without breaking. After the first three days of growth, they had ceased to make the skin itch. Orc had quit scratching, and the cuts made by his nails had healed within five hours.

Fortunately, the swellings had not appeared on the underside of the serpent body. It would have made movement across the smooth floor both painful and difficult. As it was, even its sidewinder method of locomotion did not prevent his ever-looping tail from slipping now and then.

When Los came to the doorway or his face was videoed, he refused to answer Orc's questions. He only said, "It is not a disease."

All the skin over the bumps broke in the same hour. Their contents fell onto the floor, clinking as they did. They looked like cut gems, and they twinkled in the light.

Shortly after that, Los opened the door. He stood there and laughed for a long time. Then, he said, "You're a living treasure, Orc, your own gem mine and jewelsmith. You'll be up to your ass, your human ass, in diamonds, emeralds, garnets, rubies, sapphires, amethysts, and chrysoberyls. You may even drown in them.

"Thank me, my son. Your father has heaped riches upon you, though you deserve only ashes and dung. The tale of your unfortunate fortune and strange death will spread throughout the worlds—I'll see to that—and you will become a legend to rival Shambarimem's and Manathu Vorcyon's."

For reply, Orc bent his body so that he was a few inches above the floor. He scooped up a handful of the still-wet gems, straightened back, and hurled them through the doorway. Los did not move except to make a slight step backward, then to resume his position.

As the jewels shot through the doorway, they vanished.

Orc had established that a gate was there.

"You'll see only my face on the wall from now on," Los said. "You've no way to get rid of the gems. Drown in your sea of beauty!"

He closed the door. Shortly thereafter, a small round

ceiling panel slid aside. Through the hole dropped the gems, one by one, that he had cast at Los. Orc took these and the others and dropped them into the privy hole. Ten minutes later, all reappeared from the ceiling hole.

Jim unmoored himself from Orc and returned to his room on Earth. Immediately, he began chanting. On his return to Orc, four Thoan months had passed. The Lord was taking plates piled with food from the revolving tray in the wall. He had been forced to eat and drink immense quantities to provide the energy to make the jewels. Almost all his time had been spent in ingestion and excretion. Because his hunger and thirst woke him up every two hours, he slept in spurts. If he had tried to cut down his intake to a normal diet, he would have dehydrated in less than a day and would have starved to death in three days.

The jewels were three inches thick on the floor. When Orc tried to crawl over them, he slipped and slid and had much trouble getting from one place to another. However, he had tried a new technique of locomotion recently, and it worked. Instead of carrying his human body vertically, he put it in a straight line with his serpent body. Then he cleared the jewels ahead of him out of the way with his hands.

Eventually, the gems would be piled so high that he would not be able to make a path.

The question now was whether he would die of weakness or of suffocation first. The time would come when he would not be able to get to the food tray and the water faucet. The jewels would cover them too deeply.

For the first time in Orc's life, he despaired. Death seemed to be the only exit from this room. Jim felt just as hopeless and spiritless as Orc. Also, the ghostbrain seemed to be getting larger, though its menace would cease when Orc died. At the moment, it looked as if the solution to both problems could be that.

After twelve trips, Jim entered Orc on the night that the Lord had to escape or die soon. The jewels were only several feet from the ceiling. To reach the food tray and the water faucet, Orc had to dig two wide and deep holes. These had been caving in soon after being made, thus forcing him to excavate every day. He had given up on trying to get to the privy hole. As a result, the room stank, reminding Jim of old man Dumski's outhouse pit.

The room was being monitored through wall screens and, perhaps, with other sensors. Los would be observing only occasionally unless he carried a small receiver with him. He might have stationed servants to observe the room on a twenty-four-hour basis. Certainly, he would be instantly notified automatically by machine or by an operator if his prisoner did anything untoward. However, the wall panels up to several feet within the ceiling were now covered with the jewels. But disguised monitor screens would be on the ceiling.

Orc thought of covering the exposed areas of the wall and the ceiling with his excrement. But, as soon as the monitors were blinded, Los would be called.

He scooped a hole by the wall above the faucet. That would not alarm the monitors; they had seen him do this every time he wanted a drink of water. When he came to the faucet, he gripped it. It would, he hoped, not tear out from the wall from the stress he planned to put on it. Most of his serpentine body was stretched out across the room. Holding on to the metal faucet while he exchanged hands to maintain his grip, Orc rolled around and around.

Observing this, the human watchers might believe that he was having a seizure of some sort. They might call Los. However, it would not look to them as if he were doing anything that could aid him to escape. And they would wait a while to see what, if anything, he was up to.

As he rolled, the jewels around his human body fell in and

covered him. The snake body was also soon buried, though it was closer to the surface than the human part. He then groped around with the tip of the tail until he felt one of the upright tempered-vanadium bars making a frame in front of a window. Extended a few feet more, the tail coiled around the bar.

If the frame had been welded to the metal wall, it would resist his mightiest efforts. As it was, he did not have his full strength. But, after he strained until sweat slicked his body and stung his eyes and the veins swelled to the size of tiny serpents, the frame popped out. It screeched, a sound the monitors would detect.

Though of very thick and hard metal, the faucet had bent sideways.

Now, he came up and out of the hard but loose pile over him. His fore part forming a straight line with the serpentine part, he clawed at the jewels before him while the tail sidewound frantically. He got to the window quickly. Then, he pushed himself along the wall for several feet. After he stopped, he began to hammer his tail against the window. At first, the mineralline growths under the skin softened the pain from the blows. The only hurt he suffered, and it was almost too much, was from the skin breaking over the immature jewels. But these were ripped out and off after twenty or so impacts. This caused him a greater pain. And the unbuffered slamming of the tail made him clench his teeth with agony. Blood smeared the window.

Just when he thought that he could no longer continue his weakening blows, the window fell out. Immediately, the jewels by it cascaded outwards. He writhed to the opening and stuck his tail out and above the opening. It groped around along the wall above the window until it found something upright and standing in a niche. He curved his tail around its base as an anchor. Then he extended his head and shoulders through the opening.

The only illumination was moonlight, but he could see that the object his tail had gripped was a metal statue. Now he knew exactly where he was in this huge and complex palace-city. He was on the north side of one of the first buildings erected on the lowest level. It was over two thousand years old, and his parents had been talking for a long time about tearing it down and building a new one. Its too ornate rococo style was no longer to their taste.

The palace lights came on. He saw no sign of life. The TV watchers were probably the only tenants left, the others having gone to Golgonooza. Los, of course, would have been awakened. He may already have gated through to this building or one nearby.

He tightened the tail's grip around the legs of the statue and slithered out of the window. For a moment, he was hanging face down to the full length of his two bodies. Then his mighty ophidian muscles raised him, and he twisted the snake body until he faced the wall. He rose until he could grasp the shoulders of the statue. He uncoiled his tail from the base of the statue. Almost, his fingers gave way under the weight of the momentarily dragging tail. Then he raised the latter part and coiled a length around the statue above. Thus progressing from statue to statue, he got to the roof.

As he had expected, several flying craft of various types and sizes were hangared in one corner. When he got to them, he chose an all-white craft of the Steed II class. This was large enough to accommodate his huge bulk. Getting into the pilot's front seat so that he could operate the Steed was not easy. He had to jam the front part of the serpent through the space between the two seats. Then, he had to curve it so that his human part would be able to reach the controls. Since he lacked feet, he had to operate the pedals with his hands. That made for awkward flying when the craft was not on automatic, but he could do it safely if he was careful during certain maneuvers.

He hoped that the vocal code which started the engine had not been changed. It had not. But that did not mean that the concealed self-destruction device would not explode. It could be set for automatic activation or by a radio signal from Los. Also, there could be an override which would take control from the unauthorized pilot. Then Los could direct it to land wherever he chose.

Orc was going to take his chances. He had no other choice.

None of the craft was armed or had hand weapons aboard.

Light beams sprang out from each side. They were about ten feet long and fan-shaped. Under Orc's control, they began flapping up and down as swiftly as a hummingbird's wings. The craft rose slowly, the light flashes of the Sethi engine becoming a blur. Orc turned on the radar, infrared, and headlights. The bright flashes from the side were going to be seen by anyone in his path so he might as well have a good view ahead of him.

It took six minutes of savage acceleration to put one hundred and fifty miles behind him. The lights of Golgonooza brightened swiftly as he decelerated. By now, Los must have gated to the palace, learned what had happened, including the theft of the Steed, and gated back to Golgonooza. Or he was just about to do so. He would guess correctly that his son would not fly elsewhere to take refuge while he was still part serpent.

Whether Los had gone to the palace and returned or had never gone, he was now in his new city. Orc angled the vessel steeply downward toward his landing place, the plaza by the swirl-domed towering residence of Los. As he did so, he saw his father. He was running, staggering rather, across the plaza. He was clad only in a short kilt, and he wore a belt holding a holster that contained a beamer. One hand was clasped to his side as if it hurt.

Ahead of him, her white and gauzy night robe flapping behind her, ran his mother. Enitharmon's slim legs were pumping swiftly, and she looked desperate. Although Los could have stunned or killed her with his beamer, he was so furious and, possibly, so injured that he had forgotten about the weapon. Or he did not want to use it unless he was forced to do so.

As Orc brought the Steed around in a curve to get behind Los, he saw that the hilt and part of the blade of a dagger stuck out between Los's fingers. Evidently, Enitharmon had stabbed him between the ribs, though not deeply. That meant that she had not been imprisoned in one section of the palace or had been released from it. Or his father had been lying about locking her up. In any event, his mother had found out what he had done to their son. She had intercepted him before he could take effective action against Orc. There had been a struggle, and she had slipped the blade into his side. Then, she had fled.

The Sethi wings made no noise. Los had not seen their flashing or was too intent on catching his wife for the lights to register. Orc took the craft down to about six feet above the multicolored luminescent pavement and shot it toward Los's back. Enitharmon had stumbled and fallen on one knee. That was long enough for Los, screaming, to overtake her. He clutched her by the throat with both hands as she tried to get up. She was now on both knees, her body bent backward as she clutched Los's wrists.

Before the bow of Orc's craft rammed into a point between Los's shoulders, Enitharmon had released her right hand and jerked the dagger loose from his body. He cried out with the pain. She started to plunge it into Los's belly, but he was knocked forward by the aircraft's prow, and her dagger struck his breastbone at an angle. Then his body carried her to the floor. The dagger lay close to her hand on the ground. But the impact of the bow against Los was not as violent as Orc could have made it. Even though rage filled him, it had not taken over all his wits. He did not wish to injure his mother by driving Los too hard against her. And he did not want to kill Los. Not yet.

Even so, she sprawled beneath Los. He lay heavily face-down upon her, his arms outflung. He was stunned or unconscious. Enitharmon was not trying to roll him over and away from her. She must have been stunned when the back of her head struck the pavement.

Orc raised the canopy of the aircraft. He crawled out of the vessel and to his parents. Enitharmon, looking up and past Los's shoulder, screamed. Even if Los had told her what he had done to Orc, the sight of him far exceeded the shock of the mental image. And the blood covering Orc must have added to the horror caused by his monstrous body.

"It is I, Mother!" he croaked.

He bent down and picked up the dagger from the pavement. She was silent now and staring with eyes as wide open as possible. Orc rolled the still-unmoving body of his father over and slid off his kilt and loincloth. A few seconds later, Enitharmon screamed again and did not stop for some time.

Orc had cut off Los's testicles. Then, straightening up to a vertical position, he slipped the two balls from the sac and popped them into his mouth. Cheeks bulging, he began chewing.

Rage and the legends that the ancient Lords had done this to their enemies had inspired him to do this deed. And it was possible that the serpentine part of him overrode the human revulsion at the act. Orc had become half animal in more than his conjoining of flesh with a snake.

Whatever had driven Orc to this act, it was too much for Jim Grimson. He did not have to chant to release himself from the Lord. The shock and disgust cut the mental cord, and he was back in his room. He was shaking and felt as if he had to vomit.

CHAPTER

30

"I know you're anything but pleased with me, Doctor," Jim Grimson said. "You ordered me not to reenter, but I couldn't help it. Orc was as much a drug as angel dust. I swear I'll never reenter again! Never! Not until you tell me to do it! And I won't want to do that, I can tell you for sure! I got that compulsion out of my system!

"I loathe Red Orc! I'll admit, like I told you, that I got a very funny sensation when he bit into his father's balls! I enjoyed it, just for a couple of seconds, though! That's because I was so far into being Orc I almost was him! Then I got real sick! For a moment, the sickness made me become myself enough to get out of Orc! If that hadn't happened, I might still be in him!"

Porsena's face was unreadable. Jim believed that he was really pissed off at him. He just wasn't showing it. However, his words so far had been as sharp and as hard-driven as arrows.

The psychiatrist now spoke more softly. "You've been told to call me or my staff at once if you feel your desire is getting too strong for you to resist it. You should have done that. I expect that, from now on, you will. You are, in a psychological sense, in shark-filled waters. To be precise, you're at a turning point. When a person is at that stage, he can go ahead or go back. You understand?"

Jim nodded. He said, "God knows I tried! I know now I can't make it on my own. I'll do everything exactly as you tell me to do."

"Not until the reason for the orders or suggestions has been explained to you. The patient should fully comprehend the why and wherefore of his therapy."

"I know. You tell me that every time we're about ready to go into another therapy phase."

The doctor smiled. He said, "You're astute, in some things, anyway. That's one reason your therapy has progressed more swiftly and along somewhat different lines from the others. You're ready, in my judgment, for the shedding phase."

Jim said, "But . . . but! I mean, there are some things I just have to know! Like, what about the ghostbrain? And I wanted to be there when Orc made the Earth-universe and its twin! God, what a sight that would've been, like watching God create the world! No, like being God because Orc would be doing it, and I'd be Orc!

"And I wanted to find out how Orc got his complete human body back! And there's Los! When I left, it looked like Los was dead and done with. But Farmer says Los was still living when Kickaha went into the Lords' worlds!"

"Farmer may write the sixth book in the series and enlighten you about all those. Whether he does or not, we have certain absolutely required procedures to follow. What if you were addicted to heroin and pleaded with me to allow you to keep taking it because you'd miss future highs if you kicked the habit. You do see the parallel?"

"Well, OK," Jim said slowly. "Easy for you to say, though."

"That's because I am objective."

"Yeah, I know."

"Think about Orc when he was on the island of the drug users, the lotus eaters. Do you want to be in his condition? He certainly had no craving to continue taking the drugs after he had gone through the agonies of quitting cold turkey. You went through his pain with him. Keep that torture in mind if you're ever tempted to take drugs again."

Doctor Porsena leaned forward over his desk and church-steepled his hands.

"I want you to think hard about the questions I'm going to throw at you. Consider all the angles you can think of. Orc was in Anthema, the Unwanted World. Orc's father placed him there. What does that suggest and imply to you?"

There was silence while Jim thought, his mouth twisted with the effort and his eyes rolling around. Finally, he said, "My father, I mean Orc's father, put him there. I suppose you're thinking I named Anthema the Unwanted World because my father did not want me? He sent me, I mean Orc, there because he was not wanted. That sounds good, but I didn't make up the name of Anthema. It wasn't just my unconscious mind working overtime."

For some reason, Jim's heartbeat had stepped up. He was beginning to sweat a little, too.

The doctor said, "Los loved Orc when Orc was a child or, at least, was very fond of him. He treated his son with kindness and care then. But, occasionally, he was very abusive, even then. When Orc became an adolescent and was no longer the cute and lovely infant, his father seemed to hate him."

"No 'seemed,'" Jim said. "He did!"

"That suggests?"

"My relations with my father were sort of like Orc's, weren't they?"

Porsena, instead of answering, said, "What about your visions when you were a child?"

"Hallucinations, you mean?"

"Let's call them visions. Your first attack of stigmata occurred when you were five. You were in church with your mother. The statue of the crucified Christ fascinated you. You suddenly saw it as a real man, not a carved wooden figure who was suspended by nails from a cross and whose blood was merely paint. You screamed."

"I still don't know what scared me."

"That's not vitally important. Immediately after you screamed, blood welled from your hands and feet and on your forehead. You became hysterical, your mother, also. Then . . ."

"Then there was the man I saw floating by my bedroom window when I was four!" Jim said. "And the naked green man I saw out in our garden six months later. He was eating the ears of corn! I yelled for Mom, but when she came, the green man was gone! I got whipped by my father for lying! But I did see that man! I did!"

"How do you feel about the vision you had just before you passed out in your burning house?" the doctor said. "You were naked and chained to a tree and a giant sickle was about to castrate you. Also, what are your feelings about the vision you had of the man-serpent?"

"They were prophetic. They predicted what was going to happen when I was in Orc. Sort of, anyway. They were mixed up, but their elements were true. They did happen."

"I didn't ask you if you thought they were true or what their psychological explanation was. I asked you how you feel when you think of them."

"For Christ's sake, Doctor!" Jim burst out. "I don't feel anything at all about it! I can see what you're getting at! You think I made up Orc being made into a half-snake thing because I'd dreamed about the man-serpent!"

"I am not trying to invalidate your experiences. I am merely suggesting certain parallels. The interpretations will be yours. However, allow me to point out that you deny feeling anything about it. Yet you responded with more than a little anger. For the present, we'll not go into that. You think about it, then tell me your conclusions."

Jim leaned forward, his hands holding tight to the arms of the chair. His heart was beating even harder than it had a moment ago, and he was sweating more heavily. What he felt was, he felt as if he'd like to get out of the office. Right now.

"Look, Doc!" he said harshly. But even he could hear an underlying note of pleading. "Where I went and what I saw and did, I mean, what Orc did, was no fantasy! It was all true, and I don't care what parallels there are to my life here on Earth and there in the Lords' universes! Hell, I could find parallels between my life and a thousand others on Earth! There is such a thing as coincidence, you know! No matter how crazily I might fantasize, I can do things, know things, no fantasies could teach me! Like speaking Thoan, for instance! You want to hear fluent Thoan?

"*Samon-ke fath*? Meaning, Where do I go from here? *Orc-tam Orc man-kim. yem tath Orc-tha*. Meaning, Orc was once just called Orc. Now, he's called Red Orc. If you want me to, I'll rattle off a long story in Thoan. And I'll give you the grammar, too!

"And where would I learn how to work flint into knives, arrowheads, spearpoints, scrapers, chisels, you name it? Bring me a core of raw flint, I'll shape from it any tool anybody can make from flint! How could I know how to do that unless I'd really been in Orc's mind and had seen him and Ijim work flint and then brought back how to do it stored in my memory?

"Then there's the whiplashes I brought back from the time Orc got whipped by the slave driver! Yeah, I know I've had stigmata, and maybe that's just psychosomatic stuff! But that time, I just didn't bleed from my back! The cuts made by the whip were there, too! They hurt like hell, they were real!

"Then there's the controlled wet dreams I learned from Orc! You're starting to control the dreams and delusions of the patients, but they can't hold a candle to my controlled dreams for control or realism! How'd I learn to do that? On my own? No way! I learned it from Orc!

"I could go on, but you got more than enough to make you wonder if maybe I'm not telling the truth, haven't you? And I suppose you think just because Orc cut off his father's balls I'd like to cut off my father's?"

Doctor Porsena said, "Would you?"

"Yeah, there're times when I'd've been glad to! But I swear, mad as I've been at him, I never once thought about doing that. Maybe stringing him up by them. But cutting them off and eating them—raw, for God's sake—never! So how come, if I'm just imagining Orc and what he does, did he do something I'd never thought of?"

"You tell me."

"Oh, sure, it was my unconscious mind did it!"

"And . . . ?"

"And? What else? Oh, well, there's my imagination. It's a free-wheeling extrapolator, according to Mister Lum. Takes a basic premise or fact or idea and builds logically from that. Maybe you could be right about that. But not about the other stuff. Not my speaking Thoan and working flint and, I didn't mention this before, my knowledge of biology and chemistry I couldn't have learned unless I'd tapped into Orc's mind. That can't be explained."

Jim tried to lean back and relax.

"Listen, Doctor! We can settle this! You can put me on the

lie detector machine, question me all you want, and then you'll see I'm not lying!"

"You're my patient, not a criminal. Besides, if you believe that you have actually gone into Orc's universe, the lie detector would indicate that you're not lying. But I'm not the inquisitor, and you're not on the rack. The truth or falsity of the patient's experiences are not my consideration or concern. I don't care whether they really happened or not. I accept that they did happen inasmuch as they concern the therapy. That is, what is the relevance of the experiences to the therapy? What progress or regress derives from them? Those are the only significant questions. Do you read me?"

"Sure! But . . . isn't it important, needful to science, to everybody, to know that there might be other worlds out there? Parallel universes? And at least one person, me, maybe three, since Kickaha and Wolff went there, has been there! Aren't you interested at all in that? If I can go, if they can, too, then everybody should be interested!"

"That is true, given your premises. As I said, at the moment only your therapeutic progress concerns me. It's all that should concern you. Now, Jim, I understand that your parents are coming here tomorrow to say good-bye to you. They're leaving for Texas the day after. Your father has finally consented to face you. That meeting is very important as a test of how you'll react to stress. Will you be so angry that you become violent and attack him? What will you do if he attacks you first? Will you avoid provocative behavior? And what will your reaction be after the meeting is over?"

He and Jim talked about the possibilities and how Jim could handle the situation. The psychiatrist did not expect Jim not to be angry. He did want Jim's display of rage, whatever form it took, to be appropriate.

"As you know, shortly after you were admitted here, I advised both your father and your mother to go into therapy," Doctor Porsena said. "When a patient enters treatment, his family should also enter. They refused. Their main plea was that they could not afford it. But . . ."

"The real reason was that they thought I was the only crazy one in the family!" Jim burst out. "They thought they didn't need therapy! Hah!"

"Then you'll have to learn how to handle all that appropriately and positively."

Doctor Porsena glanced at the clock.

"Just one more question, Jim. It was put to you some time ago, but I want to hear your response as of this moment. What is the main thing that you have learned about Orc's character?"

Jim hunkered down in the chair, frowning. Then he sat up.

"The night I took all those trips . . . it was a lifetime. I'd say that the main thing I learned was this.

"Orc had a lot of good qualities, courage, endurance, ingenuity, and desire to learn. He was passionate about everything he did. Oh, he was passionate, all right! But his passion was separated from real love. I don't think he really loved anybody but his mother and his aunt. And I'm not sure that that love wasn't basically lust. Passion without love is no good.

"Not bad for an eighteen-year-old blue-collar dummy, heh?"

"Not bad," the doctor said. "I don't know if you mean it when you call yourself a dummy. But we're not through working on your self-esteem."

"Another thing," Jim said. "The Thoan. My God! They're thousands of years old and like gods in many respects. But they're locked into war and conquest and jealousy and murder and torture and all sorts of bad things. They haven't progressed spiritually or emotionally in all those thousands of years. They're stuck, and there's no hope for them to get unstuck. That, I say, is like most people on Earth. They're stuck!"

The psychiatrist nodded. "I'll point out another item," he said. "Orc is to be admired for his ingenuity and wit in getting through the many obstacles in his way and in getting out of the many traps set for him. What Orc did, you can do. There are many obstacles on Earth and many traps, economic, social, psychological. You, like Orc, can use your ingenuity and wit to overcome the obstacles and spring yourself from the traps.

"And you don't have to be a dull conformist, as you have phrased it during previous sessions. You're afraid you'll be a square, part of the establishment, if you behave within certain moral and ethical bounds. But you can be a genuine individualist without being antisocial."

"Yeah," Jim said, his tone indicating that he was not fully confident. "Still, there are things I'd like to know. The ghostbrain, for instance. What was it really? I don't suppose it makes much difference if it takes over Orc. It'll act just like he would. In a sense, it'll be Orc. At least, that's what I thought. Only . . ."

"Only what?"

"Well, just before I parted from Orc the last time, I was so sickened that I didn't pay much attention to what the ghostbrain was doing just then. It seemed to have advanced on me. I mean, it had gotten a lot closer or a lot bigger, depending on the way you look at it. In fact, it seemed, somehow, to have surrounded me, half-surrounded, anyway. It was like a giant black amoeba getting ready to surround and ingest a smaller cell. If I hadn't left Orc just then, well, I don't know.

"I was thinking about it the other day. How about this idea? I was wrong thinking it came from that blue stuff floating around on Anthema. Suppose it was—this'll kill you—suppose the ghostbrain was not some alien thing menacing Orc? I mean, what if it was some kind of a shadow of Orc's brain? What really happened was that I was sensing that Orc's brain was about to take me over, and it looked like a sinister alien shadow to me? I scared myself into thinking it was a danger to Orc. But there really wasn't any alien in Orc's brain except me? And something in Orc sensed me and was going to absorb me? Orc was unconscious of this. But a mechanism in his neural system was automatically treating me as if I was an enemy?

"If that's true, then I was scared for nothing about it being a force ready to become Orc and throw him out. But I had good reason to be scared. I was going to be the victim, the possessed, or, I should say, the ingested! Only Orc was going to do the ingesting!"

"An excellent hypothesis," the psychiatrist said. "Quite possibly, perhaps most probably, that was what it was all about. I congratulate you on a brilliant solution to that problem."

"Thanks. But what does that mean? You didn't say it was the right solution."

"No," the doctor said, "but it is very probably the correct one. If you think it is, then it is. You're the person to know."

He smiled, and he rose from his chair. "Time's up, Jim. See you next session."

He flipped the intercom switch. "Winnie. Send in Sandy Melton, please."

Reluctantly, feeling that there was so much more to discuss, Jim went into the waiting room, nodded at Winnie, and stepped into the hall. It was, for the moment, empty of people. Music came down the hall from a half-closed door. When he was closer to Sue Binker's room, he recognized Philip Glass's *Einstein on the Beach*, issued by Tomato Music, a record company that dared take chances on unconventional stuff.

As he strode by the door, he glanced through the opening.

He saw Sue Binker's mantra on her wall. It was a looped cross, the ancient Egyptian ankh, formed by the Tiers series covers. One illustration, that from the British edition of *A Private Cosmos*, caught and held his eye. The background was an eerie landscape. In the foreground were Kickaha, holding the Horn of Shambarimem, and the laboratory-made harpy, Podarge. She was either attacking Kickaha or about to screw him. It was hard to tell.

Whoosh!

Subaudio sound.

Jim was hurtling through the eye of the loop on top of the cross.

The eye expanded to admit him.

Before he could scream, he was in Orc.

Behind him, or seeming to be behind him, was another unheard sound. It was the clang of an iron door shutting.

Jim knew instantly (without knowing how he knew) that the young Lord was now called Red Orc. His many slayings of Lords and *leblabbiys* had earned him that title. He was standing on the edge of a high plateau in a flickering crimson light which came from the horizon and stained the blue sky. Around him were warriors, all of them *leblabbiy*, clad in green armor and scarlet feathers, their faces heavily tattooed. They were firing with howitzer-sized beamers at the horde below. The purple rays were blowing up the forest, earth, and men; huge trees and men's bodies were flying through the red-shot black smoke.

That non-Lords were operating such technologically advanced weapons meant that the war between Orc and Los had made both sides desperate. Never before had the *leblabbiy* been allowed to use any but the most primitive weapons. The plains forces' (Los's) projectors were knocking off chunks of the cliff and precipitating groups of Orc's warriors with them to the ground four thousand feet below.

Red Orc was very anxious about the flickering crimson

light on the horizon. He thought that it must be made by a long-lost pre-Thoan weapon that Los had found during his long flight from his son. Orc now regretted more than ever that he had not killed Los at once after castrating him in Golgonooza. While Orc was attending to his mother, Los had escaped.

Through the smoke, Orc saw the wall, vengeful as an angry god's eye, speeding toward the plateau. Mountain-sized orange gouts were mixed with it, gouts that left behind them, where Orc could see through the smoke, vast craters. (The size of those on Earth's moon, Jim thought.) They would destroy Los's own Lord allies and *leblabbiy* auxiliaries before they reached Orc's army. Los, who must be far away over the horizon and operating this apocalyptic weapon, did not care. If he cracked the planet in half but killed his son, he would be happy.

Orc turned and sprinted toward a gate he had set up for escape if things did not go well.

Just as Red Orc leaped through it, Jim managed to tear himself loose by chanting the Siberian shamanic spell. He felt a pain as if he had been attached to Orc by an umbilical cord which had been yanked away from him, tearing off the tender flesh.

The pain came and went swiftly. Jim heard two other noiseless noises: a whooshing and then a clanging. He had just enough time in transit to hope that he was back in his own body.

He was not. But, though again in the young Lord, he was in another time and place. This world had belonged to Uveth the Vortex, one of Urizen's iron-hearted daughters and Los's ally in the apocalyptic struggle between Orc and his father. Orc had, after suitable torture, slain her. It was also many years after Orc had fled the cracking in two of the planet on which he had been fighting Los.

He was locked in a sexual frenzy with his own child, Vala,

named after his aunt. His ecstasy was so intense that his loins seemed to be interwoven with silken fires. A choir with voices too beautiful to be real sang around him.

Jim detected the shadowy ghostbrain, but it was moving very slowly toward him. That pace, he figured later, was sluggish because Orc was so raptured that every atom of his being was caught up in it. Jim was also entangled in the silken and fiery threads, but he made the most desperately violent effort of his life. He slipped loose.

He was in the ward hall and was just completing the step which he had started as he glimpsed Sue's mantra. His visits had taken only half a second of Earth time.

He stopped, wheeled, closing one eye so that he could not see the mantra again, and headed back toward Doctor Porsena's office. The psychiatrist would not be available because he was in a session with Sandy Melton. But he had told Jim to go to him or a staff member at once if he ever had a flashback. Jim had verbally agreed, though, in his mind, he had pooh-poohed the idea that he would succumb to the siren call of the World of Tiers.

Shaking, sweating, anxiety brooding in him like a big black bird over her black eggs, he ran to Doctor Tarchuna's office.

Jim now believed that there was a hell. It was in Red Orc in the worlds of the Lords. But a heaven was also there, though one could not exist without the other.

Jim wanted nothing of either one.

"Holy Mother!" he shouted as he banged open the office door. "Help me! Help me!"

CHAPTER

31

Doctor Porsena sat in his office and considered the next session with Jim Grimson. It would be his last as an inpatient. On the same day, Jim would start living with the Wyzaks. Leaving the ward environment would frighten Jim. Departure was often as traumatic as entering the hospital. Jim, however, was much better equipped emotionally and mentally to withstand the shocks and troubles of the "world out there" than the night on which he had been admitted.

Jim had been in great danger of being cocooned into his fantasy. A fully withdrawn patient, ceasing to respond to any stimuli outside his mind, he would have adventured inside his skull as Red Orc. Nor would he have been the Jim Grimson who was copartner in the Lord's physical and mental life. He would have been absorbed into Orc like water into a superdry sponge. Nothing of him would have been left.

After his flashback, Jim had stayed as an inpatient for an

extra week. He had not been given intensive treatment until after he was tranquilized for several days. Then, no longer taking Thorazine, he had had as many private sessions as he had needed. Neither Jim nor the psychiatrist had slept much during this period. Porsena had kept up with the regular work schedule while treating Jim.

In the meantime, The Scarlet Letterer had been caught while putting up on the wall one of his rest-room graffiti. This time, however, he had aspired higher. The wall was in Doctor Scaevola's office. The culprit was the deformed patient, Junior Wunier, no surprise to Porsena. Wunier had a very defiant attitude.

Even though he promised never again to put up his epigrams, Wunier was punished by having some of his privileges suspended. He did not mind. For a brief time, he became a hero to the other patients.

Jim's parents had not been able to make their final visit on the day scheduled. Porsena would not allow Jim, who was in no condition to handle a traumatic event, to see them. The psychiatrist was pleasantly surprised when Eric and Eva Grimson agreed to put off leaving for Texas until they could talk to him. That was over with now and with results that Porsena had not expected.

Some elements in Jim's stories puzzled and disturbed the psychiatrist. These had caused him, though he felt slightly foolish doing so, to research these elements. He had not told Jim about it, nor did he intend to. Not for a long time and perhaps never.

Jim's accounts of his adventures had faintly rung a bell in Porsena's mind. They were like chimes drifting over the horizon of a faery sea. To make certain that he had no grounds for doubt or unease, he had phoned an acquaintance, Doctor Mary Brizzi. She was not only an English-literature professor but an ardent reader of science fiction and fantasy. He had given her the names of Lords, places, and events recounted by Jim. He did not tell her that they came from a patient.

"They're from William Blake's *Didactic and Symbolical Works*," Brizzi said. "But they're also in some of the World of Tiers series, as you know. However, Farmer also writes of Lords who are not in Blake's works. Using his creative imagination, I suppose. Farmer's description of the Lords' family relationships also differs in some respects from Blake's."

And Jim's differs in some respects from both of those men, Porsena thought.

"Blake's city of Golgonooza and certain Lords, such as Manathu Vorcyon, Ijim, and Zazel of the Caverned World, are not mentioned in Farmer's series. He also has not, so far, anyway, written that Red Orc was once a man-serpent. In Blake's works, Red Orc is transformed for a while into a sort of snake-centaur. But not by Los, his father. I'll check it for you, but I think it was another Lord, Urizen, who did it. That part about Orc sweating jewels, that was in Blake, too.

"There's an interesting interlude in the latest book in the series. Kickaha sees, at a distance, an old man dressed in strange garb, obviously not a Lord. I think that that old man is William Blake, and his identity will be revealed in the next novel, if there ever is any. Just how Blake, who died in 1827, could show up alive in the pocket universes of the Lords, I don't know. Maybe Farmer will explain it in the next book. What, if I may inquire, is your interest in these two myth-makers, since you're a psychiatrist?"

"They figure in a paper I'm working on," Doctor Porsena said. "If the paper is published, I'll send you a copy."

After he hung up, the doctor sat for a long time. He told himself: Take as a premise that parallel worlds and artificial pocket universes were a reality. Premise that there really are Lords. Premise also that Blake had somehow acquired some knowledge of these. Jim's theory that Farmer had learned of them through psychic "leaks" or "vibrations" in the walls between those worlds and Earth's might have some validity—if the premise was valid. Accept for a moment that Blake had also gotten images or some kind of data through these leaks. They had formed the bases from which sprang his *Didactic and Symbolical Works.*

Blake, an acknowledged genius and perhaps a madman, had mixed his knowledge of the Thoan worlds with Judaeo-Christian theology and other subjects. The result was the *Works*, a mishmash of truth and poetry and mysticism and allegory.

But how could Farmer, an American writer born ninety-one years after Blake's death, have also tuned in, as it were, to much the same data? There were certain similarities in the lives of Blake, Farmer, and Grimson. All three had had vivid visions or strong hallucinations. Blake and Grimson had first experienced them when very young. Farmer had had them when he was an adult. He claimed to have seen ghosts on two occasions and to have had two mystical experiences. None of the three had been on drugs when these happened.

Did this tenuous connection among the three mean anything? Were there parallel universes which all three had somehow "contacted"?

No, no, no! He, Doctor Porsena, could not accept as valid either the premises or the conclusions therefrom. The most rational explanation was that Blake had originated his wild poetry with no help from vibrations, transmissions, or leaks. Farmer had based part of his series on Blake's works. And Jim Grimson had read at least some of Blake's words. But he did not remember having done so. After all, Jim admitted several times that he often read while he was stoned or drunk.

Yet . . . there were the whiplash cuts. But there was no reason stigmata could not produce incisions in flesh.

There was his claim to be expert in flint-working and to

know certain data about advanced chemistry. These could be tested.

Also, he claimed to be fluent in Thoan. That could be checked. No eighteen-year-old ignorant of linguistics could make up a language that would be self-consistent in syntax and vocabulary and pronunciation. Nor would he have a Lord word stock.

There was one disturbing fact. Porsena's keen ear had noticed that, when Jim had rattled off those Thoan phrases, he had pronounced the "r" in Orc in a most un-English manner. It had sounded to Porsena like a Japanese "r," though not quite that. And his "t" when followed by a vowel had not been aspirated. That is, the little puff of air following the consonants had been missing. That was not Jim's native pronunciation.

The doctor did not believe that Jim was faking anything. Jim really believed his stories. However, the human mind was capable of very strange and, indeed, unbelievable feats. If anyone should know that, a psychiatrist should.

If the tests were to be done, they would be carried out discreetly. It would not be good for any psychiatrist's professional reputation if his colleagues thought that he was taking Jim's claims seriously. But if it did become known that such tests were being conducted, some kind of satisfactory explanation could be offered for doing them. Such as a study of the psychological bases for the patient's delusions, their history, and so forth. That was legitimate.

For the time being, such a project would be in abeyance. What he had to concentrate on now was seeing that the patient was "cured" or in remission.

Winnie's voice came over the intercom then.

"Mister Grimson is here, Doctor."

"Send him in, please."

Jim entered the room and sat down after greeting the psychiatrist. On the whole, he looked healthy and confident.

The dark rings around his eyes were gone. He was smiling. But Porsena knew that Jim could put up a convincing front. On the other hand, he might not be frightened. He might even be eager to live with the Wyzaks and have a near-normal life. His true attitude would be revealed during the session.

"I still can't get over it!" Jim burst out. "Who'd've dreamed that my father'd suddenly be sorry for what he's done to me? I never imagined, no way, that he'd cry like a baby and get down on his knees and beg me to forgive him! I still can't believe that he really means it! Next time, he'll be the same old son of a bitch he's always been!"

"And I was overcome by emotion! I actually forgave him, and I meant it! Then! But I still hold a lot of things against him!"

"I've not treated your father. Thus, I have only a superficial knowledge of his character and his motives. But my own experience and reading of case histories convince me that such reversals of behavior do occasionally occur."

He was thinking that Eric's remorse and plea for forgiveness had a parallel in Blake's *Works*. Doctor Brizzi had told him that Los and Enitharmon had repented of their ill treatment of their son. They, like Eric, had hastened to make amends as best they could.

Brizzi had been puzzled by Porsena's questions about Red Orc castrating his father and eating the testicles. "There's nothing like that in Blake. Nor in Farmer. Where did you run across a reference to that?"

"It has to do with a fantasy of a patient of mine," Porsena said.

"Oh? Well, anyway, Los's testicles would have regenerated, grown back out, according to what Farmer says of the Lords' biological capabilities. Is your patient into Blake's or Farmer's works?"

"Somewhat," Porsena said. "That's really all I may tell you about him."

It seemed to him that the castration and cannibalism sprang wholly from Jim's wish-fantasies. Neither Blake nor Farmer was responsible for that. And it was, of course, a coincidence that both Jim's father in reality and Orc's parents in Blake should have apologized to their sons.

The doctor said, "I'm sorry, Jim. I was thinking about something. You're sticking to your determination to stay with the Wyzaks? You haven't reconsidered your parents' offer to let you live with them once they're on their financial feet?"

"No way. I'm staying here even after the therapy is complete. My father may be sincere, for now, but I'm afraid that things'll fall into the same old sordid groove after a while. I will go see them for a while someday. Not now, not soon."

In their conversation after that, Porsena stressed the difficulties and dangers the outpatient would run into.

"Mrs. Wyzak should be a stabilizing influence on you. From what you've told me, she's a strong disciplinarian. You need someone like her. But she may regard you as an adopted son, one who'll replace her dead son. She could try to smother you with love and be less strict than she was with Sam. Spoil you, in other words, because she'll be afraid of losing you, too.

"There's also the possibility that you'll identify her as your mother. You'll have to be careful about that. She is not your mother, whom you've blamed for not protecting you against your father. She's Mrs. Wyzak, a big-hearted woman who's taking you into her home. Keep all this in mind, and report to me how it's going there."

"I will," Jim said. "I believe I can make it."

They discussed Jim's "shedding" procedure, which had already started. Jim was using the technique some others had adopted. As therapy progressed, he would tear the covers off the first book in the series, then rip off pages until all were gone. After that, he would start on the second book and work through to the last one. But he would go a step further than the other patients. He would put the torn-out pages into a shredder.

Jim and the psychiatrist had agreed that he would not reread any of the series. According to Jim, Porsena did not have to worry about that. He had found it hard enough to just look at the covers without being afraid of another flashback.

"I don't ever want to go back into that evil son of a bitch!" Jim said.

Then they talked about the means the patients used to enter the worlds. Many of them thought that the mantras and chants were magical tools. Part of the therapy was convincing the patients, in the latter stages of therapy, that the means were psychological, not magical.

"There is no such thing as magic," Porsena said. "But if the patient wishes to act as if the entry methods are magical, we don't discourage that. Whatever works is OK with us. But we don't want the patients either in remission or cured to still believe that there is such a thing as magic when they are through with the therapy. Please don't tell this to any patient who hasn't progressed as yet to your stage."

When the time came for Jim to leave, he stood up, and they shook hands.

"I'm not really leaving you since I'll be seeing you once or twice a week," Jim said. "But this is kind of a farewell."

He walked to the door, then turned around before he opened it.

"I encountered many mysteries in the Lords' worlds," he said. "Most of these I solved or at least had a good explanation for. But I haven't penetrated The Mystery."

"Which is what?" Porsena said.

"If all universes except for one, the original, were created by the Lords, who created the original? And why?"

"Only the young concern themselves seriously with matters such as ultimate origins and the reasons for them. When you get old enough to know that such questions have no answers, you'll quit asking."

"I hope I never get that old," Jim said.

Porsena smiled. He supposed that the smile looked to Jim like The Sphinx's inscrutable expression. Perhaps Jim thought that his doctor was concealing the wisdom of the ages behind the smirk of the stone-headed Egyptian statue.

He was. He knew what The Sphinx knew about the ultimate mysteries. That is, nothing.

The Mysteries were unassailable in this world and in all worlds.

The most that any human being could do was to try to solve the "little" mysteries. Those were huge enough.

AFTERWORD

A. James Giannini, MD

I

On an otherwise unremarkable English afternoon, a remarkable English girl named Alice walked through a looking glass. On the other side, she found a land of fantasy and distortion. Her ability was unusual because she could enter a fantasy created by someone else and then return to the alternative "real" world. Schizophrenics and other psychotics inhabit their own world of delusion and also have difficulty reentering the real world—that common interface that humanity shares. Children can also inhabit a secret place of fantasy. While they seldom have trouble skipping across the twin planes of fantasy and reality, they do not have the ability to transport adults into their secret worlds.

It is the lack of Alice's gift that makes the practice of psychiatry so difficult. Each delusional patient is truly a master of his own universe. This universe is an entity unique to the individual. It has its own terrain, its own memory-base and its own symbolic language. The understanding of each of these worlds provides the therapist with the ability to discover the root trauma and modify the results. Unfortunately, the patient retains the ability and prerogative to alter his personal reality at any time. For some, alterations occur in a chaotic fashion, while for others it seems to occur whenever a breakthrough is imminent.

The great English therapist, R.D. Laing, developed a school of thought in which a schizophrenic's psychosis would be considered an alternative valid reality. For the initial therapeutic phase, at least, this school provided a useful model. In trying to understand the patient's psychosis, however, one had to consume a large amount of professional resources. Many times, this expenditure was wasted. The patient was sole master of his delusional scheme; he controlled its access and could alter its form.

Frustration with these inherent limitations causes many psychiatrists to rely solely on a specific class of medication, the "neuroleptics," to reduce and control their patient's psychoses. This has always seemed to me as a solution to one-half of the physician's classic problem. Dependence upon neuroleptics alone resolves the symptoms but does not remove the cause of the disorder. With the resolution of the delusional symptoms may come the disappearance of the very key that might provide insight into the damage that begat the delusion.

Alice was able to pass unhindered through an alternative universe. This was a universe of some stability. While such characters as the Duchess' child could change their shape, the underlying form of the chessboard-mirror world was stable. It is the accessibility and stability of this world that makes it an attractive alternative to the locked-off morass of each patient's separate delusional subreality. A therapeutic anodyne would then be a world with fixed reference points and a door that permits universal ingress and egress.

While completing my psychiatric residency at Yale University, I encountered many patients whose worlds were closed off to me. Their personal fears and my neuroleptic medications seemed to function as twin seals forever removing me from the dreadful fears that pushed them away from reality. It was at Yale that I conceived using science fiction or fantasy novels as the source of an alternative reality that the patient and I could explore together.

Providentially, I discovered Philip José Farmer's *World of Tiers* series. It seemed to be a tool designed for the purpose of investigating and resolving psychotic disturbances. Its "Gates" provided the access mechanisms. Its characters were a Jungian delight; an entire panoply of archetypes were available for retrospective analysis. The variety of pocket universes presented a large but fixed number of multiple realities.

In the initial approaches with "Tiers-therapy," several patients with psychotic presentation were asked to read the series. Therapy then shifted from a review of the patients' activities to a discussion of the books. Gradually, these discussions became more focused so that the patient would gradually relate his experiences with those of *Tiers* characters. When stress would occur between therapy sessions and the patient would break down, the psychotic perceptions would gradually incorporate an ever-expanding fraction of the *Tiers* system. As an adapted *Tiers* universe replaced the highly idiosyncratic forms of alternative reality, I was able to enter each patient's private world. Finally, the metaphorical means were available to conduct work on-site. It was as if I were an astronomer, who, after gazing at Mars through a distorted mirror, was finally able to walk on that planet's red sands. Once the patient and I met on a common world, meaningful therapy proceeded quickly.

In this form of therapy, I noted that adolescents and younger adults had the best results. Those who were possessed of a love for books were the most eager. Therapy was quickly engaged if these young men and women felt themselves to be misfits who belonged in another age. Some had psychoses; others were addicted to their own fantasy world. When I moved to Ohio, I found a corps of willing patients (and supportive parents) who quickly accepted the tenets of Tiersian therapy. Since these patients were comfortable with expressing themselves, I was able to utilize the powerful tool of group therapy to project ourselves into a Tiersian model.

In standard group therapy, what is discussed ("content") is less important than the act of discussion ("process"). It is after all the flow of water rather than the nature of water that gives a river its special properties and attractions. Since every patient had a unique way of relating to the *Tiers* worlds, the de-emphasis on content worked well. Because all of our group members now shared the same basic symbols and archetypes, each patient could relate to another in a way that enhanced the process. By relating to each other, the group was able to resolve the earlier conflicts of its members and gradually reenter the real world. Using the *Tiers* series as a halfway house, they moved from private reality to shared reality to that reality which all humanity holds in common.

281

II

Farmer's recreation of Tiersian therapy at Wellington Hospital captures the essence of this particular process. Tiersian therapy is currently undergoing a punctuated evolution. It has been discontinued and continued many times. Each manifestation has brought with it many refinements. As the strangely familiar Dr. Porsena emphasizes, the trick of the game is to ensure that Tiersian therapy becomes an entry into reality, not a substitute for it. Generally, our patients were able to distinguish their delusions or fantasies from reality; they simply chose to avoid reality. Tiersian therapy is not yet applicable for the profoundly psychotic individual. Schizophrenics are not candidates for therapeutic systems that utilize evolving realities.

In reading the fictional re-creation of group process and the individual reaction to it, I felt I was an observer in my own therapeutic groups. Though Philip Farmer has never observed any of these sessions, he has reconstructed them accurately. While all persons and processes are totally fictional, any of my former patients and cotherapists should feel a sense of familiarity.

Future scientific papers on Tiersian therapy will analyze the components of this technique. It is to be hoped that my professional colleagues will then attempt to replicate the methods and results of this approach. Scientific papers, while a necessary part of the transmission of knowledge, lack the gestalt of the exploration: the experiment, the analysis, the therapeutic techniques. The novel, however, while short on absolutely accurate detail faithfully reproduces the sweat and fire of scientific enquiry. *Red Orc's Rage* carries on its pages the intuitive "feel" of psychotherapeutic treatment. In it, we can truly experience Jim's emergence into reality as he takes control of his own life.

III

Alice learned to run twice as fast and so became a queen. She then was able to walk through the nether side of the looking glass and reenter England.